THE DEPTHS OF REDEMPTION

AN EARTHPILLAR NOVEL

Christopher C. Fuchs

LOREMARK PUBLISHING

VIRGINIA

The Depths of Redemption / Christopher C. Fuchs – 1st edition
Paperback ISBN 978-1-946883-02-5
Hardback ISBN 978-1-946883-12-4
eBook ISBN 978-1-946883-03-2

www.loremarkpublishing.com

ALSO BY CHRISTOPHER C. FUCHS

EARTHPILLAR NOVELS

Lords of Deception

Coming Soon:
A Light in the Depths

EARTHPILLAR HALF-TALES

The Revolution Machine
The Fourth Messenger

Coming Soon:
Arcodum
The Feuding Tower

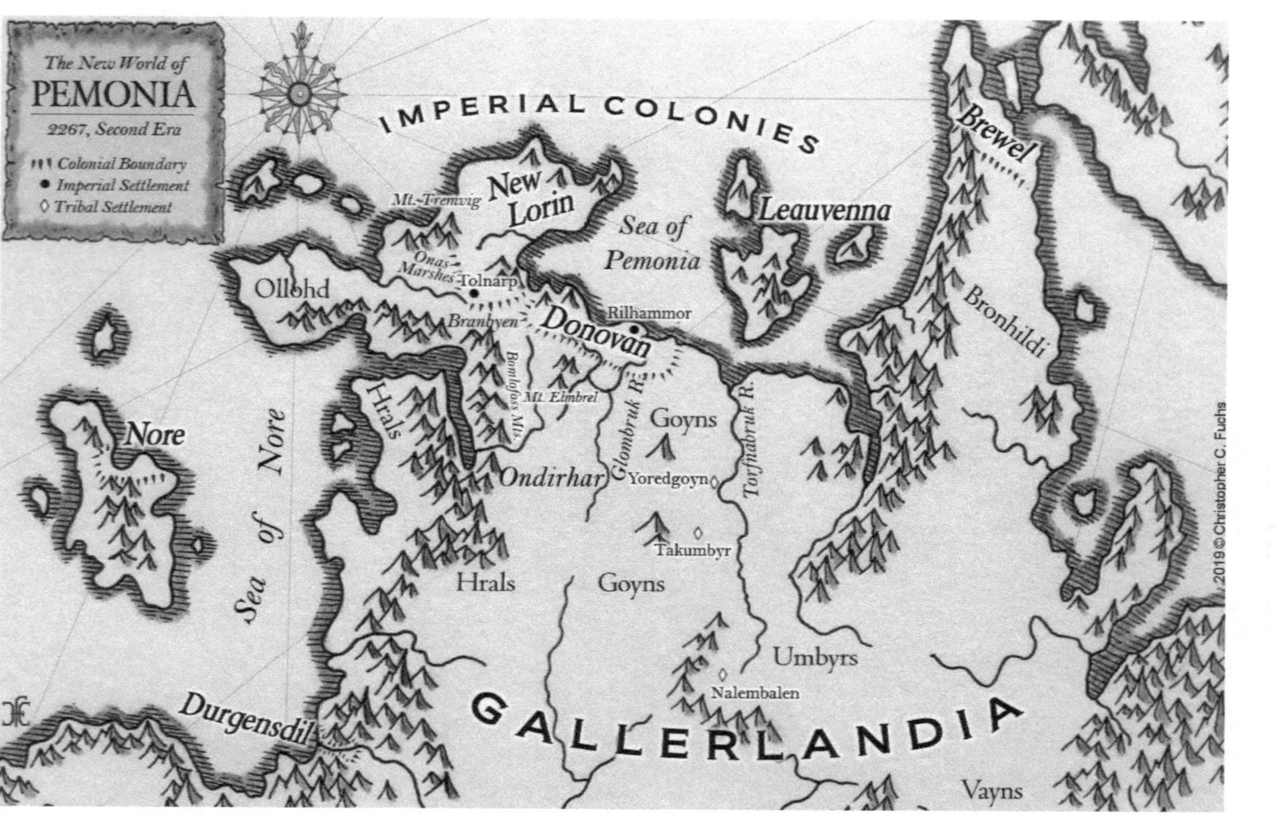

The New World of
PEMONIA
2267, Second Era
Colonial Boundary
Imperial Settlement
Tribal Settlement
IMPERIAL COLONIES
Brewel
New Lorin
Leauvenna
Mt. Tremvig
Sea of Pemonia
Onas Marshes
Tolnarp
Ollohd
Rilhammor
Donovan
Branbyen
Bronhildi
Bomlofoss Mts.
Mt. Elmbrel
Goyns
Glombruk R.
Torfnabruk R.
Nore
Hrals
Ondirhar
Yoredgoyn
Sea of Nore
Takumbyr
Hrals
Goyns
Umbyrs
Nalembalen
Durgensdil
GALLERLANDIA
Vayns
2019 © Christopher C. Fuchs

CONTENTS

PROLOGUE

Thorendor Castle, Wallevet Ministry
Harvesteve, 3032

"So where do we begin?"

"We have already begun."

"But when will I learn about the Order of the Candlestone, those ancient killers of kings? And the Crusade into the New World? And the—"

"Marlan, are you more interested in Candlestone's history than in learning how they used the sword?"

"I know how to use a sword, Master Arasemis. I want to know about ancient secrets."

Arasemis chuckled. "I presumed my students would prefer to learn warfare. The original peoples of Pemonia and the Order had a peculiar way of fighting, you know."

"I do want to know about their warfare. But I want to understand them, too. The nuggets of truth that lie in all the old tales. Hidden knowledge . . ." The young man spread his arms wide, gesturing to the bookshelves that lined the walls of the Thorendor Castle library.

"All right, Marlan. We will begin there." Arasemis stroked his long, red beard. "We must start with Rildning. You can't understand Candlestone if you don't understand Rildning. His is a tale of the struggle for survival and redemption." Arasemis leaned forward in his chair, steadying himself with his one arm. "Have you ever been to the southern coasts of Pemonia, where the modern kingdoms of Donovan and Calbria meet?"

1

"Yes, once. The white beaches and tidal marshes of Aggarwal."

"It was there, under the sandy dune fields, that I dug up an old wooden chest and found two ancient books within."

"Ancient secrets! But how did you . . . ?"

"I still had my right arm back then." Arasemis patted his shoulder nub. "It was before my tussle with the king's men."

"What was in the books?"

"They were written back when Brintilian colonists and crusaders from the Old World had scarcely delved into the deep, forested heart of the New World of Pemonia. They were buried for safekeeping, hidden for ages. In my twenty-five years as a scholar of the period, I've never seen anything quite like them. They are unique."

Arasemis paused for effect, and Marlan grew impatient.

"One of these books was the journal of a famous knight of the New Lorin Colony, Rildning. He was tasked by the governor of New Lorin to take part in an expedition into the 'heathen-infested' interior of wild Gallerlandia, the heart of the continent of Pemonia, to find allies among the natives. Previously, he had been celebrated for his courageous victories over several native tribes. The second book, written by a man named Enildir sometime after Rildning's death, is a record of Rildning's later adventures."

"Who is this Enildir?" Marlan asked.

"Our focus is on Rildning for now. Do you want to listen or chirp on?"

Arasemis pushed out of his chair and walked over to his candle-lit table. He riffled through the jumble of scrolls, quills, books, and various curiosities of foreign origin until he picked out a tattered book.

"This is Rildning's journal," Arasemis said, reseating himself. He gave his pupil the book. "Careful, it's nearly eight hundred years old."

"I never imagined something like this could be here in Wallevet."

"There is much in these lands you've been ignorant of, like nearly everyone else. Open it."

Marlan gingerly lifted the cover, exposing a map.

"This map is a copy of Rildning's original," Arasemis continued. "You see there, Gallerlandia? It was a vast tribal realm that once spanned across much of our Donovan Kingdom. Gallerlandia, right here under our feet, is where Rildning's story takes place."

Marlan scanned the map then started turning the pages. "I can't read this script. And many of these pages are torn, smeared, or burned. This one is ruined with mold."

"The script is Old Brintilian. Some of the later parts are in ancient Gali, the language of the native Gallerlanders. You will learn both of these languages and others before your training is complete."

"Why do I have t—?"

"It's what you've signed up for, Marlan. If you want to be part of my Candlestone revival, you need to know it all and understand it all. Everything from the beginning to today. For now, I will read it to you. Every day you dwell here in Thorendor, you will train in dead languages, unusual swordsmanship, and various branches of alchemy and other disciplines, with readings in between."

"I understand, master. For once in my life, I can finally direct my energies toward something I believe in, not guard duty at the lord minister's castle."

"I understand your enthusiasm. Candlestone has ever been my passion, too. Rildning's myth-shrouded life has inspired and terrified generations. You'll learn the truth, Marlan, but you'll need my guidance to harness it. Reviving Candlestone will be dangerous, as kings prefer that it remain forgotten. You must sharpen your wits, harden your heart, and, above all, maintain discipline."

"I'm honored to be your apprentice, Master Arasemis."

"Then let us begin by examining Rildning for who he really was, in his own words. Let us have a taste of that vast verdant wilderness into which he cast himself headlong . . ."

PART I

THE FRINGE

Midspring 3, 2267

The sun is slipping farther toward the horizon, and I must set quill to paper before this expedition begins. I certainly welcome this adventure, but I already have misgivings about our prospects for finding new allies and trade partners among the heathens of the interior. It is no light matter to venture beyond the frontier of the colonies, and Varesig is a fool to say so.

Both of us have fought the barbarians in their wild forests to protect the tiny foothold of New Lorin Colony. More than once I've served as a knight under his command in this corner of Pemonia, and we've seen the hardships of such perilous tasks. So his flippancy around the campfire this evening puzzled me.

Perhaps he is attempting to encourage the others on the eve of our foray. But Varesig is also a little too eager for what is surely a humble prize. His uncle, the governor of New Lorin, has charged five of us to survey the frontier and make contact with the heathens farther inland, specifically the elusive Gallerlanders.

Unlike our stronger sister colony of Donovan, our little colony has learned to make peace with the tribes out of necessity. Although we were among the first Brintilian colonies in Pemonia, New Lorin's importance is now overshadowed by other colonies' greater flow of exotic spices, furs, and timber back to the Old World.

Most of that wealth is harvested by force, not friendly relations. Why then is the governor suddenly interested in pursuing the latter? I think his scheme is unlikely to change New Lorin's position, and I have told him so. Yet he and Varesig remain enthusiastic. 'Tis a far cry from our glorious victories of days past, when Varesig in particular reveled in the butchering of the natives.

I agreed to come with Varesig because life has dulled since my injury forced the general to retire me from my commission with the colonial legion, and I thirst for adventure. But I insisted that Harsen be permitted to join us. So his village of Tolnarp, still within view of our camp this evening, was our final stop on the frontier. It is good to have such a dear friend on this journey.

The scruffy-bearded woodsman has made quite a name for himself among the merchants of New Lorin and beyond by trading with the Gallerlanders and other heathens. His success always jingles in his coin pocket when I see him, yet he retains the humble garments of the woodsman. His firsthand experience with the Gallerlanders will undoubtedly be useful, which is probably why Varesig accepted him.

For his part, Varesig, who was elevated by his uncle from active service in the legion to richly robed functionary of the governor's administration, chose the captain of his guard to join the expedition. This Rekef is a vain, piggish man who, like all of us, won his honors fighting the heathens. But Rekef, his soot-black mustache forever bent in a frown, still blames me for the death of his brother Onas.

Rounding out our quintet is Orren, an aged and eccentric scholar from the academy who shall serve as our linguist and scribe. He begged the academy to support his bid to join us. They were apparently glad to be rid of him and his contentious theories about the heathens' origins. Varesig resisted this addition, but the governor thought it a good idea.

I first met Orren after I joined the academy as commandant of swordsmanship. It was he who translated the Hral rune etched in the fateful arrowhead I carry in my pocket as a reminder of my honorable days on the fields of battle. "Blood boil," the rune says. That was the poison buried in my shoulder that kept me down for nearly four months, robbing me of my post in the army and nearly of my life.

Once an archer, Orren was also retired early. His right hand was severed by a heathen's stone ax back when New Lorin was carving out new territory on the western peninsula.

So that is our band and our duty, undertaken now at the break of spring to satisfy the eager governor. Here at the campfire our bedrolls are prepared, and we enjoy our last taste of fresh bread for the few weeks we expect to be out. We are well provisioned, with two stout packhorses tethered to our steeds. Besides our swords, bows and arrows will provide fresh game, and Harsen's foraging abilities are prized.

Not lacking anything, we have our minds on tomorrow. The initial days of crossing through contested woodland may be more dangerous than whatever comes thereafter. I've advised Varesig that we should pick a path south around the fighting, and he has agreed, assuring me he already thought of this plan.

The sun has set as I have rambled on the page. I'm no scribe but feel the need to savor these adventures, as they are fewer for me now. We sit in a quiet meadow at the edge of the vast forests of Pemonia, whose reaches are wholly unknown to us. My doubts about our task are carried away with the sun. The crisp arrival of dusk brings richly wild smells out of the nearby forest and over the grass-tufted plains to mix with the warmth of our fire.

Here we will lie a last night on the rim of the Brintilian Empire, to plunge the next day into the wilderwood, as we call the uncharted forests. It is these calm moments that are cherished by soldiers and explorers of these beautiful, unforgiving lands.

Midspring 4

t dawn we awoke in the chill air to find a convoy of
New Lorin merchants returning from business in Donovan. Several stopped to talk as we packed our
equipment, and it was clear that word of our journey had
traveled beyond the colony. One of the men cheered us on,
telling me to "kill as many of 'em as you can, like yeh used
to!" Others hooted, "Give those wild beggars the sword!"
"Conquer a dozen Mount Tremvigs!"

I did not know the men but have learned to enjoy the
honor and fame that my victories have brought me in the
name of the empire. I waved back to them and noticed from
the corner of my eye Rekef's face redden with anger, knowing the mention of Tremvig reminded him of his slain brother. He has avoided speaking to me, so I have let him be.

Our way into Gallerlandia lies through a disputed patch of
land named Branbyen. It was originally claimed by New Loriners but is one of many areas where our rivals the Donovards have asserted their power. In the middle of this
wood of elm, oak, and beech, they built a small palisade outpost that is frequently attacked by Hrals, a vicious tribe in-
habiting much of the area south of New Lorin. We have been
allied with the Ollohd and other small tribes against the Hrals
for years, attempting to quell the area with their assistance,
but the Donovards have no patience for tactics that rely on
natives. They've paid for this in lives wasted.

We rode in good spirits across the lumpy, tree-dotted plain toward the forest, which stretched well beyond view. The wood line, in perhaps the last hundred years, had swelled beyond a natural berm of earth that stretched as far as the eye could see. Harsen, who led us onward in a line, jested that as we expand our borders, so too does Gallerlandia grow and colonize the plains. The forest was "living and reaching," he said, "and we've invited ourselves into its bowels!" Varesig scoffed at this, and Rekef countered with his own sarcastic jests that I could not hear. I simply recalled the pleasing scent of the forest's cool breath during the previous evening.

Harsen led us confidently through the fringe, following a gentle deer-trodden path that weaved up and over the berm before dipping down into flat woods. The small hill continued like an earthen ring in either direction just inside the wood line, as if the roots of the whole forest had rolled the earth outward like a ripple of water. It seemed too easy an entrance into the wilderwood beyond.

Inside the ring, the forest floor was covered with small foliage, ivies and saplings taking advantage of the light from many breaks in the leafy canopy. Orren intently studied all of these features, craning one-handed from his saddle for every view. He rode a horse well enough despite his handicap and the years planted in a scribe's chair. The flatness of the ground continued among charming trees and pockets of wildflowers until at midday we reached a stream hugged by small mossy mounds.

Over a midday meal of stale bread, apples, and salted mutton pies, Harsen pulled from his tunic a hand-drawn map on old vellum. He explained that his trade with the Gallerlanders began nearby, outside his home in Tolnarp. But the skittish wild folk had ceased meeting him.

So Harsen had ventured farther into the forest to find them, encountering them at a place marked on his crude map as Beamed Boulder. This, he said, was a reference to how the Gallerlanders marked their territory. They always chose a large boulder around which they set three wooden poles that were bound together at the top with ivy.

Harsen pointed to the bubbling stream at our feet, then followed a wiggly line with his finger on the map, saying "This little water will lead us to it." He said we could reach the boulder marker by midday the next day if we had no troubles crossing Branbyen.

Orren chimed in, saying he believed only the Ollohd people marked their territory. Harsen good-humoredly answered that Orren should get his nose out of his books more often and smell the wilderness all around us. Orren thought it a remarkable sign of civilization, and I too envisioned proud Gallerlanders erecting their marker with care.

But Varesig interrupted: "It's just a big rock!" He snatched the map from the woodsman's hands. He declared no appreciation for their knowledge and sneered that he did not recall appointing Harsen to be the official mapmaker of this expedition.

The functionary scanned the vellum with nose high, then handed it to me with much pomp, saying I should have the honor. I simply returned the map to Harsen, quipping that I delegated the duty to one who was more capable. Varesig was surprised but had no retort. The good woodsman took Varesig's disrespect in stride and thanked our prideful captain.

We trotted along the meandering stream in a southeasterly direction throughout the afternoon. The swish and gurgle of the water and the lively birds and squirrels in the trees made for a pleasant ride. The horses were also content, stealing the chance to nibble at small patches of sunbathed grasses along the way.

Our pace was comfortable and relaxed, and our wariness of Branbyen faded. It was a beautiful, untouched patch of land with no sign of strife anywhere. No battle-torn views of the sort we had all heard about, so we took our time.

All of us, even Varesig, chatted excitedly about meeting the Gallerlanders. Our leader made an odd comment about shaking hands with his dagger, which he clumsily retracted, then repeated his uncle's task for us, as if reading from a script. He was most out of his depths. I had seen him on the field of battle, our swords stained with the blood of Hrals, swearing on our comrades' graves that he would forever pledge himself to the eradication of the peoples of the New World.

How odd for the governor to choose such a man, even though it was his nephew, to be an envoy to the barbarians of the interior. My doubts about our journey's success returned and I grew more watchful of Varesig, and the forest.

As the daylight dimmed, Harsen led our horses single file across a shallow spot in the stream. We soon came upon a broad knotted stump matted with emerald moss and dainty flowering plants, like an altar piece for the leafy cathedral around us. Beyond it was a carpet of the same moss perched on a small cliff overhanging a deep pool diverted naturally from the stream. In the middle of this green pad were blackened stones arrayed in a circle. This was Harsen's previous campsite. It felt as though we were in his second home, and he said as much.

We fished the pool for dinner, catching five small reddish ones Harsen called *glidiwots*. They were tasty fried up in his small pan with sprigs of wild onion and, at my request, a handful of speckle-capped mushrooms I collected nearby. I've had a lifelong love of mushrooms and long ago convinced Harsen that I knew how to find the good ones. He smiles, but he will not eat them. What breed of woodsman does not eat mushrooms?

Again producing the map, Harsen showed me our location, marked Branbyen Camp near the curvy stream line. He pointed to the general location of the Donovard palisade fort, which lay south of us. We agreed that as long as we stayed away from it, we could avoid making ourselves a target of the Hrals.

Varesig, who was not asked for his opinion but is ever eager to put his mark on things, interrupted: "Perhaps I want to visit our brethren in their borderland fort." This was absurd, and he knew it. He quickly added, "I of course approve." We ignored him and returned to the map.

Beyond our camp the wavy line of the river vanished in the southeast among many charcoal dots, and on the other side was the beamed boulder. Harsen said the dots were a large rock field, broken stones cast off the rocky foothills of the Bomlofoss Mountains, which lay well south of us. Harsen said one could see the tops of those mountains from the tree-less hills of the rock field.

Open vellum lay beyond the beamed boulder on the map, except for one angled marking. Harsen said it marked the direction of a probable lone mountain rising from somewhere deeper in Gallerlandia, but he was not sure because he had never ventured beyond the rock field.

After the glidiwots I retired to this journal to record the day while the others chatted by the fire. Varesig takes every opportunity to grill Orren about his scholarly musings on the heathens, and Rekef reliably takes Varesig's cues to jump in against the old fellow. The gullible Orren walks down their carefully laid path until they trap him in a place with accusations of heresy, then he grows quiet again. It is difficult to watch, but I am not his defender.

Everyone knows the Church teachings about the heathens, how they are the spawn of Memelos, though the devil himself remains chained in the Deeps. This has been the Church's position since the Brintilian Empire discovered the New World only three generations ago and is easy to accept when one watches how the wild Hrals live, fight, and die. Although many colonists, especially New Loriners, have been forced to seek peace with less violent tribes, the Archbishop of Pemonia has never rescinded his judgment.

Anyone involved with barbarians beyond their official duties or legitimate trade that enriches the empire risks being burned at the stake. As I understand it, Orren has caused the academy much trouble with his beliefs, which are somewhat opaque to me. Even so, he honorably served the colony, gave his hand for the cause, and does not deserve Varesig's ridicule, in my opinion. Perhaps we'll all be labeled heretics if we return to New Lorin with Gallerlander allies unsanctioned by the archbishop.

My hand grows weary of the quill, and my eyes blink for rest. May we wake to another calm day in the beautiful Branbyen.

Midspring 5

We slept late into a cloudy morning, spoiled by our spongy green turf beds and seduced by the gentle stream. I was awakened only by the smell of more glidiwots cooking. I was surprised that we would break our fast with fish, but Harsen rightly reminded me that we should eat what was freshly available and save our dried vittles for times of less plenty.

Indeed, compared to the lack of food I experienced on Mount Tremvig and in its girdle of marshes, this forest is abundant, not lacking food to be picked, scavenged, or hunted. I retrieved the kettle from one of the packhorses and fetched water. The wild dewberry leaf tea would have been superb with the glidiwots. But before we could sip, the shouting started.

Harsen quickly doused the fire with the tea. All swords drawn, we looked about us. All was quiet again until more distant shouting was heard. Harsen ordered us to break camp as quickly as possible. Varesig's feathers ruffled, but I grabbed his wrist to stay him until we reached safety. We snatched everything up into bundles on the horses then followed Harsen's lead away from the camp.

We left the path and picked a route through the brush, hearing vicious war cries ahead and echoing all around. Harsen sneaked us forward. I trusted his woodland instincts, and the horses did as well. After a while he held his hand aloft to halt our line, then an instant later we watched a mass of shrieking barbarians charge out from their leafy cover, right in front of us, spears and axes and clubs waving. "Hrals at the palisade," Harsen whispered over his shoulder. They had not seen us but were charging the Donovard fort.

When the raiders' rearguard had passed, Harsen spurred his horse forward. We darted one behind the other out of the brush. A few stragglers, surprise on their red-painted faces, raised their primitive weapons to us but were cut down by our steel as we darted through them. We rode steadily on until Harsen stopped at the top of a little wood-covered hill. None had followed us because they were intent on attacking the fort.

With smiles, we all breathed a sigh of relief. Then the haughty but courageous Rekef begged Varesig to let him chase after the horde and lend a hand to the Donovards, who would surely need it. A knight charging into the Hrals' rear, he said rightly, could panic them and break off their attack. But I countered that it would not take the Hrals long to realize he was a single man, and they would continue attacking the outpost regardless. Varesig thus declined to let Rekef loose.

At this moment we noticed that only one packhorse was with us, the one tied to Harsen's horse. Orren was horrified, the last to notice the second packhorse was not tethered to his. Harsen calmly observed that the second packhorse had two weeks' worth of supplies in its panniers. Varesig lashed the scribe with a sharp tongue. He cursed Orren's severed hand and called the scribe a "witless crippled beggar."

Wasting no time, I kicked my horse off back toward the camp. Harsen yelled for me to follow the stream back to the hill and to the rock field beyond, where I should rejoin them.

I quickly returned to the camp. No Hrals were about, but I could hear the fierce fighting down at the fort though I could not see it through the trees. I thanked God for not being one of those poor Donovards posted to such a miserable and isolated garrison. Even Mount Tremvig had not been so far outside the frontier. The Donovards would undoubtedly be slaughtered to a man, again, only to have others stubbornly replace them.

I soon found the stout mare wandering nervously within view of the camp. Catching her was easy enough, but the ride back toward my men was slow. The confusing din of the Hrals' initial charge had long passed, but I worried about being seen or caught in a new charge. Sure enough, I watched two more waves of Hrals dash through the undergrowth to cast themselves upon the fort. But I kept the stream within earshot and picked a careful route, encountering only a single Hral scout, who, very uncharacteristically for their race, ran away from me.

I passed the hill where I had left the group then followed every bend in the stream. Recalling Harsen's words that the beamed boulder and rock field were a half day beyond his Branbyen camp, I rode swiftly to catch up with them. The trees soon thinned, and the flat ground began a slight incline, turning the little stream into a pleasant cascade. Then the ground became more wrinkled and folded, as if the earth frowned at my trespass, forcing my horse to pay attention to his footing. After an hour or so, the canopy opened, and sunlight shone through. Small stones now jutted up from the earth like broken goose eggs, and they multiplied as we trotted up the incline.

After about three hours of swift riding, the forest behind me had completely given way to the rock field. Long grass waved in patches, and scattered hornbeams with crooked and fluted trunks bent around boulders planted long before the wind seeded the trees. These rocks were much larger now, as if drawn up out of the ground by the plentiful sunlight. Many were tall as men, nestled in the long grass and splotched with gray-green lichen. The stream I had followed wandered off and disappeared into a cleft in the ground under one of the outcrops.

Up the incline in the distance I could see the horses and men bunched in a shady copse of hornbeams. As I drew closer I saw their glum faces. Varesig paced back and forth. Rekef was not among them. I dismounted into the knee-high grass and tied the packhorse to a hornbeam, and all were silent. What had happened?

Harsen explained that wave after wave of Hrals had poured down on the palisade fort from all directions, cutting off their path to the rock field more than once. The heathens had realized our little band was no army and came after them. Bold Rekef made a decisive charge toward the fort to distract the Hrals, then nearly made his escape before being overwhelmed by their spears. Even the brave knight's steel armor could not protect him from their innumerable stone weapons.

Harsen said they had not attempted to recover his body but rode hard away from that place. When I looked at Varesig, expecting him to praise the honor of his best knight, he simply said. "Well, at least we have the mare."

The news of such an early loss was distressing. Rekef was no friend, but he was an honorable knight. He had always treated me with contempt though I was no more responsible for his brother's death than I was now for his. No doubt the third and eldest brother, Firkas, who had always treated me fairly, would now look upon me differently. Orren sat on a stony stool with tear-welled eyes while Varesig continued his pacing.

I asked the functionary if he wanted to continue the journey. Before he could answer, Harsen observed that the Hrals had likely overrun the fort, meaning Branbyen was again in barbarian hands. If we turned back onto the path from which we had come, we would share Rekef's fate. But if Varesig did want to end the expedition, we could turn northeast until we reached the Donovan Colony. But we might encounter Hrals on that path as well.

Varesig was undeterred and insisted we continue on, leaving Rekef's body to its fate. He displayed no emotion at the death of his trusted guard commander. He was merely agitated at the delay. Harsen pointed up the incline toward a massive boulder standing guard in the middle of the rock field. Harsen and I gave Rekef a last salute then pushed on toward the beamed boulder.

This part of the rock field was perhaps a marq in width and breadth, surrounded by forest on all sides. There was no sight or sound of heathens or animals, only the breezy rustle of the long grass crowded between the gaps of the broken rocks. Harsen slacked his reins to let his horse pick a careful path, and our steeds followed.

At last we drew up to the beamed boulder, which appeared exactly as he had described and twice as tall as a man. Its plain face and simple sapling poles was a dull reward, certainly inadequate for Rekef's sacrifice. But Orren's gloom became tempered excitement as he examined the lichen-encrusted stone. Harsen said he would find no markings or anything of note, but this did not deter the scholar from searching anyway.

Varesig looked upon the marker as he would any other rock, until Harsen announced that he would do the talking if any Gallerlanders wandered up. Orren, who probably knew much more of the Gali tongue, was annoyed. But Harsen had been here before and knew what he was doing.

The woodsman instructed us to brush our cloaks away to reveal our sword hilts. He said it was important to show we were armed, as the Gallerlanders always were. Harsen said they had never drawn their crudely hewn stone-blade weapons against him, but he still believed the plain sight of our steel was a necessary deterrent.

Harsen hauled himself up the side of the boulder, clutching one of the beams like a rope. He stood at the top and gazed out in every direction. Finally he said that if any Gallerlanders were nearby they would see him on their marker and know we wanted to make contact with them. The rest of us strolled about the boulder and waited.

Our anticipation grew as the afternoon wore on, and Varesig became impatient, insulted that his presence did not compel the Gallerlanders' immediate appearance. Harsen remained calm, and Orren eagerly scanned the wood line. For my part, I felt a bit nervous. This was not my first foray, but I felt vulnerable standing out in the open. I rubbed my shoulder, feeling the scarred tissue shift under my mail and remembering past battles.

My thoughts drifted back to Rekef's brother Onas. I had been Onas's lieutenant, one of several young officers assigned to his colonial troop sent to rid Mount Tremvig of the Hrals who had disrupted the construction of our watchtower there. From that valuable promontory we would be able to watch over the whole colony. The Hrals could do the same, if they held it. So we endeavored to build it and they often raided it.

I helped lead a fateful march up the mount to retake it. We defeated the Hrals, followed the stragglers back to their village, and left none alive. But their brethren in other villages soon swept over us, forcing us down into the marshes where my men buried their shame and anger by brutalizing peaceful Ollohds, who were themselves enemies of the Hrals. Onas was a foolish and headstrong commander, and he deserved the Ollohds' revenge, something Rekef and Firkas could never accept.

The Ollohd remain our allies to this day, but the guilt of what we did to them and even the vicious Hrals is a weightier burden to me now than it once was. I cannot help but wonder how relations will be with the Gallerlanders if we can find them. Harsen assures me their western clans are nearly as docile as the Ollohds, but, as the Donovards have discovered, the Gallerlanders are not to be underestimated. And we have no soldiers to come to our aid; we are potentially at their mercy.

Orren says the Gallerlanders are the largest tribe yet known in the New World, divided into many clans over many territories, suggesting their temperaments are as varied as the trees of the forest. The old scholar says the Gallerlanders are the key to the interior, something he did not explain but I'd like to hear more about.

As the afternoon faded into evening, Harsen squinted across the rock field with a frown, declaring that we had probably missed them passing by. We would camp at the boulder for the night. Varesig, who had contained himself reasonably well, now burst into a rage. He accused Harsen of leading us on a dead path with nothing to show for it except the loss of Rekef.

The woodsman remained calm and quiet, further maddening the functionary. Varesig intimated that perhaps Harsen had secretly untied Orren's packhorse to inflict disaster upon us. Harsen remained calm still. Varesig, his face reddened to purple, then suggested Harsen was in league with the Donovards, trying to steal the bounty of our expedition.

"What bounty?" I interrupted. We had come to the wilderness to set terms with the heathens, hardly a treasure the Donovards would covet. Harsen was the finest woodsman and tracker, and had it not been for him we would have all been hanging on the spear point of a Hral by now. Varesig stood alone in his rage, then stomped off like a spoiled child to kick rocks and fume. The rest of us lit a fire and made ourselves comfortable.

Night has fallen now. I've passed the time with a sketch of the beamed boulder and recounted the long day. Varesig eventually rejoined us. He whispered to me that he had expected me to support his decisions, as his new second in command. "Surely the great Rildning will comply with this humble request," he said. I told him that we would all support the right path to the Gallerlanders, as the governor would wish us to. He leaned back and smiled.

Midspring 5—Night

It is now the middle of the night. A bit earlier, we were all awakened by strange noises. We stoked the fire, but nothing within the light is moving except the tall grass in the night breeze. We sat and listened but were unable to tell if the sounds came from animals or men. They did not sound like wolves, but the horses were uneasy. It sounded birdlike, then ceased. We all feared the Hrals were upon us, but Harsen said we would be safe, reminding us that we were in Gallerlander territory now.

❧

The noises have not returned. Harsen believes they could have been the natives organizing their watch over us, but he has never heard such sounds before. I remember when my troop was besieged by low cries during the night upon Mount Tremvig. They were horrible sounds, like the cries of mountain lions, but we knew it was the Hrals trying to intimidate us or maybe coordinating their attack. But the sounds tonight were different.

Whatever they were, they have left us alone.

Midspring 6

arly this morning we delayed breaking our fast to look about the boulder and rock field for any sign of what had made the night sounds. But even with Harsen's expert tracking abilities, we found nothing.

Varesig reluctantly agreed to wait a bit longer for the Gallerlanders to reveal themselves. So we busied ourselves with gathering food during the midmorning hours to supplement our provisions. Harsen bagged two small rabbits with a bow, and Orren and I found several blackberry patches. We returned to the stream for fresh water and to clean the game. We took our time making a hearty stew of them, waiting until midday for the natives to appear.

They did not come. By midafternoon Harsen ventured that the Gallerlanders were not going to show themselves, though they were probably watching us day and night. He guessed that they were uneasy seeing several travelers with him and the lack of sheep or other goods he usually brought for trade. I pointed out the packhorses' bulky burden, but Harsen shrugged. At length, we broke camp and continued onward.

Harsen warned us that his map ended in the rock field. He did not know what lay ahead. If Varesig wanted to change his mind, now was the time to turn east to Donovan. Varesig, surprisingly amiable, assured the woodsman that he was prepared for a long journey and was determined to continue.

That the Gallerlanders were not waiting on the boulder was no cause for defeat, he said.

Before we pushed up the incline, Harsen once more climbed atop the boulder and neatly set out our two fresh rabbit pelts topped with a pile of plump blackberries. This, he said, was a gift of peace for the heathens. Then he pointed at the forest up ahead and said we would make for the mountain beyond.

"What mountain?" we asked. He said from the boulder perch he had seen a faint brownish-gray form peeking over the trees. It was too far away to know for sure, but Harsen believed it was a mountain named Elmbrel, which the Donovards referred to as the gateway to the deep interior of Gallerlandia, where no Brintilian had ever walked.

As we rode up the incline, Varesig took on Orren's studious attitude. From his horse he examined all the rock outcroppings within view, as if a Gallerlander would spring up from behind one. He dismounted once to heft up a large stone, turn it in his hands, then angrily shoved it to the ground. Odd, but I did not question our captain's sudden interest in stones.

We soon reached the wood line and stumbled into the source of the escaped stones of the rock field. A craggy ledge that had been hidden by the trees jutted up before us. There was no path for horses over or around the natural wall in either direction. I was reminded of the hidden berm at the beginning of our journey that acted, like this ledge wall, as a natural fortification of this vast forest. I wondered what other obstacles lay ahead and what secrets the great forests were hiding.

We chose to ride east along the ledge wall, slowly picking at its rocky terrain with our eyes, but we found no passage. When the leafy canopy grew dark, we made camp on the least miserable stony patch of earth we could find. Varesig was clearly angered by the paltry progress made today, though he spoke little.

Midspring 6—Night

We awoke tonight again to the same strange chirping noises. They were closer this time, or perhaps it was the echo off the stone cliff over our camp. We could not determine the direction from which the sounds came. The moon was brighter tonight, but we again saw nothing. The eerie sounds did not last as long as they had the night before and did not return again. If the makers of the sounds—natives or otherwise—mean us harm, I'm glad to have my trusty steel. It is the same sword that kept me alive on Mount Tremvig years ago.

Midspring 7

When we awoke this morning there was a single blackberry resting precariously on the kettle we used last night. When we looked about, we found several more arrayed in a line, a dotted path back toward the west. Following them on foot led us to a narrow cleave in the ledge wide enough for the horses to pass through. We had walked right by it in the dusk. Harsen is now sure the Gallerlanders were watching, but we're all puzzled by their apparent shyness.

He tried mimicking their night calls: *Hreeth! Hreeth! Yim-Blook!* But no voice returned the call. We returned to ready the horses, telling ourselves that sooner or later the Gallerlanders would come out of the bush. Varesig ignored me when I asked, in jest, whether the governor desired such taciturn heathens among his allies.

With the rock field and ledge behind us, we struck south. The forest thickened, and the earth leveled off again. Harsen led us, as he had previously, in the direction of Elmbrel. The ride was pleasant but unfortunately uneventful. My thoughts drifted to what lay beyond that mountain. I planned to climb it if we could. It surely harbored an unmatched view of the vastness of the continent.

We easily found a good campsite at day's end, but we were again disappointed that the heathens did not show themselves. So we busied ourselves with dinner and talk.

Over dried venison, hard biscuits, and handfuls of forest fruits and brown pearl mushrooms, I engaged Orren on what he had meant a few nights back when he said the Gallerlanders were the key to the interior of Pemonia.

He was happy to talk with me, saying this particular theory was simple. The Gallerlanders were known to control swaths of land bordering New Lorin and Donovan but also as far south as the Durgensdil Colony, which overlooked the Sea of Nore. It was possible they even controlled lands as far east as the Brewel Colony.

Harsen interrupted, saying the Bronhildi tribe near Brewel was distinct from the Gallerlanders. The scholar was a bit flustered by this challenge, saying Harsen was confused. He assured the woodsman, in a tone cherishing every detail of his expertise, that the Bronhildi were in fact a Gallerlander tribe. Harsen, smiling, continued to disagree, but Orren waved his hand dismissively. It was entertaining to see Orren, the proud scholar clearly jealous of Harsen's bookless, adventure-driven experiences, struggle to stake out a claim to tribal knowledge that Harsen lacked.

Orren continued, saying his point was that the Gallerlanders appeared to control much of what was known of the New World, except probably the scorched Far East. Since no one knew how vast Gallerlandia was, or indeed how far Pemonia stretched across the earth, the Gallerlanders could be the most powerful confederation of heathens on the continent. As such, Orren thought it wise that the governor was seeking an alliance with them. Varesig rolled his eyes and readied his bedroll.

I thanked Orren for his information. Eager to share his wealth of study, he suggested we might talk about the natives again, and I agreed.

Midspring 8

I awoke today refreshed. We expected to be startled again in the night with the Gallerlanders' calls, but we were permitted to sleep in peace. We also wondered if we would find a rabbit skin on the kettle, but our dewberry tea was left in peace.

This new region of forest was the most verdant we had laid eyes on. There were many tall, strong oaks and hickories and large bushes of wild roses. Over our midday meal I asked Harsen for his map. We were clearly well off into the blank vellum. I asked him to begin noting landmarks so we could return this way if needed. He had already drawn a jagged line for the ledge wall we had passed yesterday.

The ride was again easy, but by mid-day the forest grew dim with dark clouds overhead, and a drenching rain soon fell upon us. We rode on until Varesig ordered us to shelter under a grove of ancient yews. The spring rain was cold, not an unusual nuisance for soldiers; Varesig has grown too comfortable in the governor's house these past few years.

Even old Orren was unconcerned by the torrent and walked around the trees, talking merrily about the wood of yews, prized for making the empire's finest bows. Yews did not grow in the Old World, he said, thus colonial archers like Orren were better equipped than their brethren across the seas. He claimed the Durgensdil Colony had made its fortune exporting the wood to kingdoms throughout the empire. Varesig took keen interest, saying "At least something of value has been found on this journey!" The functionary kicked around small stones until the rain passed.

As the afternoon waned we heard the flow of water. We found a small river that meandered south, so we followed it toward its source. Unfortunately, by nightfall our path ended when the river revealed itself to be a tributary of a larger one, and we were marooned in the middle of the fork. Harsen noted this on the map as Two Rivers Camp. No longer limited to small glidiwots, we caught several larger slow-moving fish that were new to us. Green stripes, we call them. We hooked more than we could eat, so we'll smoke the rest overnight.

Midspring 9

This morning Harsen repeated his shrill *Hreeth!* calls, but still no answer. As we broke our fast we discussed whether to ford one of the rivers to escape the fork or turn back to find a different route. Varesig was adamant that we cross the smaller branch of the fork.

Harsen set out on foot to find a shallow portion while the rest of us unburdened the packhorses enough to evenly distribute the goods among all the horses. Harsen returned with the happy news that he had found a waist-deep crossing nearby. The river was not too swift, and we crossed it easily. One pouch of provisions was swept downriver, but it was nothing the fruits of the forest cannot replace.

While crossing, Harsen and I looked through the break in the trees and saw that the brownish-gray form in the distance was indeed a mountain. The lone mount boasted a rocky cliff face shrouded in gray mist. The imposing summit was barren of greenery but not high enough to keep its winter snow.

When we reached the riverbank and rested, Harsen checked the map. The mountain was surely Elmbrel, the earth gate of Gallerlandia. After nearly a week without sighting a single Gallerlander, we hope to find their tribes beyond the mount.

We continued on, keeping the river on our right throughout the day. When we camped for the night, it was clear our little band was growing weary of wandering without any sign of success. So to pass the evening I asked Orren to entertain us with a full accounting of his theories about the barbarians. Varesig protested that he did not want to hear any more of Orren's heretical nonsense.

But I insisted, saying I had not yet heard his arguments and wished to judge them for myself. Harsen also voiced his desire for some amusement. Orren, a broad smile wrinkling his face, did not wait for further objections from Varesig. The scribe soon showed himself to be an elegant storyteller, and his sudden confidence in his beliefs overshadowed his usual timidity.

The old man began by acknowledging that his views were controversial. He also professed himself a firm believer in the Messengian Church. He compared himself to the great Brintilian explorer Rin, saying Rin would never have discovered the New World had it not been for his outlandish belief that a new continent lay beyond the Edgewaters, those giant whirlpools that lurk between the Old and New Worlds.

More important, Orren said the kingdoms of the empire would not have had cause to reunite without Rin's discovery. Although the Brintilians still dominated imperial politics, the bounty of Pemonia was shared among all parts of the empire—all because of Rin's controversial theory, claimed the scribe.

For Orren, the discovery of the New World posed challenging questions to Messengianism that were mishandled by the Church, resulting in teachings about Pemonia that were misguided. He did not believe the natives were the monstrous spawn of Memelos, as taught by the priests, but rather the original peoples of the New World. They looked like us, save for their colorful body paints and leafed garments. They have similar qualities to us and they make weapons and huts as we would. Despite the violent and carnal nature of some tribes, like the Hrals, Orren believed all of the natives of Pemonia were the descendants of the Agnesci.

This last word caused Varesig to shout out "Heretic! Heretic!" but Orren did not cower. The scholar bolted up from his log seat, outstretched his arms, and looked up excitedly into the firelit canopy. His shadow was like a black giant tending a shady orchard of knowledge. Harsen and I smiled at his theater while Varesig stared in disbelief.

The old scholar continued by saying we were walking in the Agnesci's lost land of Aprelaebos, an assertion I know is condemned by all priests. I have never been as fervent in my devotion to religious matters as Varesig and other high knights are, but I'm well aware that the Messengian Church has long taught that the Agnesci and Almeric peoples were created by God as brethren, though they were divided—the Agnesci in Aprelaebos, the Almerics in Cedelaebos—to prevent their joining together and rising against the Creator. We Brintilians and other peoples of the Old World are the descendants of the Almerics. The ancient cradle of Cedelaebos still hosts the Holy Temple today.

Orren said the priests claim that the Almerics destroyed the Agnesci when the latter departed Aprelaebos in great ships to reunite with their Almeric brethren. And, as punishment for their unholy attempt to bring together what God had divided, God caused Aprelaebos to sink forever below the seas, leaving the Almerics as the sole rulers of the earth.

I remember that my grandfather, an original settler of New Lorin, had told me how Rin's discovery of Pemonia caused some Messengians to question the truth about these teachings, especially the sinking of Aprelaebos. Many questioners were branded heretics and collaborators of the Evil who is named Memelos, chained in the Deep Depths. My grandfather had witnessed the burning of an entire ship of new settlers because they came with the heretical purpose of reestablishing peace between the ancient Almeric and Agnesci bloodlines. Though he talked little about it, I knew that my grandfather had his own doubts about the teachings.

Like those early questioners, Orren asked how the natives could *not* be the children of the Agnesci. How could Pemonia be anything but Aprelaebos? The scribe went so far as to say that perhaps the great Rin himself also wondered when he first saw the natives, but could not say so himself. Orren said he has staked this claim in Rin's honor, at risk to his own life, because he believes the Almeric and Agnesci bloodlines can live together in Pemonia in the interests of a stronger, peaceful empire.

By now Varesig was struggling to contain himself. It was one thing for Orren to espouse his own heretical views. But to say that Rin, the founding father of Pemonia and devout Messengian, believed as Orren believed was too much for Varesig. Our captain took to his feet and pointed menacingly at the scribe. "Who are you to style yourself priest and re-write thousands of years of Messengian history?" he demanded.

Orren was steadfast, perhaps emboldened by our isolation in the wilderness, and countered that he was not rewriting but merely revealing what was already there. He claimed many settlers, knights, and nobles would never have braved the dangerous voyage across the seas without the high priests' exhortations to conquer this Kingdom of Memelos. The promise of crusading glory and fattened purses certainly drove some to the New World, but many were driven purely by religious duty, he said. Varesig and I were born among those powerful crusading families and needed no reminder of this. But there was truth in what Orren said.

The scribe returned his gaze to the darkened trees again. Calmly, he said Pemonia offered an escape from the repeating turmoil and rot of the Old World. Here, among the Agnesci's descendants, the empire could build a truly new world. This was why Orren so desired to join our expedition, he said, because he believed securing alliances with the Gallerlanders would lead us to learn more about all the tribes and to seek peace. He had many questions for them, he said, starting with why they sailed to Cedelaebos long ago, to their apparent ruin.

The slide of unsheathing steel cut into Orren's speech as Varesig prepared to strike him down. I wrenched the sword from him with some difficulty, earning myself an earful about disloyalty and treason, which in turn earned Varesig a cracking blow across the jaw. Harsen soon broke us apart with a hearty chuckle, saying we would not last long in the wilderness if we were already at each other's throats.

The woodsman was right. He had long made his peace with the heathens and was now playing peacemaker among us. But I did not apologize to Varesig and left him sitting where he fell, apparently stunned at my defense of Orren.

I was struck by the importance of what Orren had said, though someone like Varesig would never see it. I have been critical of what I believed to be the governor's ill-fated attempt to secure an alliance with the Gallerlanders, but I see now that our journey is indeed a broader opportunity for the peoples of the Old World to start fresh in the New, not simply acquire exotic trade. I do not know if Orren's words about the Agnesci are true, but seeking out the Gallerlanders in their own realm and on peaceful terms seems a good way to find out if such a people could be the key to the interior and a lasting peace.

Meanwhile I must watch Varesig carefully. I do not fear for myself or Harsen because Varesig does not have the courage to harm us, and he needs us out here, far from his comfortable chamber in the governor's palace. But the functionary appears to consider it his duty to enforce the Church's justice upon a professed heretic, no matter how far from the colony we are.

Midspring 10

Today marks a week since our expedition began. Everyone has grown frustrated with the lack of Gallerlanders, even Harsen. Perhaps they are watching us from afar, as the woodsman says, or perhaps they are absent from this area, since we've not heard their calls in three days.

We set out a pile of berries just within range of the firelight last night, hoping to attract them again, but this morning found they had been gobbled sloppily, perhaps by a raccoon or other night creature. Or perhaps Varesig stomped them. He has been dark and quiet all day.

Despite occasional foraging and fishing, we have eaten through nearly half of our provisions. I'm not concerned, given Harsen's abilities to find the bounties of the forest and my eye for mushrooms. But I do feel that this expedition could be much longer than we originally planned.

Harsen believes our luck will change once we reach the mountain of Elmbrel. The meandering deer paths and thick underbrush do not permit swift travel, but hopefully we will come to the foothills of Elmbrel by nightfall tomorrow.

Midspring 11

Yesterday and today have, again, been uneventful. We continued to push east and south, having parted ways with the river some time back because the rocky embankment and brambles forced us to find another path. We are now in the open forest again, which is green and lush as ever. We hunt when an opportunity presents itself, but so far a few rabbits and bush doves are the slim rewards.

The leafy canopy still hides Elmbrel, but Harsen believes we are getting close. The earth has steadily inclined and grown lumpy with many folds. Varesig, who has been lingering in the rear of our horse train, dismounted at one point without telling anyone.

I looked back as we crested a hill and saw his horse standing alone in the distance. I rode back and found our captain on his hands and knees, his head poked inside a small cave in the side of a ledge. When I asked him what he was doing, he bumped his head in surprise and was clearly embarrassed. He fumbled for words, settling on rabbit hunting.

"Did you find tiny bunnies under the stones?" I asked with a smile. At once he dropped fistfuls of rocks from his hands.

"Of course not!" he answered angrily, mounting his horse in a huff.

We rejoined the band without another word. I cannot guess what occupies his mind, but his growing interest in rocks since we left the Beamed Boulder is quite odd.

Midspring 12

Today was frightening. Our horses paced normally until we heard the howls. Harsen reacted like lightning, bolting off his horse and climbing atop a boulder to unleash a hail of arrows as the wolves descended upon us. Varesig, Orren, and I huddled our horses and defended the circle with our swords. The wolves were unlike any I had seen, with long legs and ochre fur striped with black. They were swift and leaped at us from a distance and from all directions. After we had cut down a half dozen of them, the pack retreated as quickly as it had arrived.

Harsen admitted he had never seen such wolves among the usual brown and grays of the New Lorin peninsula. The woodsman was apologetic, since he could often smell wolves or notice them tracking a horse line. But he also thought it odd that wolves would risk such large prey as us in the daylight of Midspring, when small animals were plentiful at dawn and dusk. Alas, we are truly in unfamiliar territory.

As I bound my horse's lacerated leg with cloth and ointment, I noticed the top of my own hand was gashed. It was swollen, yet I felt no pain. My companions' faces betrayed their worry. As he bandaged my hand, Harsen said we'll know within three days if I and my horse have contracted the wolf fever. I shrugged him off and insisted I would be fine, but I'm secretly troubled. The Hrals we encountered on Mount Tremvig and elsewhere had trained some coastal wolves to fight alongside them, and I had been scratched and bitten more than once. But the look of these monstrous wolves makes me wonder . . .

Before we departed, Harsen insisted that he be given time to skin a few of the beasts. Their pelts may be useful gifts for the Gallerlanders if we ever find them, he said, and their scent may help deter other packs. Varesig did not think it was worth our time, and neither did I, but there was no arguing with Harsen's wilderness sense. We did not keep the meat, however, because it reeked and we are not so needy for provisions. After an hour we continued our journey up the incline, wary of every rustle in the underbrush.

At our camp tonight, we keep a larger bonfire. I volunteered to stay up for the first watch but thankfully have heard no howling. Elmbrel is on my mind. That mysterious mountain feels so close. I have resolved that we must climb to its peak and view what no Brintilian eyes have viewed before. Surely it is a tower from which we can see the whole of Gallerlandia, if not the far coastlines of Pemonia.

The others, even Varesig, were equally excited about this prospect as we chatted over dinner. If I get the wolf fever at least I will have seen the New World from that promontory.

Midspring 13

Today was momentous, for Elmbrel stood before us when we broke into a clearing in the forest. The mountain stood proudly alone against a crisp blue sky, girdled in its own forest of beechwoods, maples, and apple trees. There were many stony paths among its surrounding hills and up its rock face.

Elmbrel was taller and broader than Mount Tremvig, but not as grand as we had imagined. It was welcoming. We stooped to fill our waterskins in a creek, then followed the shallow cascade up to the foot of the mountain. What relief to soak my swollen, tender hand in the cool water.

We dismounted and tied our steeds and packhorses to some trees. I asked Varesig if he wanted to keep the watch or climb. Already inspecting the loose rocks around us, he was shocked at the question and insisted he lead the way up. With Harsen as our guide, we started up the mountain and left the willing Orren to watch our horses.

We climbed with much energy, stopping often to take in every higher view. At first, the trees hid most of the scene from our eyes. Varesig, in keeping with his newfound interest, studied the rocky crevices and nooks more than the view. I tried not to let him or my throbbing hand detract from the excitement of seeing Gallerlandia from the top.

After an hour of climbing, Harsen said he heard something. We stopped and listened, but could detect nothing. So we climbed on. When he heard it again, Harsen climbed back down a bit to get a view of where we had left Orren and the horses. The woodsman waved us over, saying he could see the scribe jumping and shouting.

Varesig and I rushed over to Harsen's perch. There was Orren, frantically waving his hands and standing a bit up the rocky path from where we had left him. Harsen pointed. "Look! Look there, at the forest's edge!" As we shifted our eyes we caught the form of a man running into the woods.

Harsen reasoned it must have been a Gallerlander who spooked Orren, since it was the first man we've seen since the Hrals, and this is Gallerlander territory. But he couldn't be certain. He recommended that we quickly get off the mountain, and he would track the man. I was torn, not wanting to abandon the view we had been seeking. Varesig anxiously looked about the rocks as if he had lost something. Clearly he did not want to leave either, but Harsen was adamant. If this journey was to seek out the Gallerlanders, that man below was the closest we had come in ten days of travel. The natives were down there, not up on the mountain, he said.

Varesig and I reluctantly gave in. We scurried down Elmbrel as fast as we could, the three of us tripping and burdened with armor that we should have left with the horses. I cradled my throbbing hand but kept the pain to myself.

Orren met us near the bottom. As we trotted to the horses he said that a fur-garbed man with painted skin had tried to steal from the packhorses before Orren frightened him away. Orren had not seen where the man had come from, but the heathen ran east into the forest. We mounted and rode in that direction, with Harsen in the lead.

The woodsman scanned the forest floor with a careful eye. Not a single broken twig, freshly pressed moss, or turned leaf escaped him. We lagged behind to give him space, as he would often double back to regain the trail. Before long he led us to the sodden banks of a stream that carried bare footprints that even I could see. But they soon disappeared, and Harsen could not regain them. So we continued to follow the stream in hopes that another clue would be found.

As nightfall approached we found a gentle bend in the stream wherein a campsite had been made earlier. Harsen examined the circle of stones and bits of char, saying someone had slept here the night before. This excited us, so we camped here in hopes that the Gallerlander was not far. We hoped to be awakened by night calling.

Midspring 14

We were not alone, but not as we expected. As we emerged from our bedrolls this morning, we were surprised to see a rough-looking man with fern fronds in his hair watching silently from a perch on a small boulder no less than ten paces from the campfire. Before I saw him, I awoke lamenting the lack of native sounds during the night. Then there he was, a motionless form hunched upon the rock like a stuffed squirrel, dark eyes sharp and staring. After a startle, we reached for our swords, but he did not flinch.

Feeling little threat from the frail-looking form, Harsen spoke a few words in the Gali tongue. He received no response, so I attempted to greet the man in Brintilian. There was a long pause, then he answered, "Who are you? Fire stealers?"

Harsen and I glanced at each other in astonishment. The scrawny man shifted and scratched violently at his dirty tuft of sandy hair, whispering "fire stealers . . ." over and over again to himself. Clearly a Brintilian man of sorts, but he was no Gallerlander.

I felt the urge to correct his odd accusation, saying we were travelers looking for the Gallerlander peoples, not stealing his fire. The little man glared at me, then at the smoldering ashes of the campfire. Orren quickly stoked the coals. We had clearly stolen his campsite. Harsen explained that we had only stopped for the night and that the fire was still there, sleeping under the coals. We bade the man to sit and eat, which he accepted without a word.

The meal was silent and uncomfortable, as the man was uneasy with us, and we with him. He looked as though he had lived in the wilderness for years, and smelled as if he slept in a bear den. His fingers were spindly and the nails long and packed with dirt, his bare limbs lanky and scarred, his teeth half-rotted. He was barefoot, his feet canvased with calluses and grime.

He hunched over and protected his plate with shifty eyes but did not eat as if he was starving. When Harsen offered him more of our berry-studded porridge, I noticed a glint under the man's matted fur tunic when he reached for the bowl. Varesig noticed it too and put his hand on his sword hilt. I calmed the captain, and we took a closer look. It was a shirt of gleaming new mail.

No longer able to contain my curiosity, I asked him who he was. In response to my careful questions, we learned that he was from the Donovan Colony. He had been a soldier of that settlement some time ago, but could not remember how long it had been, at least six or seven years he reckoned, maybe ten. He said his name was Arvgred.

With a jesting smile I asked whether his mother had named him after the great warrior Arvgred of Durnam, the long-deceased successor of Helcirk Donovan the Founder himself. The wildman was not amused. He said in a most serious tone, "I am he, who else could I be?" Now the little hermit appeared to be a madman.

Without warning he dropped his bowl and jumped to his feet and spread his arms wide, saying all of these woods were his land, "The Land of Arvgred of Durnam!" Then he abruptly reseated himself and resumed chewing.

Varesig and I both noticed that the man's short spectacle more fully revealed the mail under his tunic. It brought a smile to my face, but Varesig's reddened with anger. The functionary marched over to his horse and went through every pouch and sack, then returned empty-handed to accuse Arvgred of stealing his spare shirt of mail. He turned to Orren, saying, "And you let him do it!"

I calmly told Varesig to sit down, that this was no way to treat the little man. Harsen piped in, saying Arvgred might help us find the Gallerlanders, and wasn't that what Varesig wanted? The captain returned to his log bench and stifled his anger. The hermit smiled at Varesig but did not confess the theft.

The wildman asked me if we wanted to find the Gallerlanders, which I confirmed. He laughed, and laughed some more, then said, "They are there!" We snapped our heads to see where he pointed, but it was only forest. "And there and there!" he continued. Arvgred said the Gallerlanders were all around, "In the trees and in the bush, even in the streams, maybe in the clouds!" And he laughed some more.

Harsen smiled, clearly enjoying the theater, while Orren was perplexed by Arvgred. Sensing that Varesig's thin patience was wearing thinner, I asked the wildman to tell us more about how he came to be so far out here in the woods. I added that we did not think any New Loriners or Donovards had come this far into the continent.

Arvgred chuckled at this, too. He said he had once led a troop tasked with scouting the lands southwest of Donovan Colony in search of a land route to Durgensdil, that cliff-hugging colony far south and west around the continent from New Lorin and Donovan. We were all astonished to hear that the Donovards, even with their characteristic aggressiveness, would attempt a land route through Gallerlandia to Durgensdil.

Arvgred's speech was halting and unpracticed, but we learned his unit had been ambushed and overrun by the natives. He alone survived, as far as he knew, but he became lost. His shame killed his desire to find his way back and he was determined to destroy as many heathens as he could before they took his life. Yet he lived still, even after allegedly killing hundreds of Gallerlanders over the years. Harsen stifled a chuckle, asking how he could accomplish this feat alone. Arvgred's simple reply was "I am Arvgred of Durnam!"

After adjusting the fern fronds in his hair, the wildman finished his tale by claiming he had killed a heathen in this wood not two days ago, and pointed to a small necklace about his neck. Harsen took a closer look, describing it as clay beads inlaid with greenish gold and woven into rough-grass twine. It was similar to those worn by Gallerlanders with whom he had traded near New Lorin. Harsen said they called the green-golden metal *electrum*, but he had rarely seen it.

Harsen jested with Arvgred that he hoped the wildman hadn't killed anyone he knew. By now Varesig was looking over Harsen's shoulder at Arvgred's necklace, staring with covetous eyes, but the functionary did not speak. Arvgred ignored Harsen's jest, saying he would finish off the heathens by raiding a village southeast of our campsite where the forest became dense and he could easily hide among the ferns. He loved the ferns, he said repeatedly.

I noticed that the wildman was eyeing our horses as he spoke, perhaps for food or flight, and an idea came to me. I told him that we would offer him one of the packhorses if he led us to the Gallerlander village of which he spoke. Varesig quickly voiced his support. But I added that Arvgred would have to depart the village without bloodshed. We wished to speak with the heathens, not fight them, I explained. Harsen suggested that the noble packhorse, with all his strength and dependability, would be a great prize.

The wildman considered our offer as he fiercely lashed and scratched at his hair. He was puzzled. "You don't want to kill them?"

I shook my head.

He shrugged and nodded, saying we must stop at his "home tree" first, which lay along the path to the village. We agreed, then he pointed to his chest. "And the shirt of mail?" I grinned, saying he could keep it if everything went as planned. I could almost hear Varesig gritting his teeth at the sight of his richly made armor being worn by the clever stinking hermit.

We packed up the camp, and Harsen transferred half of the baggage from a packhorse to our steeds to make room for Arvgred to ride it. It was entertaining to watch the wildman mount the horse. He paced around the animal as if looking for stairs. Only after putting a hand in a stirrup did he remember how to mount.

The forest was growing dark by the time we reached the tree in which Arvgred lived. Harsen and I were astonished to see him effortlessly leap up into the branches of the massive ancient yew. Orren marveled that it was the largest yew he had ever laid eyes on.

The wildman disappeared with scarcely a sound then poked his dirty face out of the flat-needle leaves above. He grinned ghoulishly down. Clearly no man had ever seen his woodland abode, and he was proud to show it off. He hurriedly waved us up, so Harsen and I dismounted and clambered up. Only with much persuasion did Varesig follow. But the aged Orren, unable to climb well with his one hand, was again content to watch over our horses.

When we at last penetrated the canopy of the lower twisted boughs, we entered a surprisingly spacious hollow portion around the great trunk, surrounded by walls of branches. Arvgred had pruned and sculpted the inner tree to fashion a chamber around the trunk, with small logs fastened together for a platform on which a little wooden bed was set. Upon the bed was a leathern blanket stuffed with feathers, thistledown, and dry grass that peeked through the rough-sewn seams.

On branches in all directions hung crude ornaments of colored stones and dried flowers, tied with long-grass twine. Dried bits of fern and the bones of small animals also lay strewn about, and more Gallerlander beaded necklaces were collected like trophies in a corner of the platform.

As we marveled at his secret home, Arvgred reached into a hidden niche under the bedframe and pulled out a roll of brown deer hide. He uncovered a few unseen items, then scrambled over to a knob in the tree trunk that had been hollowed out like a bowl and reached his spindly fingers inside. He assembled these things on the bed with his back toward us, silently touching his face. He fastened more beads to his wrists, and a metallic ting was heard.

Finally he whirled around and growled, brandishing a stone-bladed knife. A grim smile split his green-painted face. Varesig's hand crept to his own sword hilt as Arvgred withdrew the primitive-looking weapon. He explained that this costume was how we would approach the Gallerlander camp and get close to the inhabitants. The tactic had always worked for him when the ensemble was completed with grass-lined moccasins and a fur tunic that hung from a peg above his bed.

I voiced my hesitation about such a plan, but Arvgred had already made up his strange little mind. Varesig meanwhile expressed interest in the pile of greenish-golden necklaces. Arvgred let him hold one, saying the Gallerlanders considered the metal to be sacred and probably used it for evil rituals.

Harsen also examined them and handed me one, repeating that he had seen little of the electrum among the Gallerlander traders. The clay beads were inlaid with the greenish gold like the one around Arvgred's neck. The necklace I held was heavy in my hands and soft to the touch, but it did not have the brilliant twinkle or smell of gold when rubbed vigorously. It was green-hued as if cloaked in patina, but kept a faint glow when cupped in the hands.

Harsen asked the wildman if the electrum was real gold. Arvgred did not know but said the heathens did not use money. Harsen nodded, saying his trade with the Gallerlanders was always bartering, with no coins changing hands. Arvgred said the electrum, in any form, was rarely brought out from the depths of the forest by the heathens, repeating that it was sacred to them. He waved the stone blade again, noting that the heathens would not even use the electrum—or any metal—to make better weapons.

I handed the necklace back to Arvgred and thanked him for sharing his knowledge, but said we had no need to dress in Gallerlander garb and paint. We needed to meet them openly, as we were, representatives of New Lorin, rather than attempt to fool them. The wildman was unimpressed and turned away from me.

It was growing dark so Arvgred lit a lump candle of beeswax, one of several posted around the yew chamber. He sparked the flame by quickly rubbing sticks together, a method he claimed to have learned from spying on the Gallerlanders. Then he prepared to build a small fire upon a slate-tiled section of the platform, but we decided to take our meal down on the ground where Orren waited. Arvgred was pleased to eat our food again.

As we prepared the meal Arvgred asked whether it was wolves that had wounded my hand. I was surprised that he could guess this. He smiled and said that the pack of "bane wolves" had passed through this area as well, and that they roam the forests that lie within view of Elmbrel, guarding it like sentinels at a gate. He believes the mountain is cursed by the Gallerlanders and that the wolves have emerged from its crevices to protect the realm.

He bounded up into his tree and returned with a small leathern pouch. I unwound the cloth around my puffy hand, the veins now beginning to bulge. He examined it with a grimace, but declared I would not get wolf fever if I applied his medicine. From the pouch he pulled out what Harsen identified as purple coneflower.

Arvgred wetted the herb and mushed it into a paste with stones. He applied the sweet-smelling salve to my hand with cooling effect. Then he put the remainder of the paste in my waterskin and shook it, telling me to consume the remainder. "To kill the curse put into your blood," he said. The hermit hardly resembled a physician, but I had little to lose from trusting his care.

We listened to his stories of fighting the Gallerlanders as we ate. He had nearly been killed on several occasions, and he showed us one ugly scar down the length of his back, saying stone weapons inflict tearing wounds that often leave jagged shards behind. I thought of Rekef's fall under the stone-tipped spears of the Hrals.

After surviving several terrible wounds, Arvgred changed his tactics. He learned the movements of the Gallerlanders' posted watch, and he would slip into the heathen villages in the dead of night when there was no moon. He slew two Gallerlander chieftains secretly in their beds in one night, he said. I would not have believed him had he not pulled yet another trophy necklace from a secret pouch in his tunic, taken from the neck of one of the chiefs, he said. This one was decorated with intricate etchings.

Our eyes watched the firelight dance in the jewelry made solely of shimmering electrum. Varesig insisted on holding it and tried it on. The functionary asked many questions about where the Gallerlanders mined and shaped their electrum, but Arvgred had no answers that satisfied him.

Close examination revealed carvings on each square bead. The etchings were distinct from others we had seen from the Ollohd or Hral tribes. While Varesig and Harsen remained enamored with the electrum itself, Orren and I were most fascinated in what was clearly the Gallerlanders' own form of writing. I have attempted to sketch a sampling of these symbols. Despite their claim to some knowledge of the Gali tongue, neither Orren nor Harsen knew what the markings meant.

When we had grown weary of the wildman's tales, more and more embellished as the night went on, we laid our bedrolls on the forest floor. Arvgred retired in his tree. The leafy thickness of the yew's boughs did not let much of the candlelight escape, but the warm glow above us noticeably faded as he blew the candles out one by one.

Varesig quipped that the little man was like a raccoon, sleeping in a tree and hoarding his shiny treasures. Harsen agreed that he had seen nothing like it even among his most intrepid woodsmen brethren.

As the men sleep and I finish this chronicle of the day, my last thoughts are on the Gallerlanders. The farther we tread into their woods the more mysterious they become. I hope we can depend on our new friend to lead us to their village peacefully. Can he who has dedicated his life to killing the heathens now approach them without raising a weapon? I wonder the same about Varesig. Both of these men are unpredictable.

And what of the Gallerlanders? Surely they will recognize Arvgred as their marauding enemy. Even if they do not, will the Gallerlanders welcome this band of colonists?

Midspring 15

When we awoke today, my hand felt and looked much better. The hermit knew something about healing the bite of the bane wolf after all, and for that I'm thankful.

While the men packed camp, I climbed back up the tree to seek out Arvgred. He was not in his leafy quarters, so I guessed that he had climbed farther up, since we had not seen him descend. I heaved myself higher until the branches became thin, and I swayed in the morning breeze. The wildman's heavy stench told me I was approaching him.

I found him perched like a bird on the highest branch, knees at chin and toes clutching the branch. He motioned at the sky, saying the weather would make for a good journey. It was then that I spotted a mountain range in the distance to the west and south, and beyond it the distant glimmer of the Sea of Nore. These mountains were certainly the Bomlofoss, a great ridge that, along with its Hral inhabitants, had long blocked any Brintilian exploration farther inland. And there I was, peering at its eastern slopes from a treetop in the interior.

I commented on the beautiful view, glad to have seen it since abandoning Elmbrel. Arvgred was silent and avoided eye contact, as he often did when speaking or being spoken to. I asked him why he chose to build his shelter in the old yew. He was silent for a moment, as if he had forgotten my question, then he said it's what the *clever* Gallerlanders do. He clarified that the village we would visit was built on the ground, like many others, but that beyond the depths of the forest the heathens lived in trees larger than any I could ever dream of. I asked about these depths, but he proceeded to climb down without another word. And so we began our travel to the village, continuing east.

We believe Arvgred has more or less told us the truth about his past and his intentions to help us. But one cannot see his former days as a soldier in his current difficulty in riding a horse, which has proved entertaining. It has clearly been too long for him, though he still speaks Brintilian well enough. Aside from the entertainment he provides, Arvgred is adept at catching woodland animals and birds straight from the bush.

His only weapons are the small heathen stone knife and a crude hammer, merely a rock bound with twine to a short stave that doubles as a walking stick. Throughout our journey today he has caught more food than any one of us during our whole expedition, and we are grateful to him for restocking our supplies.

Watching him has also been instructive. He has shown us a new way of curing and preserving food by wrapping strips of raw meat in the leaves of an herb he calls *solin*. When asked, he freely admitted that he learned this and other techniques from his Gallerlander enemies.

The day's travel east took a southerly bent as we followed the mounted hermit. The ride was pleasant and easy along deer paths between gentle woodland hills. Arvgred explained that the area was partially bordered by a vast swampland fed by every stream in these hills. He steered us around a great bog, which he predicted we would have walked into, absent his guidance.

Arvgred told us he had never attempted to cross the swamp. He had seen mysterious lights there at night, possibly heathen campsites, so Harsen named its general location Swamp of Lights on the map. We must take care to avoid it on our way back to the colonies. I do not wish to repeat the dangerous circumstances I faced in the Onas Marshes beneath Mount Tremvig years ago.

Tonight at camp, Arvgred asked why we wanted to find the Gallerlander village if we did not want to kill them. Harsen repeated our aim and mentioned his trading with the heathens, but Arvgred could not understand. He scowled, then flashed his broken teeth and spat into the fire. "They are dirty!" he scoffed. We withheld our opinion that he looked, smelled, and largely acted the part of a heathen himself.

After a few more sneers he asked whether the colonies were still fighting the heathens of Pemonia. We told him that the Donovards were perpetually fighting the natives. While fighting still occurred in some areas from time to time in New Lorin, we hoped our expedition to find allies would help change that. He spat again at the flames. "Have you never seen their evil?" he asked. "Ever fought them yourself?" Harsen looked at me and Varesig, knowing full well the answer.

Varesig had no desire to banter with the hermit, but I wished to make him more comfortable with us so allowed myself to be goaded by him. I told him he and I were, in fact, not dissimilar in that my colonial troop had been ambushed by heathens, in my case the vicious Hrals.

I told him about the watchtower that New Lorin had endeavored to build upon Mount Tremvig nearly a decade ago and how our soldiers and masons were repeatedly overrun by the Hrals. We found our comrades' bodies in the wood that crowned Tremvig's bald, flat summit with grisly heathen runes carved on their brows and in the palms of their hands.

Brave craftsmen began the work anew under the protection of my unit, but we were attacked repeatedly. We fought bravely but were outnumbered, and our escape to the colony was choked off. So we fled down the opposite side of the mountain where we found ourselves trapped by marshes and the sea. With our pursuers close behind, we opted to hide in the scrub and reeds of the marshes.

Lacking provisions and fresh water, two of our men died quickly from disease. Another one took a bad step, and his armor anchored him to the bottom of a submerged pit. And another succumbed to earlier wounds. The Hrals knew we had sheltered in the marshes and waited us out. Every attempt we made to extricate ourselves from the muck was turned back with arrows shot from their hidden places.

One hazy morning we awoke from our soggy reed beds to find berry bunches and herbs placed upon nearby stones that jutted up just above the tainted water. With our minds dulled by hunger, we considered the food heaven-sent and ate ravenously. Though some berries looked poisonous, with bright warning colors, they were a tasty and fulfilling good omen that allowed us to identify the edible plants around us.

We were then surprised to see heathen runes drawn in oily paint on the stones beneath the food. Knowing that our commander, Onas, Rekef's brother, had little patience for distinguishing one tribe from another, I pointed out that the symbols were entirely different from Hral signs. But he was blinded by sudden rage that we had been tricked into eating "the nourishment of Memelos," as he put it. He was certain our bellies and souls were now poisoned by the devil himself.

When more of the food mysteriously appeared the next morning, he forbade us from consuming it, stomping and kicking it into the swamp. This and his other foolishness dispirited the men. We feared that the knight captain's refusal to try another escape from the marsh was resigning us to a sodden grave.

At dawn on the third day of food offering, our youngest soldier welcomed three heathens, who were not Hrals, wading across the water and bearing reed baskets piled high with exotic foods. But Onas, eyes enflamed by the sudden sight of the natives, swiftly and repeatedly hacked at them with his great sword.

Sadly, all three natives perished, and all were unarmed. It was only then that Onas accepted that their clothing and body paint, like the food runes, was not of the Hrals. But it was too late. A jarring wail of sorrow and anger rang out from the foggy reed-forests and hidden places of the marsh in every direction. The reeds rustled violently, as if the marshland itself wept for the blood spilled into it.

Then silence. When we awoke the next morning, we found Onas facedown in the dark waters, leeches clogging his slit throat. And there was no food offering. Later, when we returned to the colony, Rekef could not believe we had heard no struggle, nothing during the night. Thus his confident accusation that we somehow allowed Onas's death. He could never accept the truth.

I assumed command of the frightened men. We resolved to leave the marshes, come what may. We abandoned our armor and anything that would slow us down, then made ourselves ready. Arrows whizzed among us as we ran, felling two of my men, but we pushed on. As we found cover to plan our next run, out from the bushes sprang the friendly natives. Armed only with reed poles and yelling their battle cry, they ran toward the hidden Hrals. Others gestured for us to follow them in a different direction.

My ill and panicked men could not easily discern friendly native from Hral, and I believe one of the helpful ones was mistakenly slain by my soldiers. I could tell the difference, but what could I have done in those moments? I mustered my men, and we escaped in the direction the natives beckoned. Eventually we made it back to dry land and eventually the colony. Only five of our unit survived, including me.

Having reflected much on those days on Tremvig and in the marshes, now named for our foolish commander who perished there, we now know that we had encountered a peaceful clan of the Ollohd tribe. They repeatedly came to our aid even when met with hostility, later earning themselves a full alliance with New Lorin against the Hrals, at my urging. Orren piped in, adding that those marsh natives still have a blood feud to settle with the Hrals that is unlikely to ever be extinguished. Regardless of their determined motives, however, I have borne the guilt for the Ollohds who died by our hands.

When my story was finished, Arvgred, who had listened intently, squinted and merely said, "Fantastical tale." I was struck by the wildman's hardened heart. Arvgred rebuked me for lacking hatred for the heathens of any and all tribes. I was unfit for the wilds of Pemonia, where only the strongest and boldest survive. I told him that it may be so, but that I would choose to help build a more peaceful New World different from the tumultuous Old World if I could.

Varesig merrily slapped my back. "You sound like heretic Orren," he said. The scribe beamed with pride at the comparison, but I told Varesig that his soul was surely burdened by more crimes than mine or Orren's, even if Varesig could not feel the weight. Our commander laughed and told me to listen to the wisdom of the little wildman. Arvgred bristled and corrected Varesig by saying he was a "wilderman." The functionary skeptically asked the difference.

Arvgred shot up from his stump seat, saying he was a "wilderness man," not a mad, reclusive barbarian. He stomped over toward his new horse and lay in the grass to sleep. Varesig quipped in a low voice that perhaps the hermit was both wilderman and mad. Harsen and Orren could not stifle a chuckle, but I took no pleasure in his insulting our valuable guide. Varesig no doubt felt himself entitled because of his stolen mail shirt.

Before I close my journal tonight, I wish to write, for future eyes, that my heart still lies heavy with those events in the Onas Marshes and upon Mount Tremvig. Not only for those dangerous days and the men lost, but for the wasteful battles between the gentle Ollohd peoples and the murderous Hrals. Only later and out of necessity did New Lorin join hands with the marsh clans against their more numerous enemy, the Hrals. It is my sincere hope that we will secure a swift alliance with the Gallerlanders.

PART II

THE THICKNESS

Midspring 16

This morning we awoke in a dim light under a heavy gray sky. We broke camp after a surprisingly good meal prepared by Arvgred. He was less moody, and the scowls of the previous night were replaced with smiles displaying his ruined teeth. He was genuine enough and gave a wilderman's apology for his bitterness, saying that his manners were long ago overcome by animal instincts. Harsen told him he was welcome to travel with us and eventually return to the colonies, but Arvgred gave no response.

We continued south until we found ourselves overlooking the lip of a treeless ridge too steep for the horses to descend. It provided an excellent view of the realm despite an ominously darkened sky. Below us lay a vast sea of unbroken forest. Near the horizon was a ribbon of water that wound through the unending green.

Arvgred said the ridge marked the end of the rocky Bomlofoss terrain and that the barbarians' deep woodlands lay below. The distant glimmer was a great unnamed river, he said, and beyond it was the heart of Gallerlandia. Arvgred lowered his voice to a whisper, saying the great forest feared outsiders and grew a dense wall with watching towers around its center, so travel would become more difficult from here if we dared to go farther inland later.

But for now, the Gallerlander village we sought was a mere six hours from the ridge. The wilderman advised that we wait for better weather, as a hard rain would soon be upon us. Varesig rightly insisted we continue, since the day had barely begun.

Arvgred shrugged, and we followed him onward. He knew a narrow deer path that switchbacked through breaks in the rocks and down the ridge. We soon came to flat ground where a few trees populated the foot of the ridge. Sycamores and white oaks, poplars and lindens quickly multiplied around us. Within only a marq or so the trees drew closer and closer together, their roots entangling and branches mingling. The path was fraught with roots that knotted up in strangled bundles until there was no path at all. We were forced to dismount and lead the horses.

By now the rain had started as Arvgred predicted. It was slow and heavy, accompanied by occasional thunder muffled by the great quilts of leaf and bark above. When we paused to don cloaks, Arvgred said the rains were the first defense of the deep forest. Less light now shone through the canopy above, making it increasingly difficult to pick a path through the black pools that formed amid the pits and trenches between the root knots. We stumbled on slowly and without cheer, wondering what tricks the forest would surprise us with next.

After a while we came upon a little mound of earth pushed up at the foot of a great poplar, its old gray trunk deeply fissured like the brow of a menacing warden. We fastened the horses and climbed up the staircase of roots to sit under its shelter. We ate a meager meal, watching and listening to the steady drumbeat of the rain.

Harsen offhandedly asked Arvgred when we would turn east, but the woodsman's tone suggested he knew more than Arvgred would say. The thick woods and darkened sky had confounded my sense of direction. Harsen kept his bearing but remained concerned. Arvgred appeared to feign surprise, saying he was steering us around an impossibly dense portion of the forest. Clearly unsatisfied, Harsen shot me a worried glance.

We continued after the miserable meal, still heading solidly south by Harsen's reckoning. The rain fell harder for several hours, so we continued to trudge on by foot to let the horses ease their steps in the muck. Poor Orren lost his footing, tripped by a root bundle, and splashed headfirst into a dark pool, completely submerged.

Harsen swiftly extracted Orren from the earthen bowl. Already soaked but now muddied, with bits of turf and moss in his teeth, we shook out his boots and cloak. Arvgred stifled a grin and unnecessarily urged careful steps to avoid the traps laid by the perilous forest. After a brief rest, we pushed on.

When the remaining light faded under the downpour, Varesig reluctantly ordered a halt. In frustration, our commander demanded details of the exact path ahead. Harsen added that he wanted to know the distance to the Gallerlander village that the wilderman originally claimed this morning had been only six hours away. And why had we not yet turned east?

Arvgred flashed his teeth at Varesig, screaming that he was enlisted as a guide but not trusted for the task. Varesig, always too eager for a fight, rashly drew his sword. Arvgred drew his knife. Harsen stepped between them and calmly said that our trust had waned because the wilderman had not mentioned his long detour when first speaking of the village and had not provided a convincing explanation.

I suggested we find a dry spot to rest for the night and sort things out in the morning, hopefully under clearer skies. And so the quarrel was deferred. We found a raised bank of earth pushed up between two large oaks, which Harsen marked on the map as Rain Camp.

The ink on the page does not dry well . . .

Midspring 17

Harsen should have named this soggy place Camp of Fools or Camp of Betrayal. We awoke to find that Arvgred had abandoned us; anger and embarrassment followed. What's more, he took the supplies-laden packhorse that we had promised him as well as Harsen's horse, so a great portion of our food is gone.

We heard nothing during the night. Arvgred left a fern frond on each of us as we slept, perhaps as a warning and certainly as a testament of his skill. Orren and I were surprised, and Harsen, the expert woodsman, was ashamed that he had not detected anything. But Varesig was most furious. He hacked and cursed at the drenched earth and nearby branches until his rage subsided. The forest breathed a light wind to taunt us and the wobbling poplar leaves chuckled and winked.

When Varesig had calmed, I told him we should count ourselves lucky that Arvgred did not kill us—and particularly him—while we slept, as he did those Gallerlander chieftains. Varesig nodded soberly. I knew he wanted to blame one of us, but he didn't. We had walked into this trouble together.

Harsen took stock of our food and reckoned we had two days' worth of meals if we rationed carefully between the four of us. I noted these precious foods so we can better ration them:

Six rabbit haunches preserved in solin herb
One small bag of ale-stout mushrooms
Five solin-cured green-stripe fish
A stack of hard biscuits
Three handfuls of bitterleaf bulbs

Cheery as ever, the dauntless woodsman encouraged us not to worry. We could forage, hunt, and fish until we found the Gallerlander village, if it existed at all, though gathering food would slow us. Varesig decided we should continue the search at once then forage after two days if we had not found the village. Before moving on we also took stock of our essential remaining equipment. As with the food, there is a certain satisfaction, and certainly comfort, in seeing the items listed:

One set of bedrolls, blankets, and rain cloaks each
One set of boots and clothing each
Rope bundle
Three short swords (Harsen's was stolen with his horse)
Two knives and one hatchet
One spare light shirt of mail (mine)
One spare padded metal-scaled tunic (Orren's)
Four horses
Three candles and small bag of flints
The journal, map, quill, and inkpot in my oilskin pouch
Five waterskins (easily refilled in the swollen streams)
One cooking pot and one spoon

Harsen, gladly mounting the remaining packhorse, suggested we turn east toward the heart of the forest in hopes that the woodland abodes of the Gallerlanders would lie there. And so we struck out, though our path ahead was uncertain.

The forest was in a foul mood despite its long drink of rain, perhaps because the deluge had not foiled us. The trees huddled closer and closer together as if plotting how next to block our way and shut out the sun. Their knobbly arms reached down to us, often forcing us to duck and crouch and sometimes making it impossible to ride.

The root-strewn earth, unable to be quickly warmed by the sun hidden above the thick canopy, remained pocked with muddy pools. Slick moss covered everything. But we carried on all day until we came to a weary rest at night.

Midspring 19

Two days have passed since Arvgred's treachery, but our slog through the thickened forest has hardened our resolve. By midday our soggy spirits were lifted by the distant sound of rushing water. Surely this was the great unnamed river we had seen from Elmbrel's ridgelands. We quickened our pace, slashing through jumbled vines and brambles. It was not until we stood on the riverbank itself that we could finally see the flowing water.

We were enthralled by the sight and sound. The river was wide and swift, with scattered rapids and frothy water. We marveled at its sun-sparkled beauty, deep and swollen with the rains of the past two days. The sound of the river and the golden warmth of the sun were refreshing after our trudge through the shadowy wood. The smell of sunny banks and fresh churn cleared the mind.

We left our steeds to drink while we stepped out upon a boulder that jutted out into the flow, looking up and down the river. As we sit soaking in the sun, I am compelled to write.

From the previous ridge we saw the river cut from the south to the north, and Harsen has guessed that it empties into the Bay of Pemonia. If he is correct, the river is likely that which formed the old eastern boundary of Donovan Colony. Given this is the first river of its size we have encountered, and the pace of our journey thus far, his guess is probably accurate, and thus the great river is not nameless.

It must be the Glombruk, named in honor of Sir Glom Stimril, that ancient Almeric knight who perished while fording with his legion across a river while in service to Lord Wilhargant, father of the extinct Almeric Empire. The Donovards believe the river drains much of the Pemonian continent, but we remain ignorant of the bounds of the New World.

For this reason I'm tempted to give up searching for the elusive Gallerlanders and instead hunt for the source of this mighty river. But Harsen pointed out that it could be longer than we are ready to follow, and Varesig would never allow it. Alas, the paths we choose not to tread provide endless speculations later.

We can see no natural or manmade bridge across the river, so Varesig has set his mind to divining a way to cross it. Its deep swiftness eliminates any thought of attempting to swim it, certainly not with our baggage. Our rope is also too short to stretch across as a guideline, and there are no rock islands to skip across. We've decided to either walk the riverbank to look for a better—but probably nonexistent—crossing point, or otherwise build a boat.

It is now day's end. We spent the day walking downstream, then doubled backed southward to look upstream. But no luck. There was not a single tree that had fallen on the bank to use as a dangerous boat. The brooding forest has clearly removed any advantage for our crossing. But as night fell we found a stretch of river without rapids that lay at the bottom of a steep falls. We camped near these falls and ate the last of our provisions.

After the meal, Varesig declared that we must build a raft. We debated, with Harsen and I initially opposed to the idea while Orren and the commander agreed—for once. Harsen maintained it was an unnecessary risk when we could trek toward the source of the river in hopes of finding a safer crossing. Varesig pointed to the more tranquil waters downstream of the falls as a desirable place to put in. He eventually won me over, saying he did not intend for us to forage forever on this side of the flow. So Harsen relented.

Midspring 20

Today was backbreaking work. Harsen used the hatchet to fell birches and other saplings while Orren and I notched and roped them together. Varesig was content to supervise and mark trees for a while, then he spent all his time walking up and down the river to make sure we didn't miss a better place to put in—so he says.

He has given every inch of riverbank a closer examination than what is needed, crouching down to sift through the smooth stones and sand. When Varesig long dwelled in one spot I handed the ropes over to Orren and walked over to the commander. I surprised him and he reacted angrily, casting handfuls of stone bits into the current. It was quite odd.

What is this sudden fascination with the earth that he has gained since we left Tolnarp, an interest I had never seen him display in our previous journeys? And why be so secretive about it? My questions only worsened his tantrum. As he stomped off down the river he seemed laden with weight. None of us understand this functionary.

Building a proper boat would have taken more time and better tools, but a raft was relatively quick and easy to assemble. We needed to float the river only long enough to steer to the far bank. By nightfall our raft was done. It is large enough for all of us to stand or sit, but there is no room for the horses. We will tether one to the raft and the others behind him to help guide them as they swim.

All of us except the stubborn Varesig will leave our armor behind to lighten the load and avoid drowning. Unable to abandon his richly made armor, Varesig tied it onto the raft. We let it be, since he at least removed it from his body; we do not carry provisions or much else with us, so the weight should be fine. I still feel the whole business is risky, but we must cross if we are to continue into Gallerlandia. After dark, we used my candles to forage for berries and roots.

Around our small fire, I asked the wise Orren how the heathens would cross this river. He shrugged, saying surely they built riverboats. He told a story about how the Donovards, when first founding their colony, attempted to sail their galleons up the Glombruk. But the current was too heavy and swift, and the ships were always pushed back into the Bay of Pemonia, regardless of the wind in their sails. The Donovards witnessed Gallerlanders on both sides of the Glombruk but never saw how they tamed it.

Varesig took the opportunity to say perhaps they flew across it with wings fashioned from the breath of Memelos. His wit only succeeded in entertaining himself. Harsen offered his support to the idea that the Gallerlanders built boats, saying he had heard the Bronhildi tribe of the east made canoes from the papery bark of the white birch. Looking at our slender raft logs, it was difficult to imagine that.

Orren continued, saying that if his theories about the natives of Pemonia were correct, shipbuilding was in their blood because it was their ancestors the Agnesci who had sailed the first great ships to the Old World. He doubted the art of sailing was lost to the Gallerlanders and others, but Orren did not have an answer for Harsen's fair question about why the heathens had not sailed again for the Old World or even attacked the coastal colonies with warships.

As we prepare to retire to the warm furs of our bedrolls, my tired mind contemplates our fate upon the Glombruk. I feel very small and weak beside it. It is beautiful yet menacing, like the forests through which we've already passed. But unlike the trees, cursed to guard their little patches of a great green quilt, the river is busy and does not notice the feeble men on its heels.

I can't help but wonder what it would be like to search for its source, to see where it was small. But we must journey onward. We have agreed that if all goes wrong and we are cast into the river's jaws, we should meet back at these falls. For the first time, we knelt together and prayed to survive the crossing. Varesig led the chant, his sword hilt held aloft like the starcross of Messenger Martinus.

Midspring 21

It is with heavy heart that I write on this damp page. I sit drenched in despair, not knowing my companions' fate. I've trodden up and down the bank shouting their names, but there is no answer. The river rushes onward, cold to my sorrow. Were it not for the oilskin pouch around my shoulder, I would have nothing, not even this journal.

The Glombruk seethed at the touch of our little wooden craft, and more rain fed its monstrous body, quickly lashing us much further downstream than we wanted, well past the calmer waters we had scouted. Rapids sprang up from unseen places on the roiling back of the river, tossing and swallowing us over and again.

The horses' tethers snapped, and they were instantly lost in the foam and froth. Then the raft, after much twisting and creaking, was dashed among the rocks, and we were cast into the swirl. I never heard or caught sight of my companions. I was swept down the river, drinking and breathing the torrent until the Glombruk spat me out upon a gravel shoal.

And now here I sit, back on the side of the river from which we started, battered but unwounded, save in spirit. My companions may be floating corpses, new ghosts of the Glombruk. What can I do? What can be done?

Midspring 22

During the night I was awakened by ragged cries for help. I lit a candle and searched along the riverbank, calling out as I went. When I came closer I knew it was Varesig. I was overjoyed to find him under some bushes at the river's edge, caked in sand and half-wedged under a log.

With much effort I pushed and shoveled with my hands the sand and stones that had partially buried him, then tugged him out of the river's grasp. He could not walk and winced at every touch, so with the last of my strength I dragged him back to my little fire, where he lost consciousness.

I could see both his legs were broken. I removed his clothing to dry him by the fire, exposing many cuts and gashes in his arms and across his ribs. His head was badly bruised. He had undoubtedly tumbled against every river boulder that I miraculously missed. I placed my tunic about him then fell into a deep, exhausted sleep beside the fire.

Varesig's pitiful wails roused me again this morning. He could barely talk, and I could not understand him. I tried to set his broken legs, but the pain was too great for him, so I have let him be for now. I cupped river water in my hands for him to drink, then foraged for nearby berries and roots, but he could not eat. I can do nothing for him and cannot find the medicinal herb that Arvgred used to heal my hand. It would do no good for his legs anyway.

The only possessions that I retained are those items carried in my oilskin knapsack: this journal wrapped in leather and the map folded within it, as well as a quill, dwindling pot of ink, knife, candles and flint, and the pewter spoon. Most important, my short sword is still fastened at my waist. If I had been burdened with armor it would have surely taken me to the bottom, but the sword is life in the wilderness.

I left Varesig to sleep while I foraged upriver, hoping to see Harsen or Orren. While looking among the bushes I found a peculiar berry that I'm afraid to eat. It is thumb sized, reddish-violet, and thorny. Its juice is thick like blood and of similar hue. I crushed some in my inkpot and found the ink writes easily enough. I named them bloodberries. The pot is full, but our bellies are not, so I continued to look for food.

While foraging, I was startled by the sudden leap into the air of a buzzard and feared the worst. But the bloated carcass was that of my horse, bobbing in an inlet of the bank. I wept as I envisioned the same fate for Harsen and Orren. But I refuse to think that good woodsman would succumb.

I stooped to examine the loyal beast, finding it broken and drowned. I checked the saddle pouches but they were empty. The only useful items that remained on the poor animal were my bedroll and extra blanket, soaked, which I took. I could not bring myself to harvest meat from the noble animal at first, but my stomach would not let me leave it. With my knife I carved flesh from its haunch, then returned to the fire.

Once the blankets had dried, I gently placed them around Varesig. His face was pale but he could speak better now. I roasted the meat, and we ate as we watched the indifferent river. Varesig asked if I had seen anything or anyone, which of course I hadn't.

When we had finished I hung his clothing to dry. During the previous night I had placed them in a pile before collapsing into sleep. But now as I hung them I noticed a heavy waist pouch. He watched silently as I poured the contents into my hand: rocks, small with shiny electrum flecks. They sparkled in the sunlight that pierced the clouds above.

I turned to Varesig, and he cracked a smile. Between coughs he said he had not wished to share his finds, but that I could keep them, he certainly owed them to me, he said. What use did I have for gold out here? I replaced the ore stones and placed the pouch at his side.

This afternoon I recovered a few raft poles and bits of rope from the riverbank and fashioned a crude litter on which to drag Varesig. I resolved to head back upriver to the falls tomorrow in hopes that Harsen and Orren would do the same, as we had agreed.

Midspring 23

oday's walk was slow, as my legs have grown weary. Pulling Varesig's stretcher is made all the more difficult by the overgrown riverbank, and the forest tries constantly to push us back into the churning arms of the Glombruk.

His condition has worsened, his breathing labored and raspy. Varesig insisted I leave him behind, that his journey has ended. Though I can't do much more than make him comfortable and cup water for him, I will not leave him to the bane wolves and buzzards. We have survived too many fields of battle to lie down so easily beside the river.

There is no sign of Harsen and Orren. No horses nor raft fragments. I have called out in vain for the scribe and woodsman until hoarse. I'm also puzzled about why we've not yet reached the falls after trudging all day. I cannot see or hear them. The serpentine river carried our little raft with an evil speed . . .

Tonight we camp beside more tranquil waters, hoping this is near the stretch where we launched. But there is no sound of the falls. Sleep comes to Varesig quickly, but I am kept awake with thoughts of our lost companions. Have they gone the way of old Glom Stimril, swallowed by a river but lacking his great Wilhargantian cause?

I have come to doubt that the Gallerlanders would be of any use as allies to New Lorin. If we ever find them we'll be too far from the colony. Perhaps ours was a fool's errand, the details of which the colony may never know. Gallerlandia's forests and rivers may be silent graves for us all.

Midspring 24

We arrived at the falls by midday. No sign of anyone. Precious ink all but gone . . . diluting with water.

Midspring 25

No sign . . . Foraging . . . Unable to find more bloodberries for ink, I recalled the cloth dyers in New Lorin and pressed water-soaked lichen for a weak ink.

Midspring 26

We have watched in vain for our companions these past few days while I have tried to stay busy gathering food and wood. Varesig keeps the fire stoked and smoky with leafed branches, in hopes that they will see it. I don't much feel like writing, but it helps to keep me awake when my tired feet and legs demand that I sit.

Trapping small game is difficult. Plants, roots, and forest fruits sustain us. Varesig eats little, and I'm wearing thin. I'm considering returning to the horse's corpse for whatever the buzzards and wolves have left uneaten.

❧

It is night now, and the fire feels good. I know not what else to do. There has been no sign of Harsen and Orren here at the falls, and Varesig grows weaker by the hour. He rarely speaks now, and I know he is in great pain.

My mind now hears mocking laughter amid the gurgles of the river, and the knob holes of the trees glare at my every move. Fists of leaves shake menacingly in the night wind. I've realized why the deceitful Arvgred spoke of the forest and its elements as if they were living, thinking beings. To a wilderman alone in the wilderness, they are alive. They plot and scheme. They can kill or sustain you. Or drive you mad.

How long do we wait? Are we waiting for what will never come? It is agonizing. And where are these fabled Gallerlanders? I wonder if they dwell here at all. This expedition was not worth the cost of our lives. What hope is there? We will never leave the wilderwood.

Midspring 27

Today I returned to camp with a great prize: a small boar caught in one of my traps. This lifted our spirits. We eagerly set it upon a crude roasting spit. I had busied myself preparing the pig when I heard Varesig's little bag of electrum stones fall from his grasp.

I turned to see him slump out of the litter, but I caught him. He said he felt no pain in his legs but could no longer feel his arms and was afraid. His voice cracked and his tired eyes welled. He whispered his regrets about the electrum, but I told him it was a trifle, no harm was done.

He shook his head slightly and explained the expedition was never about an alliance with the heathens. The governor, he said, had sent him to find the barbarians' electrum. He wanted it from their mines or snatched from around their necks, wherever it could be found. And Varesig agreed to keep the secret. He wept for Harsen and "the heretic" and apologized that he had deceived us. He begged my forgiveness, and I gave it. Then he breathed out his last.

I stood slowly, in disbelief. Here was the governor's own nephew, pitifully destroyed by a wilderness he was sent into for an errand he was ill-equipped to complete. None of us were gold finders or miners, nor would we be able to steal enough from the barbarians to satisfy the governor's greed.

I angrily scooped up Varesig's rock pouch and cast it into the falls. If New Lorin was so desperate for coin then why hadn't the governor simply sent an able party to survey the realm? Why the secrecy of the expedition's true goal? Perhaps the governor wanted all the wealth for himself.

With sharp rocks and sticks I scraped out a shallow ditch then dragged Varesig into it, covering his body with stones. I said a few words, but it was hardly the ceremony that knights of his rank usually receive. At least the wild beasts will not pick him apart, as they probably will me.

I sit alone now looking into the fire and the charred remains of the neglected pig. My stomach has forgotten hunger for the moment; rather, it is filled with a sick and heavy dread. I suppose recording my thoughts keeps me sane even if these pages, like my body, are destined to be eaten by the worms of the cruel earth that is the foundation of the wilderwood.

Midspring 28

Today I have reflected much on Varesig's words. His confession fully explains why he and his uncle the governor had been so enthusiastic about the expedition, while I wavered between doubt and hope of securing a tribal alliance. Their eyes saw wealth under the forests of Pemonia that would rescue the colony, or at least fill their own coffers. It is no secret that New Lorin finds itself outpaced by Donovan and other colonies whose exotic exports to the Old World have enriched them.

But I should have seen the signal in the smoke: the governor's scheme to send Varesig to scratch among the rocks while ostensibly seeking what could have been a fruitful alliance. Orren certainly believed that he was risking his life for a worthy cause. He came willingly, the only volunteer, to help broker an alliance he believed would benefit all peoples of the New World and the broader empire. I had insisted on Harsen coming, and I'm thus responsible for his watery death. At least Rekef died honorably.

And what of me? I wish to hear from the governor's own lips why he sent our party and not the gold-finding experts and miners. But the question that I must face is what to do now. I have the map and could find my way back to the colony. But I feel I must search for the bodies of Orren and my dear friend Harsen.

So I have resolved to walk back downriver in the morning to continue the search. After that, I do not know. I could follow the Glombruk to where its wide mouth empties into the bay and hope the Donovards don't shoot this rough-looking man as I approach, or I could continue to search out the Gallerlanders . . . but for what purpose? The governor might not value a true alliance even if Orren were there to champion its many attributes. I must rest and not think on this now. My decision can wait . . .

I was awakened this afternoon by a faint thud, soon followed by another. A sudden rustle in the bushes nearby, then stillness again. I sat up, still rolled up in my blanket, shaking sleep from my head. I looked toward the river, listening for the chuckling gurgles. Another rustle and crash in different bushes. This was not my mind playing tricks.

I jumped to my feet and unsheathed my sword, expecting a hateful Arvgred or wolves to dash out, but there was nothing. I hacked at another bush when it thudded and shimmied, but again there was nothing there. Was it some wild boar or squirrel sprinting about?

My mind drifted to roast pig and my stomach howled, but I was snapped back when the coals of the fire splashed up into the air. Tongues of flame licked skyward and ash flittered up in a bubble of smoke. What evil magic was this? Had I camped upon a cursed place in the wood? When I glanced toward Varesig's fresh grave, I was punched sharply in the back, but when I whirled around I slashed only at empty air.

Panicked at this point, I ran to the water and nearly jumped in to save myself. But the water suddenly splashed up in front of me. Astonished, I looked about. There was nothing in the water, only ripples. And the falls continued their heavy dive. Then out from the swirling mist of the falls jumped a gray stone, thudding into the bank near to my feet.

At last a speck of movement caught my eye, a phantom on the far side of the river. I stood, rubbing and squinting my eyes to peer through the mist that was beginning to collect around the falls with the onset of evening. A waving form, a man, was jumping up and down on the far bank. *Harsen?*

I called out but could barely hear myself over the roar of the falls. The man pointed downriver, but I looked and saw nothing. The man sprinted downriver. Now understanding, I hopped and stumbled in the same direction, away from the noise and obscuring haze.

There was the good woodsman on the far bank, frantic, and so was I! Thankfully, he cast his last stone into the river rather than at me. We joyfully shouted over one another, jumping in tandem like two giddy hares. He had seen my campfire in the night, he yelled, but was unable to raise me because of the falls. So in desperation he tried the stones. He laughed mightily when I told him I thought a vengeful woodland spirit had come to attack me.

I told him I'd found Varesig, but that he had perished. Harsen had buried Orren also. This news greatly saddened me, for there was much more I wished to learn about the heathens from the scribe. I blamed my poor roping to bind the raft, but he answered that it was the wrath of the river, not our handiwork and probably not even Varesig's cargo of armor that was at fault. Like me, Harsen had no food. We soon felt alone together, staring at each other from our shores. Neither of us wished for the other to brave another crossing.

We foraged for ourselves and spent the evening pondering a solution. I felt guilty that I had the flints and thus the fire to warm myself at the cool riverside, while he did not. Even if he found any flint, he showed me that he lost his steel blade to strike a spark from it. I attempted to throw stones to him with flaming sticks attached, but this was futile given the breadth of the river and dampness of the air. The crude bandages on his hands suggested to me that he wouldn't be able to use Arvgred's fast-sticks method either.

❧

It's now dark, and I can't see Harsen, but I know he is there. It is a wonderful feeling to know I'm not alone in this dire place, though we are separated by the great Glombruk. As I munch on roasted bitterleaf bulbs, an idea has come. Harsen and I could now travel to Donovan by following the river together. Or we could salvage this expedition by finding the source of the Glombruk and possibly a Gallerlander village in the process.

Harsen does not yet know Varesig's secret, so he will presume our original mission must continue. When I cross the river at the Glombruk's source I will tell him the ugly truth, and then we can decide whether to seek out the Gallerlanders or go to Donovan.

Midspring 29

I was startled awake this morning by a rustle and then a thud in the bush. Grinning, I grasped a stone and returned Harsen's greeting. I could barely see him through the mist. We walked a short pace to talk—or rather shout—again.

I proposed that we travel upriver to find the source of the Glombruk, wherever that led us, because the river would inevitably narrow at some point. Surely I'd be able to cross safely at some narrower or shallower portion to join Harsen, then we could determine what to do. He agreed, and we kept the pace steady and each other in view as best we could. I would light a fire every evening to keep myself in view, and we would toss rocks to gain the other's attention when the river deafened us. Before departing, he held up a bare foot. Not only were his hands injured, but the woodsman had lost a boot to the Glombruk. The message was clear: don't hurry.

And so we journeyed southward and up the river, following it and separated by it and drinking from it. The Glombruk sustained and yet hated us. The trees continued to sneer and push but were probably content to see us plod along the edge of their domain.

Midspring 30

We continued today along our separate paths tracing the river. Our steps were slow because there was no path. Sometimes the riverbanks broadened into sandy pebble-studded flats, and at other times they were sheer mud cliffs grown over with bushes and brambles. But at least I had both boots. Harsen merely wrapped his bare foot with cloth torn from his tunic.

This trek reminded me of the time when I led my soldiers out of the Onas Marshes after our commander had been killed and the Ollohd tribe helped us escape the Hrals. We had, in fact, followed a river inland and around to the southeast of Mount Tremvig, keeping its bald pinnacle in view to our left as we sought the haven of the colony.

We had been a mere five survivors, hungry and weary. That river was a steady though winding guide, and shallower than the mighty Glombruk. We trotted along upstream—as Harsen and I were now—and the way was no less difficult. We suspected the river flowed from the grassy moors that ringed Mount Tremvig, meaning we'd have to cross the river sooner or later, as now with the Glombruk.

I recall that one of the men, Orefor was his name, had insisted on crossing when we found it was shallow because it could deepen or broaden ahead. I heeded his advice, and we crossed without incident. This was good because the river indeed deepened as it cut around Tremvig into a higher rock-sloped land.

This was not the only occasion that Orefor, wilderness-wise beyond his young age, proved of counsel. A man of such wilderwood wits, like Harsen, is critical on such expeditions. Sadly, Orefor perished a year later at the tragic battle at Port Rilhammor, a meaningless and wasteful border dispute between Brintilian colonists of New Lorin and Donovan. There is no worse death than at the hands of your brethren.

Aside from water to drink, the river around Mount Tremvig also kept us alive with its bounty of fish. This memory made me crave the green-stripes or even the small glidiwots that we had caught earlier in this journey. The Glombruk doubtless carried plenty of fishes in its currents, but we had lost our lines and hooks when Arvgred stole our equipment. Then I remembered that Orefor and others had used strips of clothing and thorns to fish until we reached the colony.

I stopped and cupped my hands to shout at Harsen. He watched as I used my knife to cut the fabric of my shirt, pulling out several long threads that I twisted and tied. I looked about in the nearby brambles, pinching off a few large curved thorns, and fastened a few on. Next I kicked up the wet soil of the riverbank to snag worms and beetles for bait.

By now, Harsen was mimicking me. We fastened our twine to long sticks and waited. And waited. Despite refreshing the bait, we had no luck. Harsen figured the spot was bad, so we continued walking and dipped our poles in further upriver. We soon caught several lavender- and silver-colored fish—small, but something.

I built a roasting fire, but Harsen had no fire. I watched as he flayed and ate his fish raw without hesitation, the hardy woodsman way. In solidarity, I kicked out the young flames and ate mine raw as well. Cold, wet, and nearly tasteless, but my shrunken belly was adequately filled for the first time since the horsemeat.

Flowertide 1

The Glombruk took a dramatically upward and craggy climb, with beautiful cascades that sprayed mist and cast rainbows in the sunlight. This incline is perhaps a sign we will soon find its source, perhaps a spring among these broken rocks that must form the lowest foothills of the Bomlofoss Mountain Range. But the rocky terrain has slowed our pace considerably, as we are forced to scramble over large boulders and jump like frogs over the perilous flooded gaps between them. And the river, noisily crashing as ever, is only slightly narrower.

By midday we noticed the trees on my side of the Glombruk gradually becoming shorter and their roots that desperately grasp at the rocky bank grown larger. Harsen pointed above my head, but only later could I find a vantage point that allowed me to see what he saw from the far side: a chain of mountaintops running west of us and parallel to the river. They were not too distant, almost certainly the Bomlofoss Range. It is my hope that the river begins among these rocky foothills.

Flowertide 2

Today was eventful, and not just because we have survived another day, nearly a month now in Gallerlandia. We began with our new habit of raw fish and scavenged roots or berries to break our night fast. Soon after breaking our camps, I stumbled across a boulder with runes hewn into its river-facing side, and Harsen found a beamed boulder directly across on his side, constructed in the same fashion as the Gallerlander marker we had seen in the rock field. But my boulder was clearly different, so I sketched the rune.

I realized I had seen something similar before. It was the sign of the Hrals. Dread poured over me as I remembered these same lines had been carved in the foreheads and hands of those masons and soldiers at Tremvig. This realization goosebumped my neck. I was now more eager than ever to cross the river into territory clearly marked as Gallerlander.

My side of the river felt darker, the trees more sinister. Unlike most of our encounters with Gallerlanders, Ollohds, and similar natives, including Harsen's peaceful trade, every contact between the colonists and the Hral tribe has been deadly. I have marked their presence this far south on our crude map as Hral Marker, for they are vicious beings to be avoided. I must cross the river soon.

Flowertide 3

As we walked our separate paths I could not silence recollections of my time fighting the Hrals on Tremvig. I remember seeing the defiled bodies of my colonial brethren, both knights and the watchtower craftsmen. The tower was not completed until years later when a larger force of soldiers retook the summit and destroyed several Hral villages found to be nearby.

Some troops from that campaign, particularly those who fought in the Battle of Deadfoot, swore on the Book of Ibelan that the Hrals were cannibals and that their chieftain was half dog. We never saw evidence of cannibalism in their villages, but these tales persist even today, and I do not wholly discount them.

After the snarling Hral chieftain was killed, the surviving Hrals largely abandoned the lands near Tremvig, and the Ollohds, whom we were usually at peace with, moved in. But the Hrals continued to use the Onas Marshes to launch surprise raids against the Ollohds and merchants traveling between New Lorin and Donovan.

To this day, the marshes are considered an impassable frontier for New Lorin. Of all the bloody campaigns in which I fought thereafter, I was glad that none of them forced me to set foot in those marshes again.

The Donovards have confirmed that the Gallerlanders are also enemies of the Hrals, so the Hrals must lack allies. I think the marked boulders that Harsen and I discovered yesterday prove that, since they seemed to serve as a warning to the other tribe. But how either of those native races could cross the Glombruk here, even if they so desired, I cannot guess.

∾

Late in the day the forest gave way to the great crags and ridges that crowded and hunched over the river. Ahead of us the faces of the mountains were now exposed, glaring down at the trespassers of their rocky realm. We stood for a moment, taking in their grandness as the lowering sun glowed on their snowless peaks.

"Harsenoss!" he shouted over the river's roar, suggesting a name for the range. But they still appear to me to be the Bomlofoss, as described by the mariners who've sailed to their east, so I'm not yet prepared to officially name them after the good woodsman. Rildningoss has a better Brintilian sound to it anyway.

I'm encouraged that the river continues to gradually narrow as we climb. I hope that it provides an opportunity to cross soon. Perhaps tomorrow we will reunite our path.

Flowertide 4

It is midday and rocky now, and our pace is that of a snail as Harsen and I continue the scramble onward and upward. But I remain optimistic that the river will allow a crossing soon. The river surely springs forth from some cloven stone here at the foot of the mountains. I tire of eating cold fish and scavenged berries and long for a roasting fire.

Flowertide 5 or 6

God or Lady Luck has smiled on me yet again. I believe it to be the fifth or sixth of Flowertide, but I'm not sure how long I've been unconscious.

The fourth of Flowertide was like any other, walking opposite Harsen. But no sooner had we found another pair of Gallerlander and Hral territory markers than the Hrals ambushed and took me. Four or five of them at least. They were beastly, with long unkempt hair and matted beards encircling cruel faces with broken teeth, and fiery red war paint around their eyes and dotting their cheeks like the pox.

When I first caught sight of them jumping from the bush, my instinct spurred me to run back downriver. But their feet were swift and silent, and they quickly surrounded me. I tried to jump toward the river, to let it carry me away, but they grabbed me with their long-nailed hands. The last thing I remember as they beat me was the view of Harsen jumping frantically, helplessly on the far bank, horror twisting his face before their arrows chased him off. Then only darkness.

I awoke sometime later in a very dim light, with foul smells and dampness clinging to my face. My bruised body was lying on loose dirt, but I could not make out my surroundings at first. A sharp pain bolted through my head when I attempted to rise, and I could feel dried blood caked above my right ear. My cry returned to me in a muffled echo, and I realized I was underground. Then silence.

I was alone, and without my possessions, in some cave. My eyes soon focused with the aid of a bit of light, a slender shaft not far away. I had been placed at the end of a tunnel, its slime-dripping rocky walls and roof arched over a well-trodden earthen floor. On the walls were Hral-carved runes, colored with dark dyes.

Most startling was the skeleton that rested quietly beside me. It was all I could do not to cry out again, for I did not wish to alert my captors if they came within earshot. The poor man—which I presumed him to be—had been dead for many years. The clothes he had perished in had all but rotted away, and his bones were long ago robbed of flesh.

Then I noticed a tiny sparkle and shifted my view to catch the light. It was golden metal, yet greenish, and it glowed ever so slightly in the dimness. I recalled Arvgred's electrum necklaces and his tales about the sacred Gallerlander metal. Surely this man was a native of that great elusive tribe. For a moment I was excited that I had finally found a Gallerlander, but felt it a bad omen that he was a dead one.

I carefully lifted the skeleton's ring from his hand and pulled the little circle close to my eye. It was unadorned, best I could tell in the gloom, save for a simple carven circle on its flattened top. It was strangely comforting to put it on my own finger, though an item of luck it surely was not, for it had not saved its owner. I thought it odd that the Hrals did not value the electrum enough to strip it off their dead captive. Perhaps they had simply overlooked the little thing.

My eyes having now fully adjusted but my head throb also returning, I stood shakily, stooping to avoid the ceiling. With my hand sliding along the grime-layered wall, I crept toward the shaft of light, beyond which I could not see. The sunbeam was long and slight, only a faint crack in the stone above.

Beyond the light was an elbow in the tunnel blocked by a rickety gate of molded wood. Either its inner wood was still strong or I too weak, for I could not force it open. Through the gate I could see that the tunnel widened into a chamber that was lit by daylight from another tunnel. I could hear the dulled river. There was also a wooden flat in the earthen chamber on which my equipment had been dumped out. But how to escape? I dared not call for help though I was clearly alone for the moment. I shook the wooden gate as violently as I could, to no avail.

Dispirited, I paced my cramped tunnel. I imagined a violent death at the hands of those heathens, or a slow starvation in their burrow. I saw myself succumbing to a mind warped by hunger, scratching at the dirt for hidden worms that would later emerge freely from the ground to consume my flesh. My head throbbed, and my heart raced. New blood trickled, tickling my ear. Then a thought of clarity.

I stared at the skeleton resting quietly, at peace in death. I apologized to him for taking his ring and for what I was about to do. I brushed away his leathern tatters, turning them into dust and exposing a femur. I returned to the gate and determinedly swung and hacked at the wood with the bone.

I bashed and thrashed until the wood splintered in the middle, then whacked it again and again until I fell in exhaustion. Satisfied that I would be able to squeeze through the break, I returned the femur to the skeleton with polite thanks. If he had not died in that foul place and lent me his leg, I surely would have perished where he lay.

Once through the gate, I quickly looked about the chamber for my equipment. Blood was dribbling onto my neck and shoulder now, my wound reopened from my exertions. I moved quickly to gather my things. The Hrals had done minor damage to my journal. Part of the map was ripped out, but I can restore it from memory. The book as a whole had been flung across the room, uninteresting and discarded.

My leather knapsack was gone, but its contents remained. The quill was in working order, but the bloodberry ink had been used to reapply color to the wall runes. I also recovered two candles (which had been chewed on), flints, and even the spoon. What a curious token of civilization to me now. But my sword and knife were gone. Tucking the journal under my arm, I looked around the earthen room for anything else of value. Seeing only Hral refuse, I hastened out.

I approached the lit tunnel carefully. The air grew fresher with every twisting turn, and the Glombruk's subdued sound lifted into a roar. I soon poked out into blinding sunlight. The mouth of the tunnel opened onto a narrow ledge, nearly ushering me straight into the angry river a few arm's lengths below. This section of the river was similar to where I had left it. But now vertical rock walls and cliffs replaced the sandy banks, and the river was constricted into falls and rapids. It was a narrow and treacherous water-filled ravine.

Above me was a rock overhang. To my relief, I quickly spotted a path up and around to the surface where the trunk of a great tree lay like a bridge across the turbulent water. But my relief melted into fear when I saw the Hral pacing back and forth across it. I stilled myself but it was too late. He had seen me moving against the backdrop of the bright stone.

Bearing my journal in my teeth, I scrambled up the rocks in the opposite direction as he ran off the bridge toward the tunnel path, brandishing a spear and yelling horribly. There was little brush in which to hide but the boulders themselves hid many crannies, all of which were death traps if I was discovered. Knowing the nimble Hral would be upon me in an instant, I risked a darker gap and flattened myself against its wall.

The Hral darted past. Then I heard and saw nothing. Taking the chance that he was the only one left to guard me, I sprang out and ran for the tree bridge and scurried across it. Hearing multiple Hrals shrieking behind me, I raced through a gap between boulders on the far bank and disappeared in the ferns and undergrowth at the forest's edge. There I scarcely breathed, like a nervous rabbit amid searching foxes.

My apparent solitude was at once calming and unsettling because I knew they could be watching and waiting for my movement. So I waited, too. But my blood loss and exertion finally took its toll. I did not awake until it was night.

Clutching my precious book, possibly the only thing that will somehow redeem this terrible journey, I waited in the darkness for another hour until my thirst and hunger prodded me. I crawled as quietly as I could through the dirt and leaves away from the river, hoping the Gallerlander territory would protect me.

I went deep into the rocky woods until I could no longer hear the water's rush. Then I foraged for what forest fruits I could find and took risks with mushrooms in the moonlight.

A cleansing rain shower woke me the next morning, and I spent much time gathering water in leaves and pools to quench my thirst and bathe my head wound. The pain had grown intense but the bleeding had stopped. Dizziness forced me to rest often and reflect on my surviving, yet again, the Hrals and gaining my freedom from them.

I studied the skeleton's ring and wondered about that Gallerlander who was not as fortunate. Then my thoughts turned to my dead companions and to Harsen. Separated again. Had he gone on, leaving me for dead after watching them take me? Or had he been struck by their arrows? These questions pained my head, and I slept.

When I awoke in the late afternoon, I found enough strength to sacrifice blackberries by mashing them into my inkpot. I wanted to eat the sweet little morsels but needed to write about my encounter with the Hral. It wasn't long before my stomach was knotted with hunger again and pulsing in rhythm with my head. Grown more desperate, I dug with my fingers and sticks into the earth, consuming worms and beetles and grubs as I found them.

I was overjoyed to come upon a cluster of hogkettles, similar to the potatoes cultivated in the Old World and now the colonies. Intending to roast the tubers, I reached for my flint but forgot my steel knife had been taken. So I chewed them raw until I was full. I fell asleep on the open forest floor, uncaring of the taste of dirt in my mouth.

That was last night. This morning I felt refreshed despite my head pain, which will probably float like a stormy cloud for some time. I sit now under peaceful trees whose leaves playfully wave down the sun's light.

My journal entry is complete, but I know not what to do next, or where to turn. But I have to believe that Harsen is alive, since he was across the river and would have hidden himself from the Hrals. I shall rest more . . .

Flowertide 7?

I am frozen with indecision, and my head burns. What can I do to find Harsen? I cannot return to the dreadful river.

Flowertide 8?

I will look for Harsen by turning northeast away from the mountains. I will not return to the Glombruk. I hope to find some sign of him.

PART III

THE DEEPNESS

Middle Flowertide

I have walked for several days, perhaps a week, I cannot tell. Counting the steps of old Father Time seems so unnecessary out here, even a burden.

This forest east of the Glombruk is more verdant than I could have imagined, and I feel attuned to its every detail. It is interesting how different it feels now. The trees are not as threatening, and I feel drawn to their whisper, even if they might still plot against my path in secret. It's as if they've come to understand me better, and I them, but I feel they're not finished testing me. The earth also feels different. It's flatter and wrinkled, far from the rocks of the brooding mountains. Both Harsen and the mountain range are now lost far behind me . . .

I startled myself today by stooping to drink from a mirrored pool fed by a silver rill. My clothes are tattered, hair matted and disheveled, beard full and crusted with berry juices and mushroom fragments, and face weatherworn. Unbecoming of a knight, but I could not bring myself to bathe.

My uncivilized condition is enhanced by being bereft of modern possessions. I have spent many rests simply examining the lowly spoon. Without this journal, I would surely forget myself. This book tells me that I've not yet spent two months in the wilderness, yet the forests have had a potent effect on my mind, body, and spirit. So much has passed, I feel. Being alone, or worse, hunted like wild game, has a profound effect as well. But the journal recovers my mind, and the quill exercises it.

Though I have a crude map of where I've been, no accurate distances are known, and my wandering is aimless. I know not where to go to find Harsen. I have stared at the map for periods of ponderous time, wondering what this continent's vast interior holds.

Indeed, how vast is it? What secrets are hidden within? How large a piece is Gallerlandia of Pemonia, and where do those elusive people live? Fingering the skeleton's electrum ring, with its simple circle engraving, I wonder about what they must be like.

I've had the idea to lay out a rabbit skin and blackberries as Harsen did in the early days to attract the Gallerlanders. I lack the patience and strength to catch and skin a rabbit by hand, but I will leave berry offerings nightly in hopes that they will come.

Middle Flowertide

No Gallerlanders or even dirty Hrals came for the berries last night. So I sit . . .

Middle Flowertide

A squirrel ate the berries . . . Must keep trying . . . The squirrels be damned! And they are too quick for my thrown stones!

Probably Bloomfade

I despair deeply at the folly of this expedition, looking in every direction and seeing the same view. It has been a long while since I last wrote. In fact, I had decided not to write again. My frustration has burned hotter with the warming weather, and I've wallowed in depression at the loss of Harsen and the lack of any sign of the natives. I sat under a drooping old ruin of a tree for three days, depressed and angry. I wished no longer to live and hurled this journal as far as I could into a nearby patch of thornbushes.

I soon fell into a profound sleep, and I dreamed of the quaint wooden houses of New Lorin huddled on the beautiful shores of the Bay of Pemonia. I could smell the warmth of home and hear the quay bells ting. I walked among the happy settlers at the autumn festival at the academy. Young knights whom I had trained were jousting while ladies looked on, and children played their games and watched the tournaments in awe.

I then stepped into the fields of freshly cut hay, but when I touched a stack, it morphed into a snarling, grasping, biting Hral. I awoke to find a rotund raccoon pawing at the electrum ring. I leaped from my sleeping place, and it hissed and fled. When I had regained my senses I laughed to my knees and felt warmth return to my soul.

That covetous little animal made me think of the treacherous Arvgred and how he lived in the trees like the natives did. I gained perspective when I considered how he had survived for many years out here on his own. I need to be more creative with my humble possessions and make better use of the many resources of the forest, as he did. I resolved to make weapons and hunt food to fully recover my strength and mind. A true wilderman, not only in appearance but in action.

My first task was to recover my abandoned journal. I searched the thorny brambles and wept upon its worn binding, clutching it like a rescued child. The pricks all over my body were a small price for its recovery, for I felt as though I had regained my very self.

I once believed that my time as a soldier had prepared me for this expedition, but I was mistaken. Though an experienced colonial knight, nothing had prepared me for the utter loneliness, hunger, and desperation of this place. Not even Tremvig.

And though I have lost men in battle, losing Harsen in these wildlands has been difficult to bear, more so than the loss of my other companions. We've always been as two brothers; now we are two small fishes in the great green sea of Gallerlandia. I still have hope that the Hrals have not captured or killed him.

I will push on and not succumb to the deepness of the forest. The battle of the mind shall be my greatest triumph.

Perhaps Midsummer

Using what I remember of Arvgred and his tools and possessions, I am teaching myself how to be at peace with the wilderness. I've identified several plants with tough fibrous stalk skins to weave rope. This has not been easy, but by cutting with chipped stones, pressing, drying, and stitching them together, I have made a few decent lengths.

With this, a twig box, and much patience, I have caught a squirrel. My first fresh meat for some time. I initially lamented that I had no fire to cook the meat, but it was good in the belly. I will continue to practice Arvgred's fast-sticks method to create fire from the wood itself, in hopes of mastering it.

Midsummer

Over the past few days, I have caught several squirrels with the numerous traps I've made. They cannot resist a feast of baited berries, and so they become my feast in turn. I've learned to skin them with my stone-shard knives, weaving their hides into a new knapsack with dry-grass twine. In this I will store dried fruits, mushrooms, and such for my journey. I have not progressed far in my search for Harsen because all my time is spent foraging and making equipment.

Midsummer

I found a broad but shallow stream flowing west, almost certainly into the Glombruk behind me. On its banks I found smooth river stones of many types and sizes. I spent much time smashing them upon each other to gain better knife shards. This proved a treasure trove, for I have been able to outfit myself with not only knife blades but a spearhead and a small hammer for whacking the squirrels and staking the traps.

I also selected many small shards for later use as arrow tips, should I ever harvest sinews from large game to fashion a bowstring. Finding a sapling for the bow itself will not be difficult. I thought of Rekef as I balanced my new stone-tipped spear in my hands, remembering that he perished at the tip of the Hrals' similar weapons. Somewhere a Hral wields my own trusty steel sword, and probably Rekef's . . .

Inspired by my long work at the stream, I chose a point on the map roughly east of where I crossed the Glombruk and named it Tool Camp. Although arbitrary, it feels good to be on the map again. Here I built a lean-to of branches and stone. I'm proud of this simple structure, the first abode I've encountered since Arvgred's platform in the tree.

Midsummer

Content with my tools and feeling better fed, I paused my work today to consider the search for Harsen. I sat in my new shelter as a soft rain shower sprouted bubbles in the stream. I scanned the map, but my eyes were drawn again to the empty vellum of the page.

I soon felt a surprisingly calm realization that my search for Harsen must end. I cannot go back to the locations on the map. Even if I were to walk up and down the Glombruk, I would have small hope of finding Harsen, and the Hrals will find me if I return upriver.

I feel a duty to carry the expedition forward, with the renewed goal of making contact with the Gallerlanders, no matter how long it takes. I feel that Orren was right about the potential for colonists and natives to live together peacefully, and my initial pessimism about the prospects of an alliance was shortsighted. My experiences on Mount Tremvig and elsewhere have taught me that such an effort is worth whatever cost I can endure in this wilderness.

Harsen was a good friend. I do not make this decision lightly, and I hope that if he survived, he followed the Glombruk to Donovan. But I feel that pushing on, without the greed-tainted conspiracies of the governor, is a worthy effort to pursue in honor of Harsen and Orren.

Midsummer

My revived determination was well timed. Not long after leaving Tool Camp, the landscape of Galler-landia changed abruptly. The forest closed, shutting out the light and stifling the breeze. The ground softened as turf and grasses gave way to damp mosses and creeping vines. The trees were older and darkened with knobs and burls and deeply furrowed trunks, and their branches reached down to scrape at me as they had in previous days.

When I doubled back to find a way around this unwelcome sight, I found my exit blocked. I panicked and stumbled into a net of thorned creepers. Tripped and entangled, I freed myself by slashing out with my knife and spear but not before being bitten by the most peculiar of plants that lay in wait upon the ground.

The light was very dim, but the vile plant appeared to have black leaves and flowers. When I fell upon it, it thrashed out with tiny teeth like a saw that drew my blood in an instant. When my blood dripped on its leaves, the flowers leaned over as if to catch it.

Sufficiently frightened, I leaped up and chopped and spear jabbed the freakish plant until I was sure it was dead. Then I felt a tree's bony hands reach down to grab my shoulders, and so I ran. Catching my breath in a small grove of hazel trees, I calmed myself but had lost any sense of direction in this sunless wood.

Not knowing where to turn and seeing no clear path, I chose a direction opposite from the bloodsucking plant and kept my spear at the ready, with measured footfalls and keen eye. The trees had taken notice of my menacing stride and drew closer to one another. They gathered more and more great vines, moss bushes, and thorn fences around themselves, girded for battle and further draping my path in darkness. The way was difficult and slow, and the tree fiends seethed as I slashed through their defenses.

After an exhausting hour or two of battle, and now covered in scrapes and punctures, I stopped upon a little mound of moss to rest. The day was now darker than before, and I could not see more than a few trees ahead. How I wished to strike my flint on some iron. A torch would be most useful in such an evil place, but lacking one, I used the remaining dim light to write of this progress, if progress it can be called.

I'm now confronted with the decision of whether to press on and risk more battles this evening, or stay on this miserable hump for a night that will surely not be restful. My ink mixture is also low, and there is no sign of any replacement in this wretched place. Of course, I can always allow the demon plants to draw more of my blood for the page.

I will rest here.

Midsummer

The night was long and my sleep fitful. Many wild and unseen beasts haunt this dark heart of the forest. I heard fierce scratching, snarling howls, and bellowing roars of every kind. Fear drove me up into a tree to escape some stalking beast.

The old cottonwood tree trembled and flailed under my touch, but I had to leave the forest floor. The unseen animal passed me by, growling and snorting with apparent disappointment. There were numerous death screams from other creatures during the night. I am thankful not to be among the prey.

There was, however, one bright note in the night's maddening gloom: the skeleton's ring on my finger. I had not noticed it during previous nights, probably because the night was not yet its blackest before I fell asleep, but in this abysmal forest, the electrum ring had an ethereal glow that was green-golden, the same as its daylight hue.

I'm no believer of the heathen magic that many superstitious colonists claimed to have witnessed, so I can only guess that this marvelous metal captures and reflects the slightest rays of moonlight that trickle unseen by my eyes through the layers of black canopy. How I want to meet the Gallerlanders and learn more about their ways, not least of all their electrum. Their simply crafted ring truly serves as my beacon of hope in the darkest of nights.

When the night did finally pass, I lowered myself to the mist-shrouded ground, but not without a thorny farewell scratch from my shelter tree. In my haste during the night I had not seen that its old knobbly trunk was wrapped in a massive vine with brown blades that slowly strangled it. Even the hulking ancient trees do not escape the slow death of the evil hiding here.

Storing a decent stash of fruits, tubers, and mushrooms in my knapsack has proven wise, because nothing edible grows here. The dark forest is without any clear landmarks, and I can only hope that I'm not turning in circles.

❧

Arasemis's Note: This portion of Rildning's journal is badly damaged. Little that is written in this section is legible. It is water-stained and smeared with dirt and blood, molded and torn. Only a few words and phrases, which I reproduce below, hint at his troubles. While Rildning's subsequent writings describe in detail what happened to him during this time when he could not write well, these fragments show that his journey nearly came to an end:

>*. . . wanderings, but I had not found . . .*
>*. . . snake or plant . . .*
>*. . . The eight days . . . same . . . into the pit . . .*
>*. . . again . . . fangs . . .*
>*. . . burning cold . . . dark . . .*
>*. . . wish . . . death . . .*
>*. . . Find me . . .*

It is also noteworthy that Rildning ceased attempts to date his writings for a while thereafter, making it difficult to distinguish one entry from another. Clearly he found it futile to keep track of the "footsteps of old Father Time," as he put it.

❧

It is with mixed emotion that I return to my journal. It must be fate or God's will that I survived, and that this book has not left me or been stolen away by creatures or the evil of the dark forest, of which I doubtless will be an eternal prisoner. I can barely read my own scribble on the preceding pages.

But the fog of my memory is clearing, unlike the dark forest around me. I do not know how long I lay here upon the sodden ground, or why the animals or the earth itself did not swallow me in my stupor.

My battle against the forest depths was wholly lost, or so it seemed. My hands still shake with the thought of how close I came to dying, for I felt the burning coldness of Death's breath upon my face and the whisper of sliding bones in my ear. However, I am still among the living, or so I believe.

My recollection is a snake or moving vine . . . some creature surely designed by Memelos that surprised me from the trees. Unlike the blood-licking black-flowered plant encountered in earlier days in this forest, this animal was far more sinister. There were several, in fact, the largest perhaps the length of three or four men.

When I came upon one of the little ones, it reared up from its belly into the air with a sharp and terrible hiss, and a frothy jet of saliva shot into my eyes. I stumbled as I tried to flee, then I lashed out with my spear, jabbing blindly in every direction. I do not remember much after that, except pitch-darkness and biting cold.

At length I regained fair vision, but only to witness the larger snake fiend coiling around my legs. I saw fang punctures in my arm and stomach, oozing with liquid the color and thickness of honey. Venom it was, and into a nest of serpents I had surely fallen.

I was stiff, lying in long murky mosses and creepers and on the threshold of death when my dull eyes caught the glint of the skeleton's ring on my finger. Its green-golden glimmer pierced the film that coated my dying eyes. My arms were outstretched, lifeless, but the ring's glow so alive.

Most peculiarly, just beyond the ring, the ground shimmied and danced in its glow, for reasons unknown. I gathered the last of my strength and shifted toward the glimmer on the ground and found my face in a warm liquid. I slurped with my last strength, feeling the coiling serpent twist up toward my chest. Then darkness followed . . .

At some point I was awakened by severe pain that pulsed from head to foot, certain the standing snakes were devouring me. I could feel the thick venom gushing through my veins. Bizarre lights and shapes gamboled in my mind's eye while convulsions rocked my body.

It was some time before I awoke fully and realized I had not been eaten. I was alive and yet without feeling. A ghost, without pain or motion, just the dark branches waving above me. Slowly, I noticed my breath, a faint rising and falling that I could not hear; indeed, there was no sound at all, anywhere.

Another period of darkness, then finally light. My strength returned, and I sat up from the muck, looking from side to side. There were signs of a struggle all around me, all manner of blood and foam and other vile waters lying about. And the carcasses of five snakes, my ankles still loosely enwrapped by the largest.

No light shone in its dirt-flecked eyes. They were profound serpents, scaled with large-ribbed coils of jade and jet. Their mouths were all agape, their fangs extended. How had they been stricken in their own nest while I survived? I was not a ghost. Frail, emaciated, cold, and wet—but alive.

I remember staring at the electrum ring, but it did not glow, for the sun had risen above the dim-lit wood. It was then I noticed the pool of blood that had been my bed. I remembered drinking from the pool and feeling the surge in my belly swell up into my heart and mind. I carefully dipped a finger in the sticky pool and traced its origin to wounds gaping in the snakes. Was it the serpents' own blood that served as an antidote for their poison? And what had pointed to this spilled medicine but the electrum ring? Not once but twice has it saved my life with its beacon.

I glanced around and discovered a multitude of eggs that must have come from the great snake. Feeling hungry, I did not hesitate to poke them with my stone knife to suck out the bitter juices. Having survived the attack of the adult, I had no fear of its unborn young. And so I filled myself with them until I was content. My instinct was to crush those I could not consume, but Gallerlandia was their natural home, not mine. Although now a wilderman, I still felt like an invader, an outsider. I let them be, choosing to let the great black forest do with them as it willed.

Feeling reborn, I climbed out from the shallow dip and breathed deeply. My hunger was sated, the pains of my head and minor scratches also gone. Renewed, rejuvenated, released. I whispered a prayer of thanks, even with the dark forest enclosed about me and undoubtedly setting its next trap. The last light dimmed with the early onset of night. I slept soundly under a scowling tree with my mind free of troubles, and no creature troubled me.

I resolved to push forward when I awoke. My steps were swift, my direction unknown yet taken in confident strides, as if I had a new instinct for the wilderwood. For the first time, I felt more a part of the forest than in it. I may have become a true wilderman, but, unlike Arvgred, I have kept my mind. I harbor no fear of the howling wolf, forest lion, or shadow hare, and I can now swoop down upon them from the trees at night to take my meals with stone spear and knife. And I certainly fear no serpents. I can even smell snake eggs from afar.

My colonial clothes long tattered and frayed, I will make new garments from the woodland animals of Gallerlandia's depths. And I will rest easy with a glance at the electrum's softness each night.

∽

Today I came upon a dark stream, the first since entering the depths many days ago. Unlike the Glombruk and other rivers whose breadth parts the forest canopy to sunlight, this stream remained enclosed in a tunnel of roots, trunks, and branches. Having no sun to light its waters and no fair banks at its edge, it remained perpetually shadowed. And it was solemn, having no rocks to dip and gurgle around.

Though thirsty, I dared not cup my hands and drink from its lifeless flow. I soon found a fallen tree to traverse it, leaving the strange sight behind.

∽

On this day I have found a whole row of bloodberry bushes. I refilled my little inkpot. More important, they have given me hope that the forest depths may soon open into the green woodland that I long for, because I've not seen these bushes since before entering the dark forest. Surely it is a good omen.

Two days have passed since finding the bloodberries, and I've found many more bushes. But only today have I seen shards of light play down through the stubborn branches, slipping though the evil gnarled fingers of the dark trees. Though small and sporadic, these glorious sunbeams are most welcome and feel warm upon my face.

One wonders if the world outside is breaking into this wretched realm, or if the darkness is spreading outward, squeezing out the light as it grows.

PART IV

THE OPENING

Luminebb

I found a rare little path and came upon a clearing in the dark forest. For the first time in a long while my lungs felt free to breathe without the constant press of forest walls and shallow light. In the center of this hollow place was a large boulder with three wooden poles strapped to it in the Gallerlander fashion. I nearly wept at the sight.

Most welcome was the sunlight that pushed through the greedy, shading boughs above the boulder, which seemed to be tended by someone. The grasses and mosses around the base of the stone were tidy and well kept. I looked around but saw no sign that someone was near. The keepers of this stone marker could not have been far. It would take regular care to prevent the dark forest from reclaiming this glade.

I patted the warm rock like a familiar friend as I walked the path set around it, then continued on the twisting trail beyond. Only a few hours' walk brought me safely to the edge of the black forest. As soon as I saw more shafts of light breaking through, I broke into a sprint and did not stop. Vines rose up to trip me, and trees launched their crooked arms to swipe at me, but I would not be slowed.

The forest slowly opened as I ran, and gradually I slipped from its shadowy grasp. My heart raced as the ground hardened and warmed beneath my thumping feet, the leather soles of my boots now worn thin. I feasted on the drier air, and the breeze bathed my face. And the light . . . O the light!

My eyes were forced shut, and I fell to my knees in thanks. I had survived the harsh, dark core of wild Gallerlandia, perhaps the inner heart of Pemonia herself.

And now I will sleep tonight under moonlight so bright that a candle is not necessary to write. The brilliance of this night sky jewel might as well be the warming sun. I do not wish to sleep through its radiance, but I must rest, here in Sun and Moon Camp. My last thought is of the electrum ring, which has led me through the depths but is now darkened like any dull ornament. Clearly, its fire glows only in the darkest of places. Where did the natives discover such a curious metal?

$\wp$

I awoke this morning in a gentle plain of broken woodland groves and open meadows. I bathed in a nearby creek then lay there in the sun for a few hours without my tunic. As I rested, I remembered Harsen. If he were alive back on the other side of the dark forest, I hoped that he would forgive me.

Reckoning I had come through the depths more or less in an eastern direction, I was now at least as far east as the middle of Leauvenna, a great island colony in the Bay of Pemonia to the north. But I was unlikely to be so far east as to be south of Arembenel, a failed colony on the mainland east of Leauvenna. The Donovard colonists were aware of a great river between Leauvenna and Arembenel, and I had surely not crossed that river or found its source. Thus, I must be south of Leauvenna, but not too far east. Alas, I am surely farther south than any Brintilian has ever stepped foot.

With the magnificent afternoon sun at my back, I will continue east. I hope to see the elusive Gallerlanders soon. Will they accept this wilderman, whose only link to civilization is a tattered journal and a pewter spoon?

Luminebb 28

This day was momentous, not because of what I discovered but what discovered me. And yes, by God, it truly is Luminebb 28, according to the newfound companions who tell me so! How time disappears in the wilderness. I was at first shocked to learn that it was already late in the summer, but my days walking the forest have been so uncertain.

Several voices woke me from my bed of soft grass under an old willow. I was frozen, fearing they were Hrals. But as the sounds grew nearer I found them familiar, and I soon heard the Brintilian speech. Bewildered, I remained unmoving. Hearing a laugh, I smiled and craved yet feared to speak to one of my own kind, but the wilderman in me kept me hiding like a panicked woodland hare. Who were they? Why and how were they here? What should I do? My thoughts raced until I became dizzy, and the throb in my ears became deafening. I scampered behind the old willow to hide.

I found the courage to peer out in time to see the men break out of the brush and into my little dell. They were three, with horses and well clad in the armor and fine equipment of crusaders. In the front walked a stocky man leading his steed, long sandy hair tied behind his head. His scraggly mustache wafted with his heavy breath as he hacked angrily at the undergrowth.

The two men behind him were mounted and rode lazily. The second man in line had a tattered banner pinned to his saddle. He seemed to be having a chuckle at the expense of the first, as the stocky man seemed weary of the forest.

The third man, with a fourth horse tethered behind, kept his composure and appeared to pay no attention to the antics of the other two. This man thoughtfully scanned the woods right and left as he rode, not fearful but observant. He was perhaps the youngest of the three but clearly the leader among them.

All three were clad in quality mail and leathern armor with thigh boots, though all showed much weathering and battle. Their leader carried the finest steel sword among them, its glittering gem-encrusted pommel and hilt signaling that he was a man of wealth.

The front man abruptly shouted a halt, so I whirled back behind the willow, certain that he had seen me. Then I realized it was my squirrel-hide knapsack, which I had carelessly left out on the grass! I could hear the stocky man draw closer as the second man dismounted. One of them picked up the pouch. After one of them commented that it was a barbarian item, they all drew their swords. I knew they would step around the willow, so I stepped out into the danger and yelled, "Wait! Wait! I'm Brintilian!"

The crusaders were astonished and stayed their swords, but the bowstring of the stocky man remained drawn. In a cautious but mild tone, the leader ordered the second man to drop the pouch and back away from me. When I showed no signs of moving, he motioned for the bowman to lower his arrow.

"Who are you?" the leader asked me. It was more than a moment before I could answer with my name. When I asked who they were, he replied that they were a raiding party, Crusaders from the colony of Donovan. "Hungry?" he asked. I nodded.

Through mouthfuls of dried venison and stale crust I told them of my journey. They listened intently, especially the leader, whose name was Hiltsfrad. But at one point Borsar, the chuckling second man, interrupted my story with a disturbing comment.

"But did you not know Gallerlandia was already our realm?" he asked. Hiltsfrad barked at him to hold his tongue, the first time I had seen the calm leader angered. He was clearly annoyed by Borsar's rudeness. Hiltsfrad apologized and encouraged me to continue. Not surprisingly, they became interested in my description of the Donovard turned wilderman Arvgred and the electrum of the Gallerlanders. I was careful not to mention Varesig's secret orders to find more electrum.

Borsar laughed mightily when I concluded by telling of my now personal quest to seek out an alliance with the Gallerlanders for New Lorin. Hiltsfrad, himself unable to stifle a grin, said as politely as he could that such a quest was doomed to fail. He added, in a more serious tone, that it was probably not in New Lorin's interest to so gravely offend their brethren in Donovan by allying with that colony's enemy. I took this thinly veiled warning at face value, resolving to hide my intentions as much as possible.

When I had finished my tale, Hiltsfrad offered condolences for Harsen and the others and also praised my skill of survival. He then told me of their perilous journey down a great river named Torfnarbruk, mightier than even the Glombruk, which was also known to him. Hiltsfrad explained that Donovan Colony had been heavily and repeatedly attacked prior to last winter.

When spring arrived, the colonists surprised the heathens by attacking their coastal villages with boats laden with men and weapons, burning their way east from the mouth of the Glombruk for many days until they found the monstrous Torfnarbruk, which had never been adequately navigated by Donovards.

They followed the Torfnarbruk inland until they came to a native town where they killed the chieftain, Torfnar. They discovered him to be the leader of the Ulgol, a northern clan of Gallerlanders. This clan and many others, he said, lived in a region of Gallerlandia named Goynland. Hiltsfrad said they lost many men in the fight but were compelled to follow their victories with more bloody raids.

They sailed slowly up the Torfnarbruk, sacking other small settlements as they found them. They soon came to

Goynland's capital city, Yoredgoyn, where the Donovards found themselves far outnumbered and soon defeated. Hiltsfrad led the survivors south, where they pledged themselves to waging the crusade from within Gallerlandia, giving their lives to this cause because there was little hope of returning to Donovan.

This smelled like the creed of Arvgred, and I wondered what made the Donovards so bloodthirsty. Hiltsfrad, Borsar, and Alvas, the stocky long-haired archer, were the only remaining members of their unit to travel this far south. A few other survivors, "cowards," as Hiltsfrad labeled them, abandoned their oaths and turned back north to seek the sea and home. But he was sure they had little chance of leaving Gallerlandia alive.

I was struck by these raiders' deep war lust but was fascinated by their revelations. This fighting in the north might explain why I had not seen any Gallerlanders, especially on this side of the dark forest. All the natives were undoubtedly drawn up to help the northern clans oppose the invading Donovards.

Hiltsfrad was no mindless brute. When I mentioned that trade between the western Gallerlanders and Harsen's folk who settled the fringe could never be conducted with the vicious Hrals, Hiltsfrad, to my surprise, nodded in agreement and said, "They are different in different places and at different times . . ." But given all that these men had done in the north, I was careful not to provoke them. And who was I to criticize, given my own history with the imperial legions?

After our long repast, Hiltsfrad asked where I would go. I replied that I would continue east. He repeated that I should avoid the carnage in the north, adding that the heathens are probably pursuing him and his men, even this far south. He said that he and Alvas had killed two Gallerlander scouts two nights prior. These scouts had killed the rider of the horse tethered to Hiltsfrad's.

The lead knight smirked, saying the heathens would not expect the next army that would follow his campaign. He had sent messengers back down the Torfnarbruk to Donovan with information about the locations of Gallerlander settlements and movements. He did not elaborate, but it was clear he expected Donovan would be sending another wave of conquerors.

I asked Hiltsfrad where they would go next. They were also planning to travel east and south, so he invited me to join them. They had learned that a great Gallerlander city lay at the source of the Torfnarbruk—"Perhaps the greatest of all the barbarian cities," he said. Hiltsfrad jested that he and his raiders would certainly perish while fighting the Gallerlanders, so why not seek out their king of kings?

The solemn faces of Borsar and Alvas told me they were serious in their oaths to strike at the beating heart of Gallerlandia, even if it promised certain death. Shuffling my calloused feet in the dirty shells of my boots, I opted to join them for now. Perhaps I could learn a bit more from them and come to understand where to find the natives.

And for the first time in a while, I would ride a horse. At first I did not care whether it was a bad omen to ride the dead man's steed, but I've since wondered about this as I consider that I am again riding with men who seek ill-gotten gold and glory in this forest realm.

As we trotted along I asked Hiltsfrad how he knew the Gallerlander names, like the chieftain Torfnar, Goynland, and the Ulgol clan. He smiled and confessed proudly that he had learned a bit of the Gali language from heathen captives when he was a warden of a fortress prison in Donovan. He fished in his pocket and revealed a tiny book, tattered as my own journal, which held his notes on their speech. He promised to share it with me around the campfire, and I was glad to accept the offer.

Harvesteve 1

My entries today will recount conversations with my Donovard companions over the past three days. They are amused that I have kept this ragged journal. I've neglected keeping it up recently, but this evening is calm, so I rest with my thoughts.

I had asked Hiltsfrad about the Gallerlander city toward which we journeyed. He explained that they had found a clay slab within the village of the slain chieftain Torfnar. The Donovards reasoned that the slab was a map of sorts. It bore a crude drawing of a colonist ship in the general direction of Donovan, and Torfnar's village was noted roughly where the colonists had found it.

This was stunning to me. Not only did the Gallerlanders have written symbols and make maps, they appeared to have a better understanding of the colonies' locations than we did of their lands. How I wish I could have seen that unspoiled clay map.

Hiltsfrad continued, saying the clay tablet was inlaid in the floor of Torfnar's hut and kept moist and soft by the map's keeper, so that it could be modified with ease. Hiltsfrad was embarrassed to admit that when his men, Borsar among them, saw the colony depicted on the clay, they stomped on it until it was ruined.

I asked whether Hiltsfrad could re-create the clay map from memory onto a page in my journal. He had already done so in his own little book and had also written down some of the symbols before they were destroyed. He was happy to let me sketch a copy, saying it was the same information that his messengers had sent back to the colony.

Hiltsfrad said they had coaxed the captured map keeper to speak the names on the map by pointing at each one. The names as written on my sketch are as Hiltsfrad heard them. The *-land* suffix is, of course, the Brintilian way of speaking about territories within the greater *-landia* realms.

I'd never heard of map writing among the natives, not even the Ollohd, who have absorbed the habits of New Loriners. I can't help but imagine the excitement Orren would feel at such a sight. Hiltsfrad was amused by my fascination with something that he clearly saw as a means to an end. I next pressed him for knowledge of the Gallerlander language.

Only when Borsar and Alvas left to forage did Hiltsfrad again reveal his little book, its pages bearing random scribbles and sketches. He confessed that in actuality, the heathens were a perpetual interest for his brother, as they had been for Orren. It was at his brother's request that Hiltsfrad had gathered words from Gallerlanders held prisoner in the fortress he commanded, and later his brother was permitted to visit with them. Hiltsfrad, his face now grave, said that the notebook was all that he had been able to salvage from his brother's studies after heathens had raided his brother's home and killed him, along with his family.

Hiltsfrad continued to learn what he could of Gali, but his motives were quite different from those of his brother. Hiltsfrad responded to the massacre with another massacre, executing nearly every native in the prison and dumping their beheaded bodies in the forest, a grisly deed he said he did not regret.

Hiltsfrad used this story to warn me that all natives of Pemonia would be a threat to Brintilian colonies, always, and that I should remember his brother's fate if ever I sit down with them. While his tale is tragic, I wonder why the Donovards have taken such a different path when dealing with the natives. New Lorin has had problems with the Hrals, but our efforts with the Ollohd tribe and others have yielded fruits of peace that the Donovards have never tasted.

Hiltsfrad told me I could keep his notebook for now. He has helped me sound out the symbols, and I have enjoyed reading the translations. Gali is very peculiar.

I also asked Hiltsfrad for more detail of the chief Torfnar and his Ulgol clan and the wider Gallerlander race, such as their chiefs and family structures. He said Donovards believe that the Gallerlanders are an uncountable people that are divided into three main groupings: Goyns, Vayns, and Umbyrs, who live in regions defined by the Donovards as Goynland, Vaynland, and Umbyrland, respectively.

Each of these subtribes encompasses many clans, which are further divided into families. For example, Torfnar was the chief of the Ulgol clan within the Umbyr tribe. The clans of the Umbyrs inhabit central Gallerlandia, named Umbyrland. Although the precise territorial boundaries are unknown to the Donovards and may not even exist among the natives, Hiltsfrad said their appearances sometimes differ. We spent several firelight hours discussing their names and structures.

Hiltsfrad judged that Gallerlander society is hierarchical, with the chief of each family, clan, and tribe holding absolute authority over his unit and being very protective of his territory. But the chieftaincies are not hereditary. "Proof of their chaotic barbarity," he said. Rather, new leaders are chosen from among all the men of the unit, usually accomplished warriors who are also noted for their skills in settling clan disputes.

This is an interesting concept that does not, of course, exist in the Old World or its colonies in Pemonia, where the divine right of kings is sacred. I think we Brintilians may have something to learn from the politics of the natives, if Hiltsfrad's observations are correct. Brintilians will not seek this knowledge, however, because we view ourselves as sitting atop the fray in the Old World. But our rule will end one day, like that of the empires before us, and the chaos will repeat itself.

According to Hiltsfrad, the Donovards also believe that the ruler of all the Gallerlanders resided in a large city in

Umbyrland, which he and his companions are seeking out. Vaynland, situated somewhere farther south or perhaps far to the southwest, is a complete mystery to the Donovards. In fact, Hiltsfrad is sure no Brintilian has ever ventured even as far into Gallerlandia as we are now.

Recalling the lone journeys of Arvgred, I wondered aloud if this was true, that perhaps other wildermen had roamed among the natives. Hiltsfrad assured me that Arvgred and I were rare oddities. He asked me to tell him more about Arvgred, so I recounted that he looked much as I did, gaunt under tattered fur tunic and weathered face. But Arvgred had been alone far longer than I and had lost much of himself to the wilderwood. He no longer resembled a proper Donovard colonist.

As when I had first mentioned him, Hiltsfrad found Arvgred's name humorous for the same reason my party did: the wilderman had taken the name and imagined persona of the famous successor of Donovan's founder. At any rate, my meager details about Arvgred were not enough for Hiltsfrad to identify the wilderman as a particular Donovard soldier. Hiltsfrad said many troops had disappeared into Gallerlandia over the years, most of them missing after a battle or taken captive by the heathens, never to be seen again.

₭

My Donovard companions noticed that my weapons were made of stone and jokingly asked if difficulties in New Lorin had forced us to resort to such primitive materials. Alvas kindly offered me a steel knife, which I declined. I recounted how the Hrals had stolen my weapons and described how I eventually learned to craft my own, having been inspired by those made by Arvgred.

Borsar sarcastically quipped that my stone weapons were a sign that I had indeed become a native. Hiltsfrad had observed that the Gallerlanders did not use metal weapons, which was puzzling. Clearly they had developed metalworking, as seen by their electrum jewelry, yet they had not adopted iron for swords and armor, to their own detriment. This was one reason, said Hiltsfrad, that the heathens would never be able to compete with steel-armored and steel-bladed colonial armies. The Gallerlanders, he added, did not even adopt the use of horses, providing the Donovards a great advantage in speed and maneuverability.

"The main reason is their barbarian stupidity," interjected Borsar. I responded that perhaps they have their reasons for not adopting metal and steeds, and that one day they may inflict surprises on colonists who were blinded by their own advantages. I added that the natives were currently outdone by our well-organized armies and tactics, but that they would probably adapt one day.

I pointed to myself, saying that I had mastered stone weapons, if ever Borsar needed a teacher. Hiltsfrad chuckled, but the grumpy Borsar remained unimpressed. "I'll sooner eat a feeble heathen tool than use one," was his ridiculous retort.

Hiltsfrad continued, saying he believed I was correct about the colonies' superior techniques of warfare. He said the Gallerlanders always used melee and swarm attacks, which had worked well against the colonies when they were newly established, grossly outnumbered, and had few permanent defenses. Arembenel was the prime example.

But the colonies that survived gained strength by building strong frontier forts and using cavalry. And when the well-trained and well-motivated crusaders came to the New World, followed by shiploads of steel swords and armor from Almeria, the Gallerlander attacks were rendered largely ineffective.

Hiltsfrad's tone was exceedingly arrogant when he spoke of these things. He later boasted of his membership in the Order of the Knights of Hovedollen, which I knew to be one of the four founding military orders of the crusaders. They answered the call of the Martinus to fight the heathens and were tasked by the emperor with expanding the territory of Donovan.

Hiltsfrad had undoubtedly served his oath courageously in northern Gallerlandia and had made it this far into the depths. But I wondered if his fate would not be so glorious in the beautiful but unforgiving wilderness that presently governed us.

Only one story is left to bring my journal up to date: that of the curious green-golden electrum. On this evening around our campfire, Borsar, always rude of temperament, asked why I fancied wearing the ring of a dead heathen prince. "Did you kill him?" he asked. "And how will that bring you peace with the barbarians?"

For a moment I was confused, then annoyed. The Donovard trio sat looking and waiting for an answer to a question they had long wondered. I carefully pinched the simple ornament and snugged it closer to the knuckle, confessing that I was a thief to have taken it. But I had not killed the man, I said, for the hand from which it was pilfered was only cold bones. I repeated my story of captivity with the Hrals, noting the part about the ring and its glow in the nights of the black forest. Then I asked Borsar why he believed the deceased native was a prince.

The gruff soldier stood from his log and unfastened a leather pouch from his belt. On the ground at my feet he dumped dozens of pieces of electrum jewelry, all manners of necklaces, bracelets, rings, and other bits. Some were carved with symbols, but most were plainly made.

He pointed proudly to his horse and said he had many bags of this treasure taken from the villages they had sacked. "But none have the circle," he said, "except Hiltsfrad's ring." I looked as the knight displayed his prize. The electrum ring was simple enough, with the bezel engraved with a circle, similar to a signet ring among our own people. He nodded and confirmed that he had taken it from the hand of Chief Torfnar, whom he had slain.

I was surprised. I had guessed that the skeleton was a Gallerlander who had been killed by the Hrals, but I had not suspected he was a chieftain. More surprising was that these crusading soldiers, who pledged themselves to honor-bound deeds for the empire, bothered to burden themselves with so much treasure if they did not intend to return home to spend it. What value did it then have in this distant wilderness, beyond useless weight?

But I kept my thoughts to myself as they sat quietly fingering their false wealth. Borsar's eyes twitched until he visited the bulging sacks resting beside his horse, to check that their glimmering contents remained safe. The silence persisted, so I retreated to my journal. By then Borsar had turned his attention to sleep and let me be.

Harvesteve 2

There are no worn paths, but our pace by horse has been quicker than what I had grown accustomed to while walking the woods alone. The great forests of this land have opened their great arms. The quaint meadows have now widened into hilly and sparsely wooded small plains. As we ride south, the land continues to dip slightly, and all streams meander and explore the low places ahead of us. One wonders if the patches of forest and plain will soon give way to a great valley.

Despite the luxury of the nice sleeping arrangement, the odd feeling of sleeping in a dead man's bedroll and riding his horse has grown. The Donovards washed their comrade's heathen-spilled blood from it all, yet I cannot help but feel uneasy. Of course, now that Harvesteve is upon us, the low ground is laced with cooler, creeping night air, and I'll be glad to have more than my fur tunic.

More importantly, I've had much time to reflect on my journey with men who intend to kill as many natives as they can before they fall, while I have wholly opposite intentions. It has been good to speak with other Brintilians, but I feel distant from the world I left and have grown wary of these men in particular. Despite our mostly friendly banter, my instincts—perhaps coming from the wilderman within— urges me to part ways at the soonest opportunity.

Perhaps my bedroll uneasiness comes from a fear that death lurks close behind this raiding party. I want no part of their bloody expedition, whether driven by the crusading spirit or an underlying greed for electrum. The usually reserved and polite Hiltsfrad is difficult to read. Borsar betrays his own chief interest regularly, while Alvas is unconcerned about any lofty goal and seems resigned to some violent fate in the nearby woods.

Regardless of their motives, I want no part of their mission or the destruction that will eventually sweep over them, perhaps sooner than they realize.

Harvesteve 3

oday witnessed a remarkable discovery.

The morning was cool and damp with a thick fog wrapped around every tree and collected in the low places. Shortly after breaking our night fast with mushrooms, dried fish, and freshly plucked pearlberries, we stumbled upon a difficult grove of elder trees that strung up nets of bramble vines and stinging briars. There was no way around the endless knot, so we resolved to dismount and cut a path through.

Luckily we found a narrow and shoulder-high tunnel path, probably cleared out by generations of pioneering deer. Also hidden in the bramble tunnel walls were plump nesting birds with big peering eyes, stubby beaks, and chestnut plumage. They watched us pass with the calm curiosity of creatures who have never before seen a man. This made them easy catch, and we plucked several from their roosts for a tasty meal.

As we came to the edge of the thorny grove, we caught sight of stonework through the breaks in the brush and fog that still hesitated to lift. They were revealed to be ancient standing stones, many of them scattered in every direction. Most were tall as a man, some waist high, but all were of a very dark stone and crusted in green and gray lichen. These blocks were roughly hewn, heavily weathered, and cold to the touch. No carvings or ornament graced their faces.

Seeing my wonder, Hiltsfrad explained that this was a Gallerlander cemetery. He had seen others farther north. We could not make out the bounds of the dour place for the fog. Borsar quickly left us and nearly skipped as he searched around each grave column. Hiltsfrad soon joined him, then Alvas with less vigor. They fanned out over the dark grass, stirring up the heavy mist like fish in a vast soup. I walked slowly behind them with our horses to keep them in sight. The burial stones seemed to stretch on forever.

At last I heard a giddy squeal from Borsar, who was now far beyond sight. We followed his muffled voice until we found him, standing before a tall, flat stone. As we came closer, the shadow of great hands reached down from the hazy cloud that hung over us, and large faces could now be seen etched in the dark stone, twisted in every manner of hideous poses.

Above the slab were poised tall crossing arches, not hands, but rows of antlers of many deer and moose, affixed to the wooden arches like branches sprouting in every direction. "A tomb guardian," explained Hiltsfrad. "Made only for the most celebrated heathen warrior-kings." By the looks of it, the deceased was great indeed. And the tomb was old, but not as weathered as many of the other smaller stones.

In short, Hiltsfrad described the Gallerlander belief that the souls of men ascended to the feasting table at Nawurihar, the heavenly hall of their pagan god that translated roughly as Great White Forest. Their souls arose in ghostly form to be remade in a heavenly body after their earthly ones lay at rest for no less than one hundred winters. Hence the elaborate protection of the great leaders' bodies, so that they could be properly at rest so as to serve in the final battle with evil. Borsar interrupted to add that the barbarians' efforts were futile, since all of them would return to the hell of Memelos from which they were spawned. Hiltsfrad nodded silently.

At this point, foolishly, I could not resist asking them if they truly believed the natives to be the children of Memelos. Incredulous, Hiltsfrad responded that he could not fathom otherwise. "Why else did our grandfathers come to Pemonia, if not to finish the great purge that was begun by the ancients of Cedelaebos?"

To this I had no answer that would assuage him, and wished for the studied, convincing words of Orren. But I did not wish to be struck down in that cemetery. Heresy, of course, remains the greatest crime one can commit, whether in the colonies or the hinterlands. Those found guilty by the holy judges are strangled or burned at the stake, a judgment that can be carried out even in the wilderness by churchmen or senior legion officers like Hiltsfrad. Luckily the Donovards were too focused on finding treasure to pay further attention to me.

Borsar smashed a small boulder against the tomb, but it crumbled without scratching the dark slab. Then he tried his sword as a lever on the massive lid. Hiltsfrad called him a fool for his willingness to snap his blade. The knight declared that we could not budge the lid of the huge tomb even if we were ten men, and certainly had no chance as four.

In a huff, Borsar sprinted to other smaller tomb guardians behind the great one. There were at least a dozen of them, arrayed in a half circle near the large one, all with similarly carved faces and reaching antlers.

Borsar clearly coveted the electrum that he knew from experience lay within the tombs. Among the smaller vaults he found one whose lid was weathered and cracked enough to wedge his sword in. Pulling himself atop it, he pushed and strained. Hiltsfrad and Alvas joined his labor. Borsar's sword soon snapped with a shattering chime that twinkled in the mist, causing him to fall from atop the grave.

Hiltsfrad did not chide him but stepped toward the breach. Borsar swiftly picked himself up from the soupy vapors and yelled at me for not helping. The others scowled. Borsar, with no regard for the gaping wound to his forearm or the loss of his weapon, climbed up again to pull at the lid. His gluttonous face boiled red with strain and anger. In a short time they pried off half of the slab to reveal a simple shallow box.

I stepped closer, hesitant to be involved in the robbing but curious about the contents. Inside were the unwrapped remains of a Gallerlander chief who had been buried in his simple leathern armor and with a stone-tipped spear.

Borsar's mouth watered. He wasted no time in snatching up the skeleton's bulky electrum necklace, dislodging the skull with his excited, grasping hands. Hiltsfrad stealthily reached in and slipped a ring from the finger bone, this one having the circular etching that signified a chieftain.

"If this little tomb has the princely ring," giggled Borsar, "imagine what lies hidden in the big one!" Borsar scooped up earrings and other small bits with a grim smile. Alvas took no electrum but angrily launched the chief's spear as far as he could throw it. Hiltsfrad was satisfied with having another ring on his hand. I stepped away in disgust. Again, these corrupted crusaders took no notice of me.

We camped for the night among the Gallerlander graves. Borsar and Hiltsfrad would not continue the journey until they had the chance to examine every large tomb in sight, picking at every lid for exploitable fissures. In the end, their efforts were mostly fruitless.

They finally contented themselves with a few small nuggets of electrum chipped off an altar stone, and even over these possessions they argued. Their insatiable desire to accumulate a worthless metal seems so unnatural in the wilderness, where survival is the ultimate prize. We have left a stain on this sacred place, and I am eager to leave, but camp we must.

As I stare at the fire that casts long shadows behind the silent standing stones, I imagine those dark pillars taking note of the colonists' actions and passing the tale to every one of their brethren mountains, cliffs, and rock fields to make our path difficult.

My last task tonight is refining the lines of a rubbing I took of a strange etching on a short column near the great tomb. A large tree or forest appears centered in the scene, flanked by crowns on both sides and surrounded by fire and snakes beyond. I cannot guess at its meaning as my eyes grow tired . . .

Harvesteve 4

"Discovery follows disaster," wrote Rin, the legendary explorer. As the father of several failed voyages and colonies and yet also the discoverer of the New World, he would know. But here with these raiders, I say that disaster follows greed.

When we awoke from our graveyard slumber, Borsar spun into a frenzy when he could not locate his share of the altar nuggets collected yesterday. He accused me and then even Hiltsfrad of stealing from him, then proceeded to give us a tongue lashing that included a traitorous oath and threating our lives.

This was not taken lightly by Hiltsfrad. The knight bolted up from his wood-hen repast without a sound, hand on sword hilt, awaiting Borsar's next move. Angered until hot faced but realizing his own recklessness, Borsar at first hesitated but then reached to draw his knife. In a blink Hiltsfrad was upon him, egregiously injuring Borsar's weapon arm.

The pitiful man fell to the fog-shrouded ground, sobbing in agony and surrender. The knight swiftly kicked him in the stomach then quietly returned to his meal, tossing Borsar's knife to me for safekeeping. Borsar is lucky to be alive.

I watched Hiltsfrad carefully while Borsar writhed in the dirt and tried to stop the bleeding. Hiltsfrad noticed my stare and, calm as ever, said, "No, Rildning, I did not take his electrum. But I should have." Then a devious thought seemed to strike him, and he approached Borsar's bedroll where he found the swordsman's missing trinkets in the bottom. Hiltsfrad held them where Borsar could see them, then deposited them in his own pocket. He told Borsar that it was payment for sparing his life, then kicked him again before returning to his meal.

I lost my appetite and looked on as Alvas bandaged Borsar's arm. Hiltsfrad's unpredictable cruelty to one of his own has caused me to carefully consider how to abandon these wicked men without being a target of their wrath.

That was this morning. It is now midday, and we have stopped to rest and water the horses. I'm glad to be out of the Gallerlander cemetery, which stretched on and on through a murky haze that seemed like it would never lift. We found recent graves as we departed the area, indicating the graveyard was still in use and potentially signaling the direction of the nearest village.

Harvesteve 5

How many times have I come so close to dying in this wilderness at the hands of the indifferent elements or the vicious Hrals, by starvation or drowning rivers, or poisoned and eaten by the beasts? And now by the hand of my own Brintilian brethren, their own foolishness, or my foolishness for having kept company with them. And now also the Gallerlanders . . .

Much has happened since we walked among the misty tomb guardians. Within an hour or so of my last writing on that afternoon, we found a Gallerlander village, as Hiltsfrad had predicted. I was glad to have finally made this discovery after so much time, but I knew we would not be welcomed.

The electrum ring felt like a lead weight on my finger, as if it was called by the earth to melt back down into the ground from which it came. It felt wrong on my hand, and I felt a similar dirtiness about all the electrum that clinked and jingled in the many pockets and sacks of those loot-burdened Donovards. I wished to rid myself of the ring at least, to cast it into the bushes and meet the natives free of my theft. But it had been a beacon in the dark places, and the Donovards carried enough stolen electrum to condemn our whole race.

We saw movement in the woods ahead. I slipped the ring off and concealed it in a pouch fold of my fur tunic. We dismounted and crouched within view of the outskirts of the village. Hiltsfrad had a devious gleam in his eyes, his mouth a curl of foul delight.

The knight calmly whispered his plan: We would take the settlement by surprise from two directions. Alvas and I were to stay where we were while Hiltsfrad and Borsar walked around to the far side. There couldn't be more than seven or eight huts, he said, and we would have the advantage, since it would appear to them that we were many. Alvas and I would rush in upon hearing Hiltsfrad's shout.

I, of course, rejected his plans as soon as I could get a word in. I told him plainly that I had been a knight of New Lorin, never under his command, and that I was here to meet the Gallerlanders, not murder them. I added my displeasure in seeing my Brintilian brethren succumb to the greed of wealth and lust for blood, which was not in the honorable interests of the colonies. And not only would I depart from them at once, but I would warn the Gallerlanders of the attack.

Hiltsfrad mustered every drop of patience as his face reddened to Borsar's hue. I admit that my lecturing the commander was unwise, but I was so astounded by him that I could not control my anger and disgust any longer. I had seen enough bloodshed while soldiering for New Lorin.

The four of us silently retreated with haste. When we had gained enough distance to speak clearly, Hiltsfrad calmly asked for one solid reason not to kill every last barbarian before they killed us. Before I could give my answer, which he had no intention of hearing, he exploded, mocking my beliefs and "petty learning."

He reminded me that every colonist knew it was heresy to consider the heathens as anything but devils, a crime he not so subtly hinted was within his power to judge. He said he had expected more from a soldier of my standing but had always been disappointed in the "soft hearts" of New Loriners. He grabbed Borsar's knife from my twine belt, returned it to Borsar, confiscated all of my stone weapons, then shoved me to the ground. Borsar stood above me, blade and grim teeth gleaming. Hiltsfrad offered to spare my life only if I would help his men with the attack, my last chance to prove which side I was on.

At that moment I shouted at the top of my lungs a warning to the village. I was swiftly and viciously boot-stomped by all three of the raiders. Then they paused long enough to listen for any reaction from the Gallerlanders. Hearing voices and the rustle of bushes, Hiltsfrad signaled to Alvas, who was quick with his flints. In no time a small fire smoldered among his pile of twigs and leaves.

Through the blood in my eyes I watched as he and the others twisted shards of cloth around his arrow tips. One by one they were lit and shot into the thatched huts. The excitement was enough to distract Borsar, and I was able to wrest out from under his filthy boot.

I looked ahead and saw the natives running about, clearly confused at the sudden burst of flames that danced upon their hovels. The Donovards laughed madly at this tragic sight, while tears streaked the blood and dirt off my face. This was my first sight of the Gallerlanders.

I took the opportunity to run, limping and weaponless. Only my knapsack remained attached to me. Behind I could hear Hiltsfrad shouting, "Flee then, but I will find you!" Borsar added something about cutting off my ring as their voices faded.

I did not get far. I ran straight into natives who appeared to have broken off their game hunt to respond to the commotion. There was no escape. They took me captive back to the village. Along the way I saw the lifeless body of Alvas, his bow snapped in two and the little fire nipping at his garments. A large Gallerlander stood over the archer, hands without weapons, his eyes glaring and his face fuming.

At the village I was cast down into the dirt of a central gathering area circled by smoldering huts. Hiltsfrad and Borsar also sat there, the dust of the ground clinging to fresh wounds. But they had not been beaten by the natives as badly as they had beaten me moments before. I also must have appeared different from those two criminals because of my furry wilderman garb. The pair held their heads low to avoid looking at the Gallerlanders, while I sat up marveling at the natives until one slapped my face down as well.

The Gallerlanders were numerous, with more rapidly appearing from the woods around the settlement. Their bodies were mostly bare, lean and muscular. Some men wore only a loincloth, others had crude leathern armor. One wore a belt with many small stone-edged knives hanging from it. The women were nearly as scantily clad, though most wore lighter versions of fur tunics and even armor.

All of the natives looked like they had swum in a river of green dye, for they were covered head to foot in many shades of green body paint, a few with brown or gray streaks. A closer look revealed much of this to be tattoo, with intricate swirled designs. Nearly all wore leather moccasins stuffed with long grass, with similar decoration or padding in bands about their head or wrists.

And then there was the electrum, fashioned into all types of jewelry. Their children, who were also permitted to view the prisoners, were similarly painted and tattooed—even a baby had bright swirls on his bulbous cheeks. And their livestock, which included woodland sheep and woodland hens, were marked with green spots or smears. The sight was something well beyond anything Harsen or Orren had ever described. I felt painfully white and unadorned, as if naked.

Their Gali language, as we Brintilians call it, was quick, and their tone confused and furious. They were clearly debating our fate while others could be seen removing their dead and wounded and burned belongings from several hovels that still smoldered. They had no means of putting out the fires that quickly devoured the stick walls of their homes.

A native in well-kept leather armor soon arrived and shouted orders. The three of us were snatched up and our hands bound tight. Then they dragged us through the village, which was much larger than Hiltsfrad had predicted. We arrived at a large oval hut and were tossed in the dirt before it. All the chattering Gallerlanders grew silent when the well-armored man raised his arm. As he quieted them, Borsar, his voice trembling, pleaded with me to plead with them to spare us. I said nothing, and neither did Hiltsfrad.

When all had grown still, the double doors of the wooden hut opened and out stepped the man who was clearly the chief, followed by others, likely his courtiers and relatives. He had a large, exposed belly but was stoutly built. He was older, with a gray beard streaked with green dye and tied in a knot that rested on his chest.

Wolf pelts draped his shoulders, and his slippers were studded with electrum beads. His head was bare except for a small circle of electrum at his forehead that hung from twine. His face was weathered and heavily tattooed. In his hand was a wooden scepter or hammer of some kind, inlaid with speckled river stones. This was pointed at us, and he calmly spoke a few words before pausing to look skyward, as if looking for a sign in the clouds. After this, we were once again hoisted to our feet.

The chieftain walked up close to us to examine our faces one by one, as well as our clothing and possessions. Hiltsfrad was first. The village men displayed the weapons and articles that had been taken from him. The chief inspected these, including the stolen princely rings, which the chief reclaimed from his fingers with a vengeful glare.

Apparently satisfied, he moved on to Borsar. The inspection revealed Borsar's belt bags full of electrum, including the bulky necklace from the broken tomb, the burial ornaments, and rings. Borsar held his wounds and smiled clumsily as he attempted to say something to the chief. But they pounced on him.

The chief whacked his scepter upon Borsar's head, then the village men swiftly beat him to death. He did not even have time to cry out. Hiltsfrad barely flinched and kept his eyes straight ahead. I tried to do the same, but their brutality was awful. All of Borsar's ill-gotten gains were then taken into the chief's hut.

Then they moved on to me. They found in my knapsack no electrum or weapons, and on me only my hide tunic, stained by wounds and weather. But after feeling through my furs they found the skeleton's ring. It did not cause the same reaction with the chief as Hiltsfrad's ring had. In fact it seemed to puzzle him. He held its rough-hewn circle up to his eye. Then he looked at Hiltsfrad, then back at me as if he was comparing our appearances.

The crusader knight stood calm and unafraid. The chief's face darkened when he tried to read something in my eyes, then he departed with a grunt. Before returning to his hut, he gave a short speech to the crowd, holding up the stolen electrum rings. They gasped and whispered among themselves as he disappeared into his home.

Hiltsfrad and I were taken and secured inside a lone hovel with a stick-barred door. We sat on the empty dirt floor, watching through the cracks as the villagers scurried about. We could see an open-air throne near the chief's hut. Trap doors were being opened from the ground before it, and a small fence was placed around the opening and decorated with flowering vines.

Hiltsfrad said solemnly that he had seen this before in villages farther north. We would be thrown into the pit to either drown or burn. I asked him if the blood and electrum had been worth it, now that we could see our fate. Holding his composure, he responded that he was ready to die because he had served the empire well and honorably in defeating the northern clans and taking their wealth. After all, he said, it was our religious duty as Messengians to purge the continent of evil.

"You, Rildning, on the other hand, do not deserve to die at the hands of the enemy," he added. "I should have killed you as a heretic when I had the chance!" I retorted that it wasn't too late, that he could avoid the pit and be strangled now by a wilderman if he wished. He laughed and said the world was changing. The Old World would rule all of the New, and the empire would do what it wills with all the barbarians, electrum, and weak-hearted wanderers like me.

He predicted New Lorin would fail and be overrun by the heathens because we spent too much time talking and trading with them and not enough time building a strong colony for Crown and Church. "But not to worry," he said, "Donovan will ultimately overtake New Lorin and herd you like sheep, just like these savages." I lunged at him but it was too late, our time had come.

As Hiltsfrad had foretold, we were tossed into the pit after having our bonds cut, presumably so the chief could see some sport as he took his seat on the throne overlooking us. But there was no water in the hollow and no firewood. We looked up expecting to see fire poured down from above but saw only smiling green-tattooed faces set in a sapphire sky.

A commotion was heard above, then the faces parted. A large basket appeared, hauled by three men. Strangely, I could sense what was next. The entire basket was cast into the pit and we heard a vicious hiss and flailing from within as it crashed to the ground. The wicker lid popped off and a huge snake of the same type I had encountered in the dark forest slithered out, spitting feverishly.

Its onyx eyes fixed upon me first, and dread filled me, for I knew the pain of its fangs and the burning coldness of its venom. And there was no spilled blood as antidote within sight. Hiltsfrad, pale faced and pressing up against the dirt wall, let slip a whimper of fear as he watched it come to me.

As the serpent approached and reared up on its ribbed belly, I closed my eyes and turned toward the wall to await death. Soon I felt the sliding puncture of the needles, then cold and darkness and no pain. After a moment I heard Hiltsfrad claw at the dirt and scream, then only silence.

Was I dead? I heard chattering above and slowly opened my eyes. There were long wooden poles with hooks dangling and fishing from above. The Gallerlanders were corralling the great serpent back into the basket. Then gasps of astonishment gushed from above as I sat myself up and rubbed the two large holes in my thigh. Venom pulsed and bubbled from the wound as before. But my sight was sharp and hearing keen as ever, my mouth dry. I was not dead. Not even sickened.

I stood up, shakily at first, as the hooks descended to loose the serpent again. But I jerked down on them, and the natives on the other end released them easily for fear of being pulled into the pit. More gasps of disbelief. I used one hook to flip off the lid and another to pin the hissing fiend to the ground. It writhed and spat at me, flinging the basket with a flick of its tail.

When I had firmly restrained it at the neck with a hook, I used the other to bludgeon it until its thrashing form fell limp. Then I took the vile beast by the tail and dragged its heavy body into the middle of the pit to display it to my captors. The weight of the great snake was perhaps two or three times the weight of a man, but my strength did not fail me in that victorious moment.

The natives were in awe, not least of all the chief. A few of the men shouted down at me, no doubt thinking me a demon. The irony of such a belief would not have been lost on Hiltsfrad. The knight's body was twisted and motionless, eyes wide open and skyward. I did not mourn him, but I took no pleasure in his death.

After a few stones were flung down at me, the chief thundered his orders, and I was spared. I held up the hook poles and was extracted from the pit. I was brought before the chief. He and others of his retinue closely examined my oozing bite wound. They looked stunned, and I could sense fear in their painted faces.

The chief motioned to the man at his right hand and spoke a few hushed words. The man, also of wolf-pelt garb, slowly drew a long stone blade and stepped toward me carefully. With wounds upon wounds, I could not run and was held fast by several of the natives. The man approached and held his knife aloft. I was sure this was finally the end. They would make sure my heart stopped beating if they had to cut it out themselves. Resigned to it, I did not struggle.

He pointed the knife at my eyes then slowly dropped the point to my neck, my heart, then shoulder. On my forearm he finally placed the tip and, grasping my hand like a vice, slowly made an incision down to my wrist. I yelled out as the dark red pulsed forth. The knife man, having never taken his eyes from mine, shouted to a nearby woman who gave up a rough grass woven sash, which he promptly wrapped around the cut. The man ordered my release, and I was dropped to the dirt, holding my arm.

Resolute, I stared back at the chieftain as he squatted to take a closer look at me. He attempted to converse, but I of course could not comprehend what he said. Then I finally understood when he pointed to my snakebite and seemed to ask questions. I pulled at the stains on my clothing to show him the snake blood, then pointed to my mouth.

The chief bent toward the largest stain and took a sniff, then looked upon me in the same fashion that Borsar had coveted the electrum treasures of the chief's forefathers. He smiled as he placed his hand gently on my arm wound, which I took to be a peaceful gesture. I now believe that the knife was the only way for them to test whether I was a demon or human flesh and blood. But the testing was not finished.

The chief and the knife man stood me up. An attendant was summoned while everyone about us whispered and murmured with interest. What a wretched sight I must have been. A moment later an old hunched man, more heavily tattooed and pierced than any other, shuffled over to us. I could only presume he was the village healer, for the chief pointed him to my snake blood stains and bite marks while speaking softly. Without a word, the old man carefully cut off a stained portion of my tunic and placed it in one of the dozens of little pouches tied around his waist.

I noticed as he reached out to me that his left arm was covered with dozens of electrum bracelets, from his shoulder to his wrist, and every finger and thumb was decorated with two thin rings between each knuckle. His other arm was bare. The healer studied me with squinty eyes, peering into my mouth and ears, parting my eyelids, and searching through my untamed hair and beard. He pinched around my neck and felt the beat of my heart with his palm. With a satisfied grunt he held his hands aloft and shouted something to the crowd, then shuffled away. I believe he officially declared me not a snake man.

The chief, who may have seen me looking at the old man's rich decorations, ordered all the electrum confiscated from the slain Donovards to be brought, and he offered all of it to me in baskets with a ghoulish smile. Clearly another test, I shunned it with as much drama as my beaten body could muster. Then I made motions to simulate the face paints and tattoos and traced the symbols in his jewelry with my finger to show my true interest: themselves.

A genuine smile crept over his face, but a quarrel broke out among his retinue. The younger wearer of wolf fur, which I judged to be the chief's son because of their resemblance, was joined by his father in arguing against several others. The apparent leader of the opposition was a tower of a man who wore a necklace of heavy electrum blocks and boar tusks, with tusks also in his earlobes. In my mind I designated these men Chief Wolf, Prince Wolf, and Boarmaster.

At length they came to some conclusion, with Boarmaster eyeing me skeptically. He ripped the knapsack from my hands and gave me a shove, escorting me back to the jail hut with his friends. I was not so gently placed within the hovel, and for a while he stood watching through the gate, unblinking.

I sat down quietly in the dirt and gave him nothing to watch, so he soon stomped off with a grunt. Other attendants, men and women, came to clean and dress my many wounds. They were gentle and smiling and looked upon me with curious stares. I smiled back, but they could probably sense my unease.

As day faded into evening, Boarmaster returned, growling, with a woman who provided a wooden platter of food. It was the roasted haunches of some small animal and a collection of nuts and berries, among them bloodberries, which I had long presumed inedible. The pair left as I ate. Soon after, Prince Wolf appeared with my knapsack and all its contents, including my precious journal.

He handed the bag to me with a broad toothy smile, and in thanks I offered him my food. His friendly demeanor shifted to worry. He pinched some bloodberries and threw them down, smushing them into the ground as he gave me a stern look. I repeated the act with the rest of the food and he approved it all with a smile. I suspected, as I'm sure he did, that Boarmaster had attempted to poison me. Before Prince Wolf left, he held my bandaged forearm with care and spoke a few words, apparently an apology for the wound it had been necessary for him to inflict. I smiled and nodded.

I sat alone eating the food, which was plainly made but nourishing, and contemplated the momentous day as it drew to a close. I was now the sole Brintilian for a distance of probably three thousand marqs or more. I had finally found the elusive Gallerlanders despite nearly perishing at their hand, as my electrum-thieving companions had. These crusaders' exploits in the north made me wonder whether the New Lorin governor had heard tales of the electrum from the Donovards, then tasked his nephew Varesig to find it. What folly, if that's how it had all come about.

I hope my present confinement is short-lived so I can learn about these tattooed people, these original folk of Pemonia, as Orren would say, whom I have endured so much to meet. I proudly marked this place on the map as Chief Wolf's Village.

For whatever reason, I have found it difficult to turn my mind to thoughts of how to secure an alliance with these natives. Perhaps it is because I'm so far from the colony, or maybe the wilderness has taken its toll upon my mind. Regardless, it is my first day among the Gallerlanders, and I'm happy to have survived it. I must stay on guard for the likes of Boarmaster, who clearly thinks me evil. Hopefully I will have plenty of time to assess these natives and learn their ways and words before deciding whether to negotiate anything on behalf of New Lorin.

With my bloodberry inkpot replenished but the sun's last rays losing their luster, I must stow the quill and rest this weary body.

Harvesteve 6

I was removed from my wooden cell this morning at dawn. Boarmaster and Prince Wolf both supervised the rebinding of my hands and the rough-grass rope collar that was placed around my neck. The prince's face was unsmiling but gentle, while Boarmaster was pleased with my primitive fetters. One of his minions held my leash, which was jerked from time to time for his entertainment.

I saw the Gallerlanders drag the mangled bodies of Hiltsfrad and Borsar into the woods, probably to rot with Alvas. Although I do not mourn their deaths, I do not approve of not burying those Messengians and leaving their corpses to the ravens and wolves. But I reminded myself that despite my bonds I remained alive, and was in no position to protest. I wonder what fate awaits this poor body, puzzled as to why the Gallerlanders have neither killed me, too, nor set me free.

All around me the Gallerlanders suited up in fresh tunics and leather armor cuirasses of intricately painted designs. It was clear we were to march through the forest, but to where? And I was not the only captive: two men that I could easily identify as Hrals were wrestled from a hut and bound as I was, then brought over to our group. They had been beaten, possibly tortured, and they were to be forced to march barefoot, although they are probably accustomed to this. They snarled at the sight of me, but a swift jerk on their neck ropes, on which they were tethered together, silenced them.

The Hrals were so much more vicious than the Gallerlander tribe, and not because they were leashed like dogs. The Gallerlanders had shown restraint with their captured Brintilians who had unleashed fire on their village, even if their ultimate judgment was death in the snake pit. By comparison, the Hrals, in my experience, had never shown any hint of restraint or compassion. The Gallerlanders also communicated with one another more civilly. Not Brintilian manners, mind you, but lacking the constant barking and spitting of the wild Hrals.

The final preparation before our departure was the bringing of food bags by a group of women. This was quite a ceremony. I saw again that they were just as painted and tattooed as the men, head to foot, but were graceful and adorned with the beautiful flowers and colored leaves of the hidden forest. Most had emerald eyes that shone brighter than the electrum, their fair hair flowing and interwoven with gleaming grasses. Every one of them wore sets of electrum beads in each ear, and some had lip or cheek piercings.

They brought the food in solemn silence, laying it before us and stepping back from the provisions. They then drew out their own long stone knives, spears, and bows and held them high in the cool morning air with a shrill chanting song of farewell. This was most impressive, and every man in our party watched the ceremony with a certain pride. Everyone looked skyward for a moment, as Chief Wolf had done upon our arrival. Then the men shouldered the bags, and we marched.

Chief Wolf led the convoy, which numbered about a dozen men plus we three captives. He was followed closely by Prince Wolf and Boarmaster. The journey out of the village was easy, as the path was well stamped and flat, dipping slightly downward.

The mild terrain did nothing to help the holes that widened in my boot soles. More than five months they have lasted in this wilderness, and for that I was grateful. But now the wilderman in me covets the softgrass-stuffed moccasins of the natives. Apart from evident comfort, their footfalls are quiet, merely a breeze on the forest floor. Perhaps they secretly laugh at the awkward clomp of my weatherworn boots.

We marched a solid six or seven hours before resting, neglecting our morning meal—or perhaps they ate before rousing me. So I had grown light-headed and eager to eat. Food finally came in the form of a fresh grainy flatbread. On this was smeared what could be called jam. This was served to me with the word *afban*, which could mean "jelly and bread," or perhaps "food," or "here, idiot." I repeated the term and won a snicker from my captor, so it was likely the last.

Thankfully, our rest was long. Perhaps this portends another intense march. I begged freedom for my hands, and finally won it, to bring out my journal. From the moment I opened it, half the group crowded around to watch the quill flit across the vellum. Some noted my use of the bloodberry ink with foul grimaces, but most were intrigued by my writing.

At one point Boarmaster stomped over and ripped the book from my hands, sniffed it disapprovingly, and aimed it at the nearby stream. Before he could throw it Chief Wolf shouted at him with hideous anger. Boarmaster threw the book back at me instead, clearly embarrassed but still disgusted.

A Hral took the opportunity to spit on the big brute from his seat in the dirt. Boarmaster swiftly backhanded him so hard that he rolled into the stream, then Boarmaster skulked off. I'm sure that to him I'm of the same ilk as the Hrals, maybe worse.

I must end here, for we prepare to move again.

❧

It is now dark and we have finally stopped. The march was exhausting, with the terrain steadily inclining. Harsen had always kept a manageable pace, and I certainly did not march myself while alone in the woods. I have not done a forced march since my days in the legion. But even then my feet did not bleed as they have today. So much for being a true wilderman. My feet, long used to the well-made and comfortable boots of master cobbler Craine back in New Lorin, have finally succumbed to the wild earth.

As soon as we stopped for the night a fire was lit. It was a curious sight that I would like to watch again. Like Arvgred's fast-sticks method, which he said he had learned from watching the natives, one of the men took from his sack a straight, smooth stick and a boat-shaped strip of wood. A handful of ready tinder was placed in the boat. The peculiar-smelling stick stood on end in the tinder-filled boat, then it was quickly rubbed back and forth between his palms. With a spark and small plume of smoke we gained a nice campfire.

As the night meal was prepared, Prince Wolf released my bonds with only a sniff of protest from Boarmaster. The Hrals were not afforded this freedom, so I deemed myself the favored captive whose fate was hopefully better than theirs.

We munched on more afban and grilled rabbit. I pondered how to continue charming my captors, beyond the smiles and the simple flick of my quill. I reached into my pouch, which made Boarmaster nervous, and withdrew a candle. Certain that it was evil or poison, Boarmaster snatched it and prepared to strike me.

Again he was shouted down by the chief and his son. The brute tossed the candle to Chief Wolf for inspection, which took but a moment. Oddly, like the Hrals in the skeleton cave, the chief even tasted it. With a puckered face and waxy smile he handed it back to me, assured it was harmless. Now here was a brave and witty chieftain.

I took the gnawed candle and let the campfire light the wick while many firelit eyes watched. A torch was certainly nothing foreign to the Gallerlanders, but the sublime glow of beeswax, with its steady control and slow burn, was enough to captivate their weary minds. Even the Hrals watched silently. I passed it to Prince Wolf to hold. When it had traveled full circle around the fire, dribbling itself only on Boarmaster, I propped it by my journal and wrote in peace.

Harvesteve 7

We continued the steady march, finally locating an incline into forested hills. The Gallerlander men are stoic on the trail, talking rarely and only then apparently to discuss the path when a fork or crossroads is encountered. In these moments they seem to make decisions based on consensus, perhaps to avoid errors or in deference to rules of counsel, despite a familiarity with the way ahead. Peculiar to watch, since I have been trained in military units wherein it is not customary for the officer in charge to consult with lowly foot soldiers.

It is during these rests that the Gallerlanders' jovial nature comes out. The Hrals have none of these lighthearted characteristics. Even the sour Boarmaster has his hearty chuckles, usually at the Hrals' expense.

When we rested in a small dell, I pointed out my worn boots to Prince Wolf and showed interest in his moccasins. He nodded with a grunt and pointed up the trail ahead and spoke, as if to tell me "wait a while longer." But I was struck by a sudden realization that his nod of affirmative understanding was obviously the same gesture used by Old World peoples.

I thought back to Orren's teachings. How is it that we could be separated by the seas for thousands of years and yet the natives of Pemonia could share this simple sign? It is a small thing and one could argue they have absorbed mannerisms from the colonies. But we share so many other characteristics that could not be so quickly learned by natives sheltered in the depths of this broad continent, not to mention our identical physical forms. I believe that Orren was right: the peoples of the Old and New Worlds surely share a common origin, namely God's hands.

As I have written previously, it is heresy to believe the natives of Pemonia are the descendants of the Agnesci, the ancient and supposedly extinct brethren of my Almeric ancestors. The scriptures tell us that God separated those two original tribes of man, planting the Almerics in Cedelaebos, the heart of modern Almeria. And the Agnesci in Aprelaebos, clearly meaning Pemonia.

Every Brintilian child knows those ancient stories of that first fateful meeting, when the intrepid Agnesci crossed the seas and landed upon the shores of Cedelaebos. The Messengian Church teaches that this *invasion* breached the sacred separation, and that the Agnesci were utterly destroyed by the Almerics for that blasphemous sin.

Thus the teachings reason that the New World must be populated by the evil creations of Memelos because there were no Agnesci survivors. But if anyone could sit with them as I have, even as their captive, they could not deny that these natives must be the descendants of the Agnesci, not the spawn of Memelos.

When I learn the Gali language, there will be so much to ask them. Surely they must know their own lineage better than our faraway priests and scribes pretend to.

We continue the march.

ᢒ

We settled into camp this evening a bit shaken. Not long after returning to the path we crossed over a little stream. Beyond it were small wooded hillocks where bane wolves, as Arvgred had called them, were lying in wait.

Luckily Chief Wolf was not at the head of our line, because the first poor soul was quickly killed by these wolves. I presume the Gallerlanders have an eye for these beasts, judging from their leaders' wolf-hide clothing, but they did not smell or otherwise detect the wolves before the attack. And we heard no howling.

My captors reacted quickly once the silent hunters were upon us, and I have never before seen anything like it. These Gallerlanders of the depths did not fight like the natives of the north and east. Prince Wolf literally ran up into a tree, straight up its trunk, and disappeared. A moment later he pounced down from the branches onto the back of one of the long-legged beasts, burying his stone blade into its skull.

Boarmaster's techniques were equally impressive. Hidden on his back under his tunic were two wooden poles, which quickly attached end to end to form a double length nearly equal to his height. It had no blade or point. He used it to vault his body from ground to tree and into the wolf pack. In and out he rushed among them, breaking their bodies with his own. His muscular, bulky build appeared graceful and light.

Chief Wolf's skill was in his wrists. He had a hidden quiver of the most peculiar arrows, yet needed no bow. The arrows were made of stone, with circular handholds rather than straight shafts. The sharp outer edges would bite into a tree even after passing through the living bones of a wolf. He launched these throwing rings with precision, felling any wolf that approached him or the helpless captives.

All of the Gallerlanders had such odd weapons that I lack good words to describe, and all of the weapons were hidden again as soon as the last wolf was killed. Clearly they had no use for metal weapons, but more impressive was their fighting style. I'm still puzzled at how they could move themselves like that.

Harvesteve 8

After yesterday's wolf attack I was too stunned to write much. I could not remove my gaze from the Gallerlanders. I still cannot comprehend their technique, particularly running up into trees.

In the colonies, as in the Old World, the armies with steel swords and heavy armor win the wars, particularly those that have mounted cavalry. But these natives have none of that, not so much as a rusty iron knife. And while the crusaders and other knights have a refined, highly disciplined fighting style, none leverage their surroundings in the way that Prince Wolf and Boarmaster do. No armored knight could run up into a tree or vault by pole into his enemies.

Fascinating, though I cannot help but doubt how useful those skills would be on an open field of battle when facing a veteran squadron of cavalry. Nevertheless, impressive. As a teacher of the sword, I wonder how many colonial soldiers could or would be willing to learn such exotic maneuvers.

Now I must write about another attempt on my life by Boarmaster, second to offering me bloodberries to eat back in the village. As the battle with the wolves closed, he approached me with fire burning in his eyes, but he turned at the last moment to kill the last of our enemies.

He could have vaulted his huge form, crushing into the Hrals and me, but he stepped slowly and deliberately. The sudden and noiseless bolt of one of the chief's throwing-rings, which was a hair's thickness from severing Boarmaster's moccasined toes, was enough to freeze his steps.

With another circular blade ready in his hand, Chief Wolf stared Boarmaster down until the brute departed from us. I carefully pulled the blade ring from the ground to observe its polished gray surface. Even while holding it in my hands it was difficult to believe something cut so thin was made of stone. I handed it to the chief with a thankful nod.

After the fight great care was taken in recovering the fallen tribesman. There was talk among the Gallerlanders that concluded with one of the men shouldering the deceased before walking back toward Chief Wolf's Village. We were within a day of that settlement, but that hearty fellow would be carrying dead weight equal to his own, alone.

I thought back to the elaborately carved drawings and etchings in the Gallerlander cemetery, and the carefully arrayed tomb guardians. Clearly death was something that was taken seriously by the Gallerlanders, probably with much ceremony. We Brintilians would have buried him here in the ground where he fell, but the Gallerlanders sought to return the dead home. No such honor would exist among the spawn of Memelos.

۶

This evening we did not have to camp in the forest. Chief Wolf's Village was shown to be just over two days' swift march to another little hamlet. We were greeted near the outskirts of this village by smiling children, tattooed in the same leafy paints.

To impress their guests, the children held their stick toys high in the air, then proceeded as a team to stack and balance them against each other to form tall structures. Some sticks were bound to others with twine at their ends, making moveable joints that could quickly form triangles or squares. They were efficient at forming this scaffolding in the bare dirt or grass, then quickly tearing it down and raising a different shape elsewhere. They were like little craftsmen or builders, yet this was their play.

Upon entering the village, the true wonder stopped me cold. There, hunched along the edge of the path ahead, was a wooden waterwheel that dipped into a stream running between two hillocks. These people were indeed builders.

Harsen had never mentioned that such contraptions existed among the Gallerlanders, and I had never heard of anything like this being built by any native tribe, certainly not the Hrals. As we walked by the creaking machine I could see women and men tending to the crushing of seeds by a stone wheel inside, no doubt making flour for afban or similar bread.

Prince Wolf noticed my stare and smiled. We soon approached the hut of the village chieftain, who was much less adorned than Chief Wolf. He seemed of a similar age, but his hands were calloused and worn, clearly less of a scepter holder.

The chiefs conversed amicably as the sun's light faded in the trees and a cool air crept out from thick woodlands nearby. Chief Wolf, his son, and Boarmaster then entered the chief's hut while I was led to an empty one and the Hrals to another. The villagers brought me tasty grilled fish by torchlight and permitted me to light my candle to write of the day's discoveries.

Later I heard a bit of commotion outside. I peered through the stick walls to see Boarmaster exit the Hrals' hut. The guard posted there appeared to pose objection to Boarmaster's visit but he was promptly backhanded. Boarmaster's sly, half-lit face looked in my direction before departing, the glint of his grim smile easily visible. Perhaps he was just checking on his captives, but given his treatment of the guard, I sense something else is afoot.

Harvesteve 9

oday has been odd. Except for a food delivery at dawn, I have been left alone in the spare hut. The activity in the village appeared routine, with villagers hunting, weaving, cleaning, stitching, and tending the watermill. Members of Chief Wolf's convoy have simply walked lazily to and fro, as if they are waiting for something. This is puzzling, given our rush to arrive here.

Since I have time to reflect, I will comment on the little pocket book that originally belonged to Hiltsfrad's brother. Luckily I never returned it to the crusader, otherwise it would be rotting with him in the woods.

As noted previously, its many random scribbles are difficult to decipher, but I've managed to learn some Gali words. Most of it is transliteration and translation with few actual Gali symbols, probably because Hiltsfrad's brother focused more on learning the sounds from Hiltsfrad's prisoners and less on Gali writing, but I'm striving to learn all I can from it. For example:

hal	tree
har	forest
ond	dark or black
wuru	light or white
sogon	snake
dem	land

dembal	slice of land
dembalir	world (literally all slices of land)
parin	spirit
thuran	king
thur	day
gra	to walk

It is now late afternoon and I've finally witnessed something out of the ordinary in this little village. There were a few shouts, and some people, mostly Chief Wolf's men, gathered in the middle of the village. A moment later one native, apparently a lone messenger, trotted up to the group from the woods. Chief Wolf greeted him warmly. The chief of this place also came out of his hut to greet the panting newcomer, and he brought from his hut several curly reeds that they puffed like pipes.

They all sat down with blue-gray smoke curling about their heads. Finally, as if the formalities were complete, the messenger unfolded a stiff leather packet. This was interesting, even from a distance, to see that the Gallerlander language was written down and not merely etched in stone or electrum as I had thus far seen it. Whatever was on the note excited all of them and caused them to hurry about.

It is nearly dark. Perhaps the morning will bring me understanding of the Gallerlanders' excitement, for I cannot guess what is in store for me.

Harvesteve 10

I awoke in the night to hear a muffled yell, so I crept quietly to the door and peered out. In the moonlight I saw the guard of the Hrals' hut slump to the ground and two forms run out. I alerted my guard, who had surprisingly not woken from his slumber. He ran to the hut but the two prisoners were already gone.

I watched as my guard and several others ran into the forest after them. Intermittent shouts could be heard in the woods, and it was a while before they returned. Prince Wolf had gone with them, his garb and face easily recognizable under a lit torch. I could see that they had recaptured one of the Hrals. The captive was kneeling, head down and hands bound. The last Gallerlanders to emerge from the woods came empty-handed. The second Hral had escaped.

Prince Wolf shouted until Boarmaster arrived. The vile man exited his hut slowly, yawning as if he had heard none of the commotion. Prince Wolf castigated him, pointing to my hut and the Hrals'. Clearly Boarmaster had been in charge of prisoner security. There was no way for me to tell the prince that Boarmaster had paid a suspicious visit to the Hrals and had abused their slain guard last night. But I reckoned the prince knew this fellow better than I.

When the tumult calmed and the single Hral was returned to his cell after a beating, I curled back up under the fur and rough-grass quilt. In the morning I awoke to food brought by Prince Wolf. He also surprised me with a lightly worn pair of moccasins, a wonderful gift for my tired feet.

I did my best to show my gratitude. He had remembered my request, surely a good sign that danger did not await me at our destination, wherever and whenever that might be. The prince spoke and pointed to my guard, then the Hrals' hut. He smiled and nodded, as if to thank me for sounding the alarm during the night.

The word from the messenger must have been enough to spur us to continue our journey. We left later this morning, turning south. I wondered if we were still traveling in the direction of the Gallerlander capital, where Hiltsfrad had said their king of kings dwelled.

The woods along our path quickly thickened. Though nothing compared to the black forest, this new forest was dense with plants I had never seen. Many dark-hued purples and browns and burgundies mixed with the verdant greens to create a mystical forest, and I don't think it is the transformation of early autumn but rather a new realm of Gallerlandia that we entered. So when we paused for our midday rest, I sketched a few of the more unusual specimens alongside long-trusted and tasty ones like pearlberries.

My sketches drew a few chuckles from the natives. Chief Wolf, who puffed away on the curly pipe given to him by his fellow chief, gestured with a broad sweep of his arm toward the forest and canopy above, as if saying, "You are in no danger of losing them."

I took the opportunity to show interest in his pipe, which he was initially hesitant to share. He finally permitted me a puff, which twisted Boarmaster's face in disgust. The smoke was intense at first then smooth, with a complex taste of pepper, crabapple, and licorice.

I exhaled the blue smoke and instantly craved more. But the chief plucked the pipe out of my reach. The Gallerlanders had a good laugh. But not Boarmaster, nor the Hral. Chief Wolf pointed at the pipe and said, "*Tabakat.*" He gestured to my drawings to signal, clear enough, that it was derived from plants.

It is curious that tabakat is similar in pronunciation and in use to our own tobacco in the Old World, and is perhaps another piece of evidence linking our peoples. Also, I can imagine my fellow colonists trading for this concoction. We have not yet been able to cultivate tobacco in the colonies, for unknown reasons. Perhaps tabakat could serve as an exotic substitute.

As Harsen would have attested, it would certainly not be the first unusual item adopted by colonists and exported to Almeria for large profit. But what would the natives take from us in return? What could we give them that they don't already have? They're self-sufficient and have no need of our finest goods or trades, even metalworking.

Unlike the Hrals and Ollohds, the Gallerlanders know how to build machines like watermills. We colonists could show them how to build bigger structures like castles, but what use do they have for such forts in their vast forests? They can handle our common enemy the Hrals fine on their own. So how would any alliance with New Lorin benefit them? What can the empire offer them that they do not have here in these verdant depths? Certainly not peace . . .

We marched all day until nightfall and rested well.

Harvesteve 11

Today did not go well, as Boarmaster's suspicious behavior back at the village has been exposed. All was well until our midday rest and meal. There was no sound, no warning. As I contemplated asking Chief Wolf for another smoke of tabakat, I was snatched into the bush.

I could smell the stench of a Hral as a stone blade pressed to my throat. Chief Wolf and his men burst through the bushes into the little clearing where the Hral held me. I was puzzled by Boarmaster's expression, which was pleased at first, then dumbstruck. He must have expected to find my body, but instead he was confronted with demands from the Hral who had escaped from the watermill village.

I remained as still as possible, feeling blood trickle from my neck. I was confident that Chief Wolf and his son would not have walked me this far only to see a Hral cut me down. But it was soon clear that whatever the Hral was demanding was not going to be given to him.

Chief Wolf and his men calmly turned stone-faced, as if they expected lightning to strike their enemy at any moment. My confidence soon melted away, and I feared they had resigned me to my fate. I could feel the Hral trembling with desperation. His hideous breath fogged my face, and his nails dug into my arm.

Then a sudden waft of air lashed my cheek, and the Hral fell dead behind me, his blade nicking my throat a little more on the way down. My eyes caught the shuffle of the Galler-lander archer who had ascended a tree behind Chief Wolf. I knew the arrow had missed my own head by a thread.

I didn't have much opportunity to thank Chief Wolf because he and Prince Wolf berated Boarmaster for some time. It was clear to all of us, I think, that he had arranged the Hrals' escape, even at the expense of one of the village guards, to kill me. But his plan went wrong when the Hral did not act as Boarmaster believed he would. I can only guess that the Hral attempted to bargain a guarantee for his freedom or perhaps that of his friend, still bound. Whatever the case, the Hral's delay provided Chief Wolf and Prince Wolf enough time to save my life and end his.

Although Boarmaster endured the most severe tongue-lashing I had yet seen delivered by the chief and his son (which he passed on by kicking the remaining Hral), what was his real punishment? He was not bound or sent home, nor was he ostracized by the rest of our group. He was clearly important enough to receive nothing more than a verbal reprimand. I resolved to keep my distance from him.

PART V

THE HEIGHTS

Harvesteve 15

The last five days have been the most terrible, the most wonderful, and the most eventful of this expedition since it began in the fringe fields of Tolnarp nearly six months ago. I've had much time to organize my thoughts while separated, yet again, from my journal. So I will start from the beginning.

In the late afternoon of the 11th of Harvesteve, our march through the vibrant forest ended. The watermill hamlet and its hilly woodland corridor was a gateway to what can only be described as a city in the trees. Surely no Brintilian has ever laid eyes on what was revealed to me, for such a tale would have spread far and wide only to be disbelieved by those who had not seen it with their own eyes.

Clustered dwellings perched like moored ships upon a sea of leaves and vines high up in massive trees. They were like pillars holding up a vast green dome. Their great trunks were of such girth that fifty or sixty men standing hand in hand around it would scarcely complete a ring. A man could easily hide in the deep grooves of its mottled taupe and umber-hued bark.

The climbing heights of the great boughs of these giants carried the city up beyond our sight from the forest floor. There were no settlements on the ground, and those in the trees were not the humble hovels of Chief Wolf's Village. They were large wooden structures grouped like colonies of mushrooms, some shaped like arks that gently bobbed up and down on the breeze.

Vine ladders and rope bridges linked one grouping to another. Natives could be seen upon these skyward paths lighting lanterns that hung out over the sides of the bridges. The upward city was alive with activity, more Gallerlanders than I had ever hoped to meet. How wondrous was their creation! Surely this was the place where the king of Gallerlander kings dwelled. Even my captors were taken with the sight, so I guess they do not journey here often.

Our approach to the treetop city was signaled by Prince Wolf, who bellowed a peculiar chant or code—perhaps the announcement of the arrival of his father's clan. We were greeted by a distinctly different call from above and met by three natives who appeared from the shadows, one in front and two at our rear. Prince Wolf was recognized by the man in front, who promptly sheathed his stone knife while his two companions relaxed their bowstrings.

After a moment of talk and gestures toward the prisoners, our convoy was led on a little fern-lined path through the brush to the foot of one of the endless giant trees. All of the Gallerlanders climbed up ropes and ladders except for Boarmaster, who accompanied the Hral and me.

Still bound, we were made to sit on a wooden platform with a local guard. When he whistled, the platform leaped off the ground, and we were steadily hauled up, dangling by ropes tied to each corner. This frightening ride lasted several minutes throughout which Boarmaster and the Hral glared at me. They were no doubt tempted by the opportunity to kick me over the edge.

At the top we saw that six stout Gallerlanders had done the hauling. Large toothy gears crafted from thick layers of oak were connected to the handles that they had turned to coil the rope upward, similar to a capstan used to weigh anchor aboard a ship. Like the watermill, it was surprising to see these tattooed natives making use of these mechanisms in the deep forest.

These tree dwellers stared at me without paying any attention to the Hral. Most were hulking, bearded, and covered with swirled designs. One had a tattoo of a great tree on his back, with reaching branches spread across his broad shoulders. All of them were curious and puzzled by my presence.

From this entrance we were led single file through a network of bridges that swayed violently with every step. The natives swayed with it in perfect balance. Though I was not used to such devices myself, the Hral was particularly unnerved and had to be coaxed and prodded at every step. I tried to shake my fears to make myself the easy captive.

As we walked the bridges, I noticed that our climb had elevated us far up into the city. There were tree huts above and below us now, at every level of the endless canopies of the great forest. With the onset of night, the wide-open spaces that hovered between the trees became populated with glowing insects and curls of smoke from evening-meal fires. Calming smells of roasted meat, sweet fruits, and spicy tabakat swirled around our perilous walk.

We finally spiraled around a great knobbled tree and walked up a ramped bridge toward a regal complex of houses, at the center of which stood a grand chalet crowned with a timber dome with flame flicker in every hole-cut window. Every surface of its beams and walls were covered with intricate carvings or plated with hammered electrum.

The size of the chalet swelled as we drew closer, revealing itself as an eight-level structure built up the trunk of a tree with a burst of branches in every direction above the dome. The building looked as though it had sprouted from the ancient tree itself.

We were taken up to the doors of this grand tree hall, which were studded with circular electrum shields rimed with gear-toothed designs. The doors were opened and our escorts said their farewells to Chief and Prince Wolf. Inside they were greeted by a tall and graceful Gallerlander woman who seemed to expect our convoy. I have named her Lady Emerald for her gemstone eyes, and I will write much more of her.

Her flowing chestnut hair was interlaced with electrum beads and framed a gentle face. She is most beautiful woman—native or Brintilian. She wore a fur and grass-quilted gown that flowed light and airy despite the wild material. Her arms were bare but tattooed with sharp designs and electrum bracelets at the elbows and wrists. Her warm smile and soft words greeted Chief Wolf, who clasped her slender hands between his plump palms. The lady bade us to follow her deeper into the great hall.

The place was cavernous, with living tree boughs standing like columns along the central path and stretching their fingers out along the dome above. Mossy planks guided our feet toward a great throne that perched in a low-slung bough as a bird in the hand. Sitting upon it was, surely, the king of all Gallerlanders.

He watched in silent stillness, as did his many courtiers, who hailed from many different clans, judging by their varied dress and tattoos. The king himself was clothed in beautiful painted leathern armor lined with furs of brown bear, black marten, and silver fox. A cape of the same furs was tied loosely around his neck.

On the king's head rested a magnificent electrum helmet, the only raiment I had seen crafted wholly from the precious metal. This helmet sat upon a crown of ivy, with small bits of curly vine poking out on either side of his head, similar to the laurels worn by ancient Almeric kings. Deer antlers reached out from the top of the helmet, wider than his shoulders were broad.

On his feet he wore grass-stuffed moccasins, each tipped with many sets of eagle talons. His silver-gray beard was streaked with jade paint, and beads of electrum were woven into it on either side of his jaws. Despite his age he was youthful in expression, with wide eyes and a strong build.

As we approached the throne, Chief Wolf and Lady Emerald stepped forward, with Prince Wolf and Boarmaster behind. It seemed to me that the lady introduced the chief to the high king, who now descended from his perched throne to clasp his hands with the chief's. The high king smiled with warm welcome. The two were like old friends, engaged in warm conversation while the court watched in silence. Only the easy creak of the branches in the evening breeze accompanied their mild banter.

At last we captives were called forth, the Hral first, accompanied by Boarmaster. The high king's face darkened as the wretched prisoner slinked close. For the first time the

Hral appeared humbled by his situation. But this did not last, for when the high king bellowed at him he screamed and hissed and spat. He was dragged away kicking and shrieking by attendants into a side chamber. Then Prince Wolf guided me forward.

Chief Wolf launched into an engaging tale to the high king and his court, waving his hands in sweeping gestures and regularly pointing at me. At one point I recognized his imitation of the serpent pit and my victory over the foul beast. Chief also pointed at his own electrum ring, then to me, which I thought odd, but then he produced the skeleton's ring from a pouch and held it aloft.

The high king's face darkened again but was touched with sadness as the skeleton's ring was presented to him. He studied it somberly, then my eyes met his, and he quickly looked away. He cradled the ring in his hands, and then tightened a fist around it. He pushed aside his apparent grief and pointed me toward the chamber into which the Hral had been banished. Chief and Prince Wolf tried to speak, but they were silenced. When a devious smile curled upon Boarmaster's ugly face, I knew this was not good.

As I was taken from Prince Wolf's custody by guards, I realized what must have happened. The skeleton, which I had supposed to have been a Gallerlander, and which the Donovard raiders assessed to be a prince, must have been a close confidant or relative of the high king. When I looked back, I saw Lady Emerald place her delicate hands over his tightened fist. He released the ring to her, and she held it close to her heart. I tried to speak, but my words were as meaningless and unnoticed to their ears as the creaking of the planks and branches.

The guards pushed me roughly into the side chamber, wherein we dipped into a dark staircase. Down below was a narrow room with vine ropes attached along the walls. They had finished securing the Hral and had prepared a place for me.

As I was bound to the wall, hands above my head, I noticed the floor planks were spaced such that the night breeze flowed up into the room from the black void below. The Hral writhed and tore violently at the vines with his broken teeth, but their skins were fibrous and tough. He could not free himself, so I did not try. After a while his exhaustion calmed him.

As I sat pondering my fate, I heard a weak whisper from the dark end of the room. It was very faint at first, but I made out the voice of a man, a Brintilian. Then the voice spoke a familiar name. I cocked my ear toward the voice and asked, "Is it you?" A pause, then came the weak reply. "Yes."

I could not see him, for the guards snuffed out the torch, and only a little light peeked through the slats above. But he was somewhere in there, sharing my dark cell. I closed my weeping eyes, my soul suddenly unburdened with the guilt of having abandoned him in the woods. When I could speak, I confessed to him how I forced myself to think that he was dead so I could survive in the depths of the dark forest. Harsen jested that he was nearly dead for sure, then coughed out a broken chuckle.

He could not talk much, but did his best to say that he was caught in a battle between Hrals and Gallerlanders not long after we were separated at the Glombruk. He reckoned the Gallerlanders believed he was aiding the Hrals, so he had been imprisoned here for a long time with other Hrals. "They're dead, and we're not far behind."

I told Harsen what had befallen me since the Glombruk and noted my hope that my new friends, Chief Wolf and his son, would intercede on our behalf with the antlered king. Harsen sputtered a laugh and mocked the word *friend* to describe what he called the "Memelos kin."

I was disturbed to hear my old companion refer to the natives in this way, for he had always been sympathetic toward them, even when I was not. He would never have agreed to join this expedition if he believed what he said now. But I could tell he was in pain, so I told him to rest. We would talk when it was light.

❧

The morning of the 12th brought a difficult sight. Harsen was ragged, more so than I, and deathly ill. His color was pale, and various weeping and unhealed wounds dotted his arms and legs. He was wholly uncared for and there was no telling how long he had suffered in this way. Like me, he had the unkempt hair and bony gaunt form of a new wilderman, but he seemed on the edge of dying.

Harsen kept his eyes shuttered and breathed weakly, not answering my call. Only the clamor of the guards and the smell of warm afban and freshly picked melonberries roused him, but he would not eat. I begged him to accept nourishment, but he replied, "It is too late." He drifted back into a half sleep, and so I left him in peace, staring through the slats down to the forest floor far below, where strolling deer looked like roaming ants.

Around midday Prince Wolf arrived with Lady Emerald, concern fixed upon their faces. The prince had clearly come to check on me and paid no attention to Harsen or the Hral. Crouching near me, Prince Wolf took the skeleton's ring from the lady and held it out with spoken words. Although I could not understand him, I thought it prudent to simply point to the Hral. This was the best I could do to convey who was responsible for the death of that lost Gallerlander.

Prince Wolf seemed to understand I was not culpable. I hoped that my repeated and genuine disinterest in electrum during their trials of me would prove my innocence to the antlered king. But I knew my life was ultimately in the hands of a ruler who would do what he willed to sate his grief and anger.

Another night nearly passed in the treetop prison before Prince Wolf and Lady Emerald returned to me. They came in secret under the cover of night and without guards but were accompanied by a young Gallerlander. He was considerably shorter in stature than most others of his race, but no less tattooed. A knotted wooden club hung at his waist, but otherwise he wore only a leather and broadleaf loincloth and grass-stuffed moccasins.

Though unremarkable in his appearance, the young man would turn out to be a rare treasure. I do not have to conjure a name for him like Short One in this journal because his real name was soon revealed: Pagdorat.

Pagdorat was skittish at first, clearly uncomfortable with being in the little jail, but Lady Emerald urged him toward me. I was utterly shocked to hear him say "Hello" as if he were a Brintilian colonist. It was astonishing to hear that simple salutation from the lips of a painted native. I returned the greeting, then waited, and he waited.

After an awkward pause, he proceeded to tell me, in decent Brintilian, how he had been schooled by a Donovard priest as a child on the island of Teshdembal, which the colonists now call Leauvenna. His people, the Teshi, cousins of the mainland Gallerlanders, were nearly wiped out by the Donovard settlers, so he and others came to Gallerlandia to seek shelter. That was how he came to be here, talking to me.

I expressed my regret and condolences at hearing of his peoples' troubles, taking care to note that I was from New Lorin, where we had good relations with many natives in western Gallerlandia. Pagdorat was unimpressed but nodded politely, saying that the woman, meaning Lady Emerald, wished to know what became of her husband, the wearer of the ring I had stolen. That was a humbling moment. I half-wished I had never escaped the Hral river tunnel if it meant I wouldn't have to look into her sad eyes.

I told Pagdorat the tale of my capture by the Hrals and my escape from their cave using her husband's leg bone, saying I did not know why I took the ring, perhaps because it was a comforting light in the darkness. I added that its glow certainly aided me in the darkest depths of the forest thereafter. But I expressed my gladness that I could at least tell the lady and the high king what had befallen their prince, sad as it was.

After relaying all of this to Lady Emerald and Prince Wolf, Pagdorat told me, to my great relief, that they believed my story and would secure my release. I quickly took the opportunity to plead for the life of my old companion, but the Teshi man said that Harsen was condemned as a "spirit thief." I protested, demanding that his crimes be explained, but the trio were eager to depart. And so they left and the night was again quiet. I slept little, wondering what they thought Harsen had done and what the new day would bring.

At dawn on the 13th, Harsen and the Hral and I were unbound from the walls and led back up to the main hall. There, the antlered king sat in his tree throne with grave face. The courtiers around him hummed with anticipation.

Our guards released us into the custody of six men robed in long red fox furs studded with electrum plates that were etched with many symbols. Upon their heads were fitted small antlered helms of wood, their faces tattooed in sharp designs. Each man carried a staff with a blunt electrum orb at the top end and a stone-tipped point at the bottom. Quickly joining these men was a seventh official with similar garb and staff, but he was distinguished by the glimmering electrum-flecked paint on his arms and face.

We were escorted by these ceremonial-looking priest-warriors to a wooden door behind the throne. I held Harsen's arm around my shoulders to help support him, as he could barely stand, much less walk alone. The high king led all the court outside, followed by us captives.

The doors opened to reveal a beautiful day, with sun streaming through the highest canopies of the giant tree forest. Outside was a spacious balcony where all the court could gather. The edge of the platform was fenced with tied beams except for one area that resembled the gangplank of a ship. At the entrance to the plank was an archway carved with symbols. Two priest-warriors stood ominously on either side.

The high king walked to the balcony's edge and looked skyward for a moment, watching the clouds pass by the break in the canopy high above. Then he began a speech with his back still turned to the people, his arms spread wide over the open leafy chasm below. The ground far below could not be seen, for the foliage of the lower canopies obscured the view. The balconies and bridges of other tree huts within view of the high king's chalet were crowded with Gallerland-ers watching the ceremony.

The high king ended his speech by turning back to face the condemned. The Hral was jabbed forward by the priest-warriors. He fought and kicked, but it was no use. Hands bound behind him, he was led to the arches and passed under. At the point of a stone-tipped staff he was prodded off the edge. His scream stained the breezy sun-filled air long after his tumbling body punctured the leafy canopy far below. I felt the blood drain from my face. Even after the echo of his death cry faded I found it difficult to breathe.

I was next. As they began to urge me forward, Lady Emerald walked out calmly before the high king and crowd and began her own speech. The priest-warriors halted me while she gave her testimony.

She was respectful and soft-spoken at first but gradually became passionate. She held up the skeleton's ring and gestured to the fallen Hral below. And several times she pointed to me and referred to me as "Ringding," which was close enough. Her speech was captivating, though I knew not her words.

Prince Wolf soon joined her and Chief Wolf after him. Their chorus was impressive. They weaved their words in a moving performance, dancing between sorrow and anger to concern and happiness, until finally they returned the floor to the antlered king.

He was clearly touched by their efforts because he approached and loosened the priest-warriors' grip on my tattered tunic. With a steady stare, he calmly spoke my pardon and ordered my bonds to be cut. I was then handed over to Chief Wolf. I cannot express the relief I felt in that moment, after watching the wretched Hral plummet and knowing I would follow him down. But I could not yet celebrate the efforts of my new friends because Harsen was being dragged toward the arches.

I reached for Pagdorat, frantically telling him to say something, anything that could delay his execution until the situation could be explained. Harsen was carried steadily closer. I reached for Chief Wolf and Lady Emerald, their worry and confusion at my panic finally stirring the chief to raise his hand to stop the ceremony.

Harsen was close now. I darted out to save him, but was blocked by those electrum-gilded red furs. So I fell to my knees clutching the high king's taloned slippers, begging that he spare the woodsman. Pagdorat translated, telling the high king Harsen was with me on our journey to seek out the Gallerlanders in peace, and that we were not Donovard raiders. I added, through Pagdorat, that Harsen was known in the western forests for peaceful trade with the clans there, and that he could not be deserving of this sentence.

The high king slowly lifted his hand to stop the march on the plank. Harsen was already near the edge and looking down into the hypnotic sway of the green sea below. The ruler spoke, saying through Pagdorat that by sparing Harsen, the two of us would be bound by a single fate. Further crimes committed by the one were shared by the other, and also the punishment. I swore that we would cause no harm, and they released him. All the air rushed out of me and I dropped my head with relief as I heard Harsen call out with joy.

That evening Harsen and I were lodged in a room adjoining the guest chamber that was occupied by Chief Wolf and his clansmen. Lady Emerald arranged for servants to care for Harsen. His wounds were tended with a smelly white salve and bound with pressed grasses and aromatic leaves, but he remained bedridden. I congratulated him on his decision not to learn how to fly with the birds. Humorless and tearful, he expressed his gratitude and apologized profusely that I had been caught up in his crimes.

Harsen confessed that the Gallerlanders had caught him picking over a battlefield where the Hrals and Gallerlanders had fought, his pockets and arms overflowing with the electrum possessions of the fallen. Like the Donovard raiders, Harsen could not resist the whisper of great wealth. It mattered not that he was far from the colonies, the only place where it would be of any use.

I said as much, and told him about the greed of Hiltsfrad and Borsar and how they died and how I nearly died with them. He accepted this, saying he regretted what he had done. He promised to keep his hands off the Gallerlanders' sacred metal.

We agreed that Harsen needed to rest. We had survived many trials and finally found the natives. I had much work to do while he recuperated. We slept in peace that night, well fed and warm in our fur beds as the autumn winds grew colder outside.

On the 14th, our fourth day in the tree city, I spent many hours with a patient Pagdorat and kind Lady Emerald, presenting myself as an ambassador of sorts from New Lorin. This is when I learned that beautiful woman was named Eniri.

I could scarcely know where to begin because I was eager to ask them so much. I started by expressing my deepest thanks to them, particularly Eniri, for saving my life and that of my companion, and for sharing their time with me. I briefly told them about myself, my past in New Lorin, that I had come to their lands seeking an alliance. Eniri was unconvinced. I added my personal interest in learning from them so that our peoples could live in harmony on the new continent.

Eniri, through Pagdorat's translation, expressed her gratitude in my helping them learn the fate of her husband, Gofalnig, who had also been the eldest and most favored son of the antlered king, Gratgofa. She recounted how her husband had been captured by the Hrals while out hunting and was never seen again.

I offered to one day lead the Gallerlanders to the cave where I had been jailed with Gofalnig's remains, so that his bones could be recovered and buried in their rightful place under tomb guardians. Eniri smiled warmly. She showed interest in my crude map and my battered journal, its pages growing full of many inks.

My written words meant nothing to her, but my illustrations of native symbols, plants, and other things caught her eye. She was amused at the drawing of the Beamed Boulder and the Gallerlander symbols that I had copied, particularly the one from the pillar in the graveyard.

I tried to make clear through Pagdorat that I was very eager to learn their language, writing, history—anything they would share with me. She nodded and assured me I could fill many journals, but that Gratgofa's permission would be needed for me to stay in the treetop city, which was called Nalembalen.

She said the high king would not allow it unless he saw some benefit, especially at a time when the Donovards were pushing south deep into their forests and burning their villages. I told her that perhaps my experiences here could help find a way for peace, including with the Donovards.

Pagdorat became agitated, reminding me of what happened to his people on Teshdembal (Leauvenna Colony) and elsewhere in the north at the hands of the Donovards, even saying Gratgofa had a right to kill Harsen and me in retribution. Once he got this off his chest he calmed down and became embarrassed.

Pagdorat had every right to direct his anger at Harsen and me, but he was conflicted. He obviously had learned a lot about Donovard culture in addition to the Brintilian language, but had not forgotten his loss. He apologized, saying that many of the natives here were uneasy about our presence, given the Gallerlanders' history with the Donovards.

Pagdorat acknowledged that relations with New Lorin might be different, but he said the inhabitants of Nalembalen did not make a distinction between the colonies. To them, we were the pale tribe that abruptly appeared from the sea and stayed, building settlements that brought fire and bloody steel into the forest.

Pagdorat was right, and I realized that I no longer believed in any effort to make genuine the governor's false quest to seek an alliance with the Gallerlanders. So I told Pagdorat that there was more I wanted to tell him and Eniri.

I told them about how my grandfather's family had sought a new home across the seas to escape the endless turmoil of the Old World, a vast realm that was doomed to the repetitive cycle of peaceful union and widespread war since ancient times. This curse between the many fractious kingdoms of the Old World could never be broken, I said. Borrowing from the teachings of Orren, I explained that the Brintilian Empire had revived the ancient Agnesci craft of shipbuilding to relearn how to tame the wild deep waters and sail to Pemonia.

Eniri's eyes widened when I mentioned the Agnesci. When I asked if she wished to say something about them, she shook her head vigorously. Pagdorat urged me to continue, saying that as a child he had seen the great Brintilian ships pass by Teshdembal. I said the ships continue to come and go because the coastal colonies were still owned by the faraway kingdoms of the Old World. This was an odd concept to them.

I continued, telling them about how the New Loriners had usually lived at peace with the Ollohd and western Gallerlanders, though I was guilty of helping to lead many battles against them for the colony's expansion in my younger days. When I added that we had allied with the Ollohd tribe and fought together against the Hrals, Eniri said that this cooperation would need to be conveyed to High King Gratgofa because it would help win his approval for me to dwell in Nalembalen for a while longer.

I was grateful for her suggestion but said New Lorin, like Donovan, ultimately sought to expand their wealth and territory at the expense of Gallerlandia. In the end, New Lorin would be as harsh toward the Gallerlanders as the Donovards were.

I told her everything about our expedition, the hidden guile of the governor and Varesig in pursuit of electrum, Hiltsfrad's raiders, all of it. Her expression shifted from confused, disappointed, and pleased during my tale, and she and Pagdorat discussed it at length. I confirmed to her that I did not seek their electrum, and that their wondrous forests had changed me. In truth, I said, I was no ambassador for any colony. The Gallerlanders were already masters of their domain and needed nothing from the empire.

She accepted all I had told her, then asked why I had done so. I could not say why exactly, except that I did not want their world to change. The colonies would do much to change Gallerlandia, anything for the benefit of the Brintilian Empire. She asked what I, an accomplished son of that empire, would do now. I did not know, except that my desire to stay in the tree city was genuine. We continued to talk all day, answering each other's questions until Pagdorat was exhausted.

That evening we dined in the antlered king's great hall. The feast commemorated the visit of Chief Wolf, who I learned was a distant cousin of Gratgofa's. The death of the Hral was also celebrated. Interestingly, the Gallerlanders had a special term for the Hrals, *turserkgyn*, meaning "shrieking lion warriors."

The tree-limb tables overflowed with wild game including forest hares, venison, and pheasant. Baskets of honeyed and herb-crusted afban sat within easy reach, as did stacks of mellonberry cakes and many varieties of autumn forest fruits. It was the best food I had eaten in a long time. Lacking cutlery, the Gallerlanders ate their meal with fingers and slurped from bowls and mugs, but politely enough. I did the same.

The natives made merry with many kinds of drink. There was heavy brown mead, black currant wine, and a frothy beer made from the roots of a plant that sounded like *chaurik*. My favorite was the woody ale with mint sprigs that floated atop.

Wisps of tabakat smoke also curled about the scene, puffed by the women and men alike. Between the smoky swirls came the music of fifes and the chatter of merry courtiers, and even gruff Gratgofa was engaged in hearty banter and laughter that filled the hall. A woodland feast fit for any king.

As bellies filled with food and minds slowed with drink, Eniri discussed my request with Chief Wolf. Then they proposed to Gratgofa that Harsen and I be allowed to stay in Nalembalen, and mentioned New Lorin's friendship with the western natives. After some questioning and consideration between gulps of wine and puffs of tabakat, the high king granted my request, but only for as long as Harsen needed to recover. Although this was not ideal, I graciously accepted his answer and was determined to make the most of it. I also plotted how to keep Harsen ill and in bed, even if he only appeared to be so.

The merrymaking continued and the fifes and stump drums elevated their tunes. My eye was caught by Eniri, her every movement graceful and her sharp tattoos framing her emerald eyes. She soon bade me to follow her out of the smoky hall. She took me by the hand and we easily slipped away from the crowded revelry of that night.

Into a side chamber we went, then upward to the second and then third floors of the great domed chalet. Finally we came to a small dimly lit hallway where the oaken plank walls formed an archway overhead. Here she signaled to step softly.

We approached a closed door on which she placed her ear for a moment. Satisfied at the silence, we crept to a second door and entered a little room. Inside was a small library or archive, lit only by the moonlight that flooded in from two small circular holes in the wall.

Eniri wasted no time in singling out an elaborately carved wooden orb of a box, gilded with electrum and balanced on a single foot of eagle talons crafted of the same metal. From a little pouch at her waist she withdrew a key of solid electrum and unlocked the spherical chest. These items were fascinating in themselves, as was the Gallerlander use of a lock and key contraption, but not as captivating as the tattered roll of parchment that she plucked out.

With a glint of mischief in her eyes, she unfurled a bit of it to reveal faded symbols similar in shape to other Gallerlander writing I had seen etched on electrum and at the tombs—which she had seen in my sketches. Unwinding it further, she said, "Agnesci sheeps," and fluttered her hand like the waves of the sea. She was trying to say the scroll was about Agnesci ships.

My curiosity now enticed, I reached for the parchment. She held it away from me, shaking her head mischievously. She pointed to the symbols again, then pointed to her lips. Then pointed to the symbols again, then touched my lips. I guessed that I was being told to learn her language first.

Eniri quickly rolled the scroll back up and restored it to the peculiar orb chest. What wonders lay in that document that no eyes of Almeric blood had ever seen? She stepped closer to me. Her moonlit eyes gleamed like wild diamonds as she again pointed her slender finger to her lips, then to mine. Her lips parted, and I craved her touch.

But the sudden creak of the floorboards startled us. We pressed our backs to the wall near the door in case someone walked in. After they passed outside, she took my hand and we escaped back down to the great hall where the merriment had bloomed into a style of sweeping music my ears had never heard.

In addition to the primitive but cheerful-sounding instruments, the men and women who danced in the hall had tied wooden bells to their wrists and ankles. Even gruff Gratgofa's bells rang as he clapped from his throne. But when he saw Eniri, she departed from me and joined her father-in-law in the dance.

I kept near Chief Wolf and his son to watch the festivities and felt myself under the oppressive glare of Boarmaster. The names of these three, I soon learned, were Yelgoram, Owerdir, and Arbardir, respectively. Pagdorat was pleased to inform me that Chief Yelgoram thought the name Rildning was humorous.

&

Finally, my fifth day since arriving in Nalembalen was today, the 15th. It was a morning of rest and for me, much writing in my journal. My friends also departed before midday. Chief Yelgoram embraced my hands as he had done with the high king and Eniri, and, according to Pagdorat's translation, he gave me a fine farewell, calling me by my new honorary name, Parinsogon, meaning "snake spirit."

Yelgoram extended the invitation for me to visit his village, Takumbyr, at any time. Wishing there was some way for me to repay his mercy and generosity, I reached into my knapsack and pulled out the metal spoon I had long carried. I presented it to him with a demonstration of how to use it, and he accepted my lowly gift with fascination.

To Prince Wolf, Owerdir, I gave the half-burned, half-chewed beeswax candle and told him through Pagdorat that he had been a trusted light for me, the one who protected and guided my feet. He put his hand on my arm where he had wounded me, and Pagdorat said he would remember my bravery. That meant a lot coming from this bold native.

And finally, in an attempt at goodwill, I gave Boarmaster Arbardir the length of rope I had made while alone in the wilderness. My gift of peace was thrown to the ground with a grunt. I thought perhaps he misunderstood my gesture to mean to go hang himself, but Pagdorat explained that Arbardir would be staying in Nalembalen in the service of Gratgofa, and that others from Takumbyr and other villages would come here too if more Donovard raiders continued to push south as expected.

So, said Pagdorat with diplomatic charm, Arbardir would not yet need the rope gift. Arbardir crossed his arms and sniffed at me. With that, the wolf-clad natives set off for home. I was sad to see them go.

Pagdorat walked me around Nalembalen during the afternoon. It was exhilarating to climb the ropes and walk the swaying bridges unbound, as one of them. I had grown fond of Pagdorat and already owed much to him for helping me to speak with my hosts.

When I thanked him he surprised me by saying that my journey had inspired him to do what he could to help bring our peoples together. He said I should not so easily give up on my original mission of seeking an alliance for New Lorin. As his Teshi people knew too well, resisting the colonies was near impossible for the natives, he said, though he did not often share that truth with them. An alliance could still be a door to peace.

I replied that perhaps he was right, but that the wilderness had taken away my attachment for my old home and its ways. I was no longer a knight, and had left no wife or family behind. I wanted what the Gallerlanders had: their own self-made peace, here in the unspoiled heart of Pemonia.

Pagdorat said the world was changing, which reminded me of Varesig's words. And I suppose they are both right, but my mind is made up. Instead of a hollow alliance, if there is a way to help the Gallerlanders resist the colonies, I will help them find it.

Pagdorat was encouraged by this and vowed to translate for me, teach me, and travel with me until I needed him no more. I thanked him for his selfless kindness and replied that I would always count him as a friend.

Pagdorat is but one example of the kindness I have found here in Gallerlandia; despite my origins and the present threat of the Donovards in the north. Neither Pagdorat nor any of his kin owe me anything, yet they have extended a strong hand of friendship to this stranger in a short time. And the beautiful Eniri continues to captivate my mind.

As we explored the passages of Nalembalen's giant trees, Pagdorat explained that the city was very old and had always been the greatest city of the Gallerlanders. I learned that Gratgofa was indeed high king, or more properly namnak, over all of Gallerlandia. He ruled over three *thuran* (kings) who in turn ruled separate Gallerlander territories.

Goynland in the north and west was the smallest. Umbyrland was the central and largest realm. The dark forest called Ondirhar—through which I had passed—bordered both the Goyns and the Umbyrs. The third territory was Vaynland in the southeast. The treetop city of Nalembalen and its environs were collectively called Balanland and lay at the heart of Umbyrland. Balanland was the realm ruled directly by the high king.

Each of Gratgofa's three underkings ruled one of the three tribes and was elected by and from among their clan chiefs. For example, Yelgoram was the chief for his clan, one of many who answered to the king of Umbyrland. Yelgoram ruled the many families within his clan but was also elected from among these families. Thus, no chieftaincy or kingship was hereditary, and even the high king himself was elected from among the clan leaders.

But Pagdorat said that many of the families of the high kings and underkings ruled for generations because the electors repeatedly confirmed their suitable qualities. I find this novel, given such politics are wholly unknown in the Old World, where dynasties rule outright until toppled by another. But the Gallerlanders' method is genius in its simplicity. I cannot help but wonder, however, if the Gallerlanders may also be vulnerable to distortions and usurpers among their chiefs, as we are in the empire. I will have many questions about this.

After our exploration of Nalembalen, Pagdorat agreed to teach me the Gallerlander alphabet. He explained that there were many dialects of Gali, including his native Teshi, because Gallerlandia and its people were so vast. But there was a common set of root sounds and corresponding written symbols that comprised the core alphabet. He warned that learning would not be easy but that he would use the same teaching methods used by the Donovard priest who taught him Brintilian as a child. I was eager to learn, so we practiced until nightfall.

It is now late, and I'm utterly exhausted from what has unfolded since my arrival in the treetop city and from recording these events on the page. I'm grateful that my path has led me to Nalembalen, great capital of these great people, but I of course survived many perils to arrive here. A new chapter of my journey has begun. Or rather, the true journey has only just begun.

Midautumn 12

I have spent nearly a month putting basic Gali sentences into practice with Pagdorat and Eniri. Even Harsen, who has recovered well over the past few weeks, is impressed and says I have surpassed his own Gali abilities. I have begged the good woodsman to remain in bed until I figure out a way to stay in Nalembalen longer. He has grudgingly agreed to act the part of invalid.

The Gali language is difficult indeed, and there is so much to learn. The thought of what the lovely Eniri might reveal in the ancient Agnesci scrolls also tickles my mind. Poor Harsen is also understandably a bit jealous of my exploration of the treetop city. Nalembalen rivals the largest cities of Almeria, with inhabitants living from its highest reaches to its lowest rungs and out to the edges of Balanland.

I have also learned more about the society here. The people of Nalembalen and wider Balanland hail from about twenty clans, suggesting that hundreds of clans probably exist in Gallerlandia as a whole, wherever its borders lie. These seem to be among the most powerful clans of the area:

Mandegar—Gratgofa's clan, of which he remains the chief
Edryngyn—former rulers of Nalembalen
Tamtur—Eniri's clan
Dorngyn—clan of the head priest-warrior
Hangodir—protectors of Balanland's northern fringe

As described by Pagdorat, there is no true nobility among the Gallerlanders. But those families who do attain leadership positions are permitted to distinguish themselves by physically altering their tattoos. Originally curved and circular, new ink is added to the tattoos to make them appear sharper and with jagged angles. This is considered honorable, to show that the ruler and his immediate family have won the trust of their people.

Pagdorat said that anyone caught sharpening the design of their tattoos illegally has the tattoos scraped off with pumice stones until scars are certain to obscure the tattoos. I have seen such dishonored persons, but very few. Pagdorat informs me that his people, the Teshi, have the same practice. Pagdorat's own skin displays a mix of sharp and round paint, denoting several close relatives who held elected positions.

I have concluded that religious beliefs are more important to Gallerlanders than politics. One evening I was able to sit down with Eniri and Pagdorat to learn more about their spiritual life. Eniri was happy to share this with me, explaining that life in the forests revolved around a single god, Wurumnak—whose name roughly means Great White One—and the many blessings bestowed by him upon his people.

When asked to describe Wurumnak, she said he was the "spirit father" and "life giver," and that no other gods sat with him in Nawurihar—meaning Great White Forest—which I interpreted to be heaven. I asked if Nawurihar was above the earth, since the Gallerlanders gazed skyward from time to time. Eniri explained that Wurumnak placed "sky omens" above us to help show the way. Although finding the sky while in the forest was often difficult, looking to the clouds before making important decisions was critical for the Gallerlanders. Perhaps this is comparable to prayer in the Messengian Church.

Of course, Brintilians, especially colonists, believe that the natives are sun-worshipping pagans at best, or at worst demonic folk spawned from Memelos. To hear Eniri's soft voice tell of their single god was a true revelation, though one Orren had claimed all along. On the other hand, she described the Hrals as pagans, with deities and rituals for the sun, moon, trees, and so on.

Eniri said that the words of Wurumnak had been passed down through the ages by the Graparins (spirit walkers), those fox-furred priest-warriors who had cast the Hral to his death. Their teachings held that Wurumnak had created the first men and women, and that our souls rest with him in Nawurihar after death.

This fact of the natives' belief denounces the actions of the Messengian Church, which has condemned more than a few Brintilians as heretics for believing what I have now heard from the mouths of the Gallerlanders themselves. How heretical they would think me at home!

Eniri continued to describe Wurumnak, saying that he tended to Haldembalir (the Tree of the World), which grew at the center of the Great White Forest in heaven. She recalled my sketch of the tomb symbols and made me show it to her again. I opened to that page, and she seized upon it, pointing to the central tree. Excited, she used the drawing to illustrate her story.

There in Nawurihar the souls of the virtuous will dwell, she said, led by the twelve Thuraniparin (spirit kings) who were the greatest rulers and warriors during their natural lives. They were represented as crowns in the drawing, protectively encircling Nawurihar and the Tree of the World. The twelve shall be the chosen vassals of Wurumnak, she continued, their spirits preserved to help defend the white realm from the consuming flames of the devilish Ominchar, who is clearly the Gallerlander version of Memelos.

According to her tale, Ominchar hates the peace of Wurumnak's white forest and hastens the day of the final battle between good and evil, called Thurondsogon, meaning the Day of the Black Snake. This is the day that Ominchar will transform himself into a giant serpent and seek to devour the Tree of the World with fangs of flame to birth a wicked world anew. The flames of Ominchar and his snake form were clearly recognizable as viciously encircling heaven in my sketch of the tomb etching.

Eniri said Ominchar's evil could be overcome if enough souls of brave and honorable Gallerlander kings joined her god in Nawurihar, rather than succumb to the wicked ways of Ominchar during life. Just as Wurumnak sought virtuous souls to lead that final battle, the coils of the great snake would be numbered by the evil souls, and the length of his fangs by the words and deeds done against Wurumnak, and the power in his jaws strengthened by the spilled blood of innocent life.

Ultimately, Eniri said that Demfrebra, as the snake form of Ominchar is called, is destined to perish under Wurumnak's electrum sword. To hide the sword until the End of Days, and to assure the loyalty of his created people, Wurumnak entrusted the holy weapon into their hands by driving the sword deep into the Tree of the World, where it scattered into shards that melted down into the earth.

In life, the people must gather and protect the electrum so that the sword can be reforged in the afterlife and strike down the dark serpent in that final battle, when all souls awake. The sword is also depicted in the etching, in full unbroken form, within the heart of the Tree of the World.

Eniri's tale made the sacredness of the electrum very clear. I could now understand their reaction to seeing it in the greedy hands of outsiders. Though the metal adorns some Gallerlanders' bodies as jewelry and decorates select homes and tombs, it is neither traded nor does it convey wealth as minted coins, as we from the Old World would do. Neither is the electrum, nor any metal, used to craft weapons and armor—with the exception of Gratgofa's antlered helmet—probably in deference to its holy purpose.

They mine the electrum from the deep earth only to gather their god's buried sword and fulfill the destiny of heaven. This also explains the hidden glow of the electrum, for it must be found by Gallerlanders, especially in the darkest of times and places. It is for them to cherish and protect in life, and it shall be their protection in the afterlife. For these natives, the electrum is symbolic of duty, goodness, and life itself.

I dare say that my own God of Messengianism bears similarities to Wurumnak. Both of them are single and all-powerful deities who wield mighty swords. The people of both cultures have a choice between the good and evil paths of life, and are harkened to join the righteous and honorable in a final battle.

And Ominchar, like Memelos, is a vile shape-shifting crea-ture who will not rest before gaining as many wicked souls for himself as he can. Ominchar's transformation into a ground-dwelling serpent is similar to Memelos being chained within the depths of the earth, where he drives up snakes, lizards, and other foul beasts to infest the good lands of Crea-tion.

Here I wish to record a poem recited to me by Pagdorat, whose Teshi people share the Gallerlanders' beliefs, because it beautifully conveys those beliefs in their own words (though translated into Brintilian).

Woe be to Ominchar,
In all his many forms,
And to his gathered souls
Harvested among men,
For End of Days beckons.
Thurondsogon will be his final reckoning!

The mighty electrum sword
Of Wurumnak, hidden
Deep in Haldembalir.
Scattered electrum pieces
Re-forged into one.
Thurondsogon will be his final reckoning!

Twelve greatest kings of men,
Thuraniparin, as
His chiefs of honored men,
Shall defend the white trees
Of Nawurihar, to
Save from Ominchar flame and Demfrebra fang-teeth!

On thunder they will roar
To triumph over he
Who becomes the serpent
Of blackest black, venom
Most consuming of souls.
Demfrebra destined to consume Nawurihar!

Should men's strength fail on Earth,
And glowing gold lay dark
Under mountain roots, then
Woe to man for failing
Pledge of Wurumnak to
Final fight with serpent-fiend, he who hates all life!

And so the fate of the
Haldembalir and all
Souls within are saved by
Wurumnak's boundless strength,
And Demfrebra lives not,
Should man reject all Ominchar evils in life!

The stories of my friends have poured forth like cool waters to quench my thirsting mind. I urged Eniri to continue, perhaps with the origins of the Gallerlanders, a request that made her visibly nervous then quiet.

Pagdorat conveyed that I asked what is known by only the Graparins. Those priest-warriors are the stewards of traditions, history, and religion. When asked why the information is so secret, his reply was "It just is." After a moment, Eniri and Pagdorat engaged in a lengthy conversation in which it became clear to me that she was attempting to persuade him of something.

Finally, Pagdorat declared with some frustration that Eniri had sworn him to absolute secrecy, and that he was not to repeat any of what he was about to translate. Neither would Pagdorat reveal to anyone her telling me these things. When I asked why she was taking such a risk, Pagdorat confessed that it was because she "favored" me. Eniri blushed, and the Teshi rolled his eyes. I grinned but said nothing, hoping to ease her embarrassment.

Eniri began by saying that the Gallerlanders, like all people in the Tree of the World, were created by Wurumnak, who would reclaim them at the End of Days, except those who followed Ominchar. But all Gallerlanders believed that speaking openly about such hefty religious subjects was forbidden because it was the sacred domain of the Graparins.

People believed that an uninitiated person speaking about these things provided an opportunity for Ominchar to twist the words into inaccuracies that, unbeknownst to the untrained speaker, blasphemed Wurumnak and would literally lengthen the fangs of Demfrebra. Writing down the teachings provided a similar opportunity for corruption. Only the disciplined and highly trained Graparins could retell the histories of the Gallerlanders. Eniri said they were careful to pass down the teachings without changing a word.

Pagdorat briefly interrupted to say that nothing Eniri had said was secret. She quickly hushed him. What was not well-known outside of Gratgofa's great hall, where the Graparins also lived, was that some of the histories had in fact been written down but kept hidden in their archive. She gave me a knowing glance as Pagdorat translated. I thought of the scroll in the wooden orb.

Eniri said that among those writings was a story about the Agnesci Seafathers who had discovered the second of three great branches of the Tree of the World. This meant the Seafathers had found another continent of Wurumnak's creation, that is, Cedelaebos. The Old World. She said they found it after many long journeys sailing through sea *and clouds*.

The people that the Seafathers found there, the Almerics, were considered Wurumnak's people and thus their brethren. Most of the Agnesci people, riding a wave of religious fervor sparked by their discovery, left Aprelaebos to live alongside the Almerics and teach them about Wurumnak and the Tree of the World.

But the encounter between Agnesci and Almeric was under ill-starred sky omens, she said, for the Agnesci who made it across the seas were eventually slaughtered by their newfound brethren. All of the Seafathers were captured and killed, and all their ships burned. Only one ship of survivors escaped and made it back home across the seas, where the small number who had stayed in Aprelaebos learned the sad fate of the many.

The tragic tale was recorded on a scroll kept by the Graparins, the one Eniri had allowed me to peek at. She claimed that the first keepers of the scroll all the way down to the present Graparins were forever charged with hiding the tale because the ancient Agnesci wished for their children and later generations not to know about Cedelaebos and the Almerics so as to prevent a similar catastrophe. They also did not want the bloodthirsty Almerics to follow them back here to Pemonia.

Eniri said the Agnesci were so distraught and ashamed of the great loss that the clans who had built the ships were banished to the forests south and east of modern-day Gallerlandia, taking their knowledge with them. This exile, she said, along with the passage of time, was why the history was easily buried. The Graparins subsequently came to control the religion of the Gallerlanders, so that the secrets of the ancients could be kept hidden to avoid repeating the past.

Eniri's tale begged many more questions, and many had gathered on my lips. Why was *she* permitted to have this secret knowledge? Why did she break the laws of her land to tell me? What had happened to the shipbuilding natives who were banished?

Pagdorat was clearly shaken by her revelations. Confused and frustrated, he refused to translate further and had many questions of his own. She spent much time whispering and consoling him. I cannot imagine what it must be like for him to hear what she said, even as distant as we are from those times.

We of the Old World know well the legends of the first meeting of the Almerics and Agnesci. But whereas our timeworn tales paint the Agnesci as an invading force that blasphemed God with their voyage across the seas, the Gallerlanders have carefully preserved quite a different story.

Eniri's tale has made me feel more of an outsider than ever before. Though I'm not responsible for how my Almeric ancestors treated her ancestors, my hands have certainly contributed to that ancient struggle as an invader of their world. And yet they do not see me as a threat, and Eniri shares their inner secrets.

I crave the details that must be hidden within the Graparins' archive. I wonder if Eniri's aim is to find a way to set the world back in balance. After all, it is tempting to think those fragile age-old pages could crush the ignorance of the imperial priests and conquerors, who know no truth of the Agnesci.

But the powerful do not bow to ancient writings, and they would sooner snuff out this candle of knowledge than see its light shine. The Brintilian Empire would never acknowledge these natives as the other half of mankind, because that would mean we share the same Creator.

I'm grateful to Eniri and wonder why she has chosen to share so much with me.

Frostfall 1

Winter has come early here in Nalembalen, and how fantastic it is to see the great tree city cloaked in snow. The tree hearths are warm and welcoming, as is the spiced ale of the Gallerlanders.

Harsen has fully recovered over the past few weeks, but with Eniri's help we have won approval from High King Gratgofa to stay until the thaw of spring. Unfortunately Harsen has grown restless in this place that I find most enchanting. He longs for home, but for now he contents himself by joining the hunting parties and learning how to play the natives' musical instruments. I have spent many hours in study, often with Eniri and Pagdorat, but also alone. I have come a long way in learning Gali in a short time, but have a long way to go still.

I have also made an effort to closely watch the Graparin priest-warriors, especially during feast gatherings. They are a peculiar bunch. By tradition there are exactly a dozen of them, perhaps to serve as an earthly reminder of the loyalty of twelve Thuraniparin (spirit kings). Knowing now what Eniri said about their sacred duties regarding the hidden scrolls, it has been difficult for me to resist the temptation to creep up and take another peek in their archive.

Eniri told me that the Graparins serve for life and that the high king chooses the head Graparin from among the twelve. When one among them dies, the Graparins vote on a new inductee. They are not permitted to have wives or families because they must be wholly dedicated to their duties, which include burial rites and interpreting sky omens, both of which I have witnessed. New Graparins tend to be trustworthy young men who have shown an interest in the histories. To refuse the invitation to join the twelve is considered a great shame, and few have resisted the call.

I have not discovered the names of all the Graparins, but their chief is named Talimnat. He was the one who presided over the Hral's death. The eldest among the twelve is Hegdir. Eniri told me he is the most studious and learned, so he is the keeper of the sacred scroll. A third Graparin is Dirdayn. Like Talimnat, Dirdayn appears to dislike Harsen and me. Outsiders, Eniri reminded me, are viewed by the Graparins with utmost suspicion given their secret responsibilities. Dirdayn, the one who led me to my execution, has kept a careful eye on us ever since.

I've already detailed the Graparins' decorative electrum and fox-fur garments. No other Gallerlander is adorned with as much of the sacred metal as they are, but the interior of Gratgofa's great hall is equally decorated with electrum ornaments. The winter hearth fires make all of this metal glitter and shine, casting a foggy glow among the tree branch columns of the hall. The finely carved woods throughout the chalet are equally pleasing to the eye.

The richness of Gallerlander carpentry and goldsmithing are unparalleled among any I've encountered in Pemonia and are more exquisite than most works found in the colonies. Yet the goldsmiths in Nalembalen are few while the carpenters are many. Surprisingly, the goldsmiths occupy the lowest rung of Gallerlander society. Despite their skill in crafting the holy metal, viewed as the shards of Wurumnak's own sword, they are regarded as unclean for reasons I do not understand.

Pagdorat said the goldsmiths and miners are primarily from a clan named Maluram, who have dwelt in the mountain caves of Vaynland since ancient times, when the Gallerlanders were divided and leaderless. When I asked whether they still mine electrum in Vaynland, Pagdorat, a Teshi outsider himself, confessed he did not know.

Pagdorat said he was told that only the Maluram know where to dig and how to craft the metal. There are no other cleavers of the earth among the many Gallerlander peoples, he said. This may also be a reason why these natives have not forged iron armor and weapons for themselves. If the Maluram are the only metalworkers, and their focus is on gathering and shaping the electrum of Wurumnak, they have no time or need for dull iron ore.

Still, I cannot help but wonder how the Gallerlanders will defend themselves from the steel claws of Donovard raiders. These natives have such a rich past of inventiveness and know how to build certain contraptions, but what chance will they have if they use primitive stone blades and spears against steel-clad mounted knights?

Frostfall 17

A messenger arrived on the evening of the 15th amid a heavy snowfall bearing dreadful news for my gentle hosts. The man arrived in Nalembalen exhausted and frozen but carried important information to High King Gratgofa immediately. Another Donovard army, larger than any previously encountered, had invaded from the north, pillaging and burning villages as it pressed toward the treetop capital. Gratgofa sent word to the chieftains of the area, summoning them to a council to be held the next day.

During the night of the 15th, numerous families from the north began arriving to seek shelter. Many more have followed since. Gratgofa ordered preparations to be made at once to receive and care for them.

By midday of the 16th, the refugee flow was staggering. First small bands of survivors, scouts, and warriors arrived. Some of the latter were from villages that had been spared the carnage but whose chieftains offered them to assist the high king's collective defense. Many women and children followed, then the wounded, piled in carts pulled by men and women trudging through the snow. Eniri organized quarters for them in the tree hovels and fur-skin tents hastily set up on the forest floor with fires to warm them.

Harsen and I have been told to stay out of the way and preferably out of sight, for fear that some survivors might seek revenge. So we watch silently from the balconies and bridges. I wish to help these poor people but know my untattooed face would do more harm than good.

When the flow of refugees started to slow, Gratgofa held a council with the great men of Nalembalen and the clan and family chiefs who had arrived. The council first partook of a solemn welcome feast, which Harsen and I were allowed to attend. Interestingly, this caused no problems beyond a few surprised glares and grumblings. Pagdorat translated some of it for us, since I could not easily comprehend the dialects.

The feast concluded with a formal meeting of the council. For the newly arrived chiefs, the original messenger repeated his story about the Donovards breaking into northern Umbyrland, forcing survivors to flee south toward us here in Balanland. These refugees said a colonial army named the Frontier Corps had pushed south well past Yoredgoyn, which I remembered was the Goynland capital that Hiltsfrad's men had failed to capture. The Frontier Corps had marched through three waves of Gallerlander counterattacks without stopping. The invaders felled other great cities and were soon to be upon Nalembalen.

The chieftains were bitterly divided on how best to counter the crusaders. Most bickered among themselves, some shouted curses at others, and a few were disheartened and advocated fleeing south to Vaynland.

I wondered how the Frontier Corps knew about Nalembalen, hidden deep within Gallerlandia. Then the hair on the back of my neck stood on end as I recalled Hiltsfrad's discovery of the clay tablet map earlier in his campaign, and the translation he forced out of a captive. The knight had told me that he sent couriers with this intelligence back to Donovan Colony before he continued his raiding. Hiltsfrad had even shared a copy of the map for my journal.

Hiltsfrad had predicted that his information would avenge his death and that others would follow to complete his work. Thanks to the forethought of this dead knight and the trails left by the fleeing natives, the Frontier Corps will know exactly where the high king of the Gallerlanders dwells. I never doubted Hiltsfrad's words, but I was stunned that these crusaders had marched to Nalembalen in the middle of winter, through a woodland realm with no proper marching roads to speak of.

And how could the comparatively small Donovan Colony muster another large army and penetrate this far into the forests so quickly? I can only guess that they have received reinforcement ships from Almeria to man and equip this new Frontier Corps. Its name betrayed the motive and goal easily enough. The campaign was clearly meant to expand the colonial territory at the expense of the natives.

A hefty, blond-bearded Umbyr chieftain named Urgamdir, who had participated in some of the heaviest fighting in the north, stepped forward to address the council. The Frontier Corps's general plans, he said, might be learned from a colonial soldier that his clan captured before fleeing.

Urgamdir said they had brought this soldier to Nalembalen for Gratgofa to question. It was then that I noticed Boarmaster Arbardir's steady glare at me, knowing that he suspected Harsen and me to be spies. I wanted to question the prisoner myself, but this was not the time to make a request.

The council grew rowdy with all this news, and it worsened as the spiced ale and dark wine flowed. The newcomers had not eaten much during days of cold escape, so they filled themselves with hot food and drink. Eventually they decided that all the chiefs of Nalembalen, greater Balanland, and southern Umbyrland should be summoned to the tree city for a great council to determine how resistance could best be made.

Runners were dispatched from the great hall with fresh provisions for their pouches. It was temping to offer to accompany one of these messengers to witness other parts of Gratgofa's realm and help where I could. But the situation was too dangerous for exploring, and I knew my involvement would likely be forbidden.

❧

Today is the 17th and we have seen the flooding in of countless broken and tired families and many wounded and dying warriors. Many more refugees than before. From sunrise through sunset they plod the once snowy and now half-frozen muddy paths into the tree city. Few ready warriors were among the later flows, and all carried with them stories of massacre and fire.

Harsen and I are doing our best to lay low, but there was a moment this evening in the great hall when we couldn't avoid their ire. An enraged chieftain from the north grabbed Harsen by the throat and would have strangled him were he not saved by one of Gratgofa's chieftains. Despite our appearance as rough wildermen we are now everywhere met with vicious eyes and gnashing teeth. I cannot blame them. They have every reason to hate us.

When the pace of survivors finally slowed to a trickle, I was summoned to the great hall. There, the antlered king sat upon his tree throne and pondered the heavy burden now placed upon his shoulders. He was accompanied by several chieftains as well as Eniri and Arbardir. With Pagdorat at my side, Gratgofa wanted me to tell him about the colonies. Why had they come to his realm? What did they want?

I recounted to him the story I had earlier told to Eniri, about how the peoples of the Old World sought an escape across the seas from the unending upheaval and war in Almeria. My ancestors had revived the shipbuilding of the Agnesci to cross the waters and seek a new home, but unfortunately the empire simply brought the violent habits of the Old World with them.

The high king stirred at my mention of the Agnesci and looked about him at the faces of those who were listening. I realized my mistake in mentioning the Agnesci. His people certainly knew of their own ancestors, but Eniri had said they did not know about the Seafathers' travel to the Old World because this was the secret Graparin knowledge. Gratgofa cut off Pagdorat's translation and quickly shifted the conversation back to the present colonies.

I explained that I was not from Donovan, but rather New Lorin, where relations with western natives were usually peaceful. In attacking his realm, I said the Donovards were seeking more territory and would do anything to conquer it. I added that even my own colony had fought with the

Donovards because of their boundless desire for new land and wealth.

The high king asked if I would fight them again. Without hesitation I said yes, if permitted to help. He asked if I would help question Urgamdir's prisoner about the coming of the Frontier Corps. I nodded. As proof of my solidarity, Eniri reminded Gratgofa of my having risked my life to warn Yelgoram's village about Hiltsfrad's impending raid.

The high king nodded, but Arbardir laughed himself into a rage. Eniri quelled him, but it was clear Boarmaster still harbored deep distrust of me and that he had probably attempted to fill Gratgofa's ear with many falsehoods since our arrival.

The remainder of the evening passed with more passionate debate among the chiefs about what could be done. Harsen and I sat at a side table and watched. Before we retired for the night Eniri told me that Gratgofa would again seek my advice when the great council was convened.

Frostfall 19

Yesterday I met with the captured Frontier Corps soldier, whose name is Siglef. The chieftain who captured him, Urgamdir, insisted on being present. Pagdorat also accompanied us, despite my improving Gali, so that I could more easily communicate with Urgamdir and the guards.

Siglef was kept in the same small jail chamber linked to the great hall that Harsen and I had been held in. The irony was not lost on me or Pagdorat, who jested that I was no doubt glad to be returning to the cell as a questioner and not a prisoner.

Siglef was alone in the cell with one guard from Urgamdir's clan. I requested that the captive's hands be loosed from their vine chains, and Urgamdir grudgingly ordered it so. I also provided Siglef with afban when I sat down with him, presuming that he had not eaten in some time. He was a young soldier, perhaps not more than twenty years.

Siglef was surprised to see an unpainted face and hear me speak his language. And he surprised me in turn, as he was not a Donovard but rather a New Loriner. He might have recognized me were it not for my rough wilderman appearance, but when it was clear to him that I was not a native, he was at once relieved and confused.

Siglef asked if I was a prisoner, too. I did not answer him directly but gave him that impression. He wanted to ask me many questions, but I told him he needed to answer my questions first if he was to have any chance of leaving this place . . . a comment I asked Pagdorat not to translate for Urgamdir, to avoid angering the chieftain.

Siglef said that about three months ago he had been transferred from a New Lorin border post to a new regiment that was sent to join a new legion being raised in Donovan. There was pride in his voice when he said he was glad to have been among the men chosen to gather in Donovan as part of the new Frontier Corps, to join in "the hunt for the forest folk of Memelos." It was the first united army, Siglef said, and he believed it to be the mightiest army ever assembled in the New World. Even famous knights of the crusader military orders of Almeria had been sent to join and help command the corps alongside the colonial knights.

As I noted earlier, crusaders like Hiltsfrad were employed by Donovan to expand the territory. But the Frontier Corps was clearly a more focused effort. And I knew that the colonial legions would not be permitted to join ranks with the crusaders unless the emperor had given his blessing.

Next I queried Siglef about who commanded this new force. His swift response was Hilsingor of Ned Gollen. This name required no further explanation. Hilsingor was not a colonist. He was a Brintilian from Almeria who was notorious for his ruthless military genius. It was Hilsingor who put down the Arukan Rebellion in Ned Frosel and smashed the Kingdom of Arukia itself to preserve the Brintilian Empire. So I was not surprised that the emperor had sent him on this mission to the colonies.

Siglef said that Hilsingor arrived in Donovan with a flotilla of eight hundred ships brimming with knights, horses, pikemen, archers, and infantry. I said he was surely jesting. But the captive insisted Donovan had been chosen above the other colonies for a massive push into Pemonia. Even if Siglef had inflated the number of ships, I was certain Hilsingor would travel with a large force of veterans who would be well equipped to confront any number of Gallerlanders.

Siglef again wondered aloud why I was with the Gallerlanders. He guessed that I was not a spy for the colonies, since I did not know about the Frontier Corps. I saw no reason to continue the charade, so I told him that I journeyed here originally to seek an alliance on behalf of New Lorin but would not return. I wanted to learn about the natives, whom I found to be as human as the two of us, and help them.

Siglef glanced at the bulky strong Urgamdir, whose bright blond hair was shaggy and streaked with green paint that linked into the braided beard on his chin. He asked me if Urgamdir or Pagdorat could understand Brintilian. I responded that Pagdorat could, and I asked him to do his best not to insult my friends. The soldier's face twisted with disgust, saying the corps would trample the evil giant trees of this place like grass, and that I would be among the slain for my treachery.

As with Hiltsfrad and Varesig before him, I did not expect to cure this young soldier of his ignorance. I asked what the Frontier Corps would do next. Siglef laughed and said that was no secret. Hilsingor knew of the treetop capital of "Nimbalin," meaning Nalembalen. Siglef said the legions were marching here to take their prize. What prize, I asked.

"The electrum, of course!" he said. The Donovards believed the natives had a great hoard here, tucked away in or under the trees. I told Siglef that the rumor was false, that the Gallerlanders did not value the metal the same way we did. There was no hoard. Siglef laughed again, saying Hilsingor had "good information" to the contrary. He declined to elaborate, or perhaps, as a lowly soldier, he could not. But it's clear to me that if Hilsingor did receive Hiltsfrad's map, the dead knight's courier must have passed on wild tales of the raiders' electrum treasures as well.

As this point Siglef declined to answer any more questions. I thanked him for talking with me and conceded that he was probably right: the Frontier Corps might destroy Nalembalen and perhaps me with it. But he would be the first Brintilian to die here. I described the demise of the Hral, the long fall to the frozen ground below. I told Siglef that I would try to convince the Gallerlanders to spare him and that if he provided more information it would certainly help.

Siglef smirked, declaring himself already dead. Whether he would be executed by the barbarians or die fighting them, it made no difference to him, he said. At least he had given his life in the pursuit of ridding the continent of the "Memelos infestation." So he would not talk to me anymore. Besides, he said, there was no way to stop Hilsingor's legions. Again, Siglef was probably right. The corps would soon be upon us.

As the guard returned Siglef to his vine chains, I told him that I would not take pleasure in seeing a fellow New Loriner die at the hands of the natives. I had seen others suffer the same fate and wished he had taken a different path. He countered that his path had been honorable and in service to the colonies and the empire, while mine was traitorous and heretical.

I told him it would not always be this way, that if the empire wanted to stay peacefully in Pemonia they would have to find a way to live with the natives. Brave and defiant until the end, Siglef said the only peace with the empire was to submit to it, and once again he was right. The empire had never bowed to anyone.

Later in the evening I relayed Siglef's information about Sir Hilsingor and the corps to Gratgofa, along with a request to spare Siglef's life. I knew the news about the enemy would disappoint Gratgofa and that he would not spare Siglef, but I felt compelled to try. The prisoner's information made me wonder if the Gallerlanders could defend their capital or if they would have to evacuate. I doubt they would abandon their magnificent city, so perhaps a great capital like Nalembalen has defenses besides its soaring heights that can withstand fire and steel.

Gratgofa was interested in every detail I knew about Hilsingor, including his personal behavior and manner of fighting, suggesting the antlered king intended to meet him in combat. Gratgofa is certainly a bold ruler who would stand against an impossible enemy to win his place among Wurumnak's Spirit Kings. I recounted all the tales of Hilsingor's famous exploits, but unfortunately I did not know enough about the brutal commander to satisfy Gratgofa.

As for Siglef, he took the plunge at midday today. He met his end with a stout heart and chin up and practically marched himself under the arches. He was a braver man than I was when the Graparins took me forward by my arms, and I did feel like a traitor when Siglef fell from the plank. I had to remind myself that Siglef was not unlike most colonists and especially the inhabitants of old Almeria, who would see him as a martyr for Messengianism and the empire.

Harsen was bitterly distressed at the sight of Siglef's silent plummet, and he accused me of failing to save him. I worry much about the woodsman these days, for neither of us are as we once were.

❧

This evening I spent time walking the bridges between the boughs, their lamps swaying with each careful step. I wish to continue my Gali studies with Eniri, but she is tending to the refugees. So I pondered what the next few days would bring, sometimes looking up to see if I could understand the Galler-lander omens in the night sky.

When the cold finally numbed my mind, I turned toward Gratgofa's domed chalet and fixed on my warm quarters within. But as I approached there was someone walking the bridge toward me. It was Eniri, and she wanted me to follow her.

We walked into the great hall where Gratgofa and his chieftains were talking and drinking. None of them was the least bit interested in us. She led me into the royal sitting chambers above the great hall, where we seated ourselves among rough grass rugs and fur pillows. Numerous wall lamps cast a soft light in the room.

She surprised me with a sudden embrace. Sensing her concern, I shifted to hold her more comfortably. Her tenderness was the only thing that could calm the unease that was hourly growing here among the treetops. Proving that I was not the only student, she simply said "stay" in Brintilian.

I told her in my broken Gali that I would stay in Nalembalen, and asked her what Gratgofa would do if he saw us now. She jolted away at the sound of his name and looked at me with those mischievous emerald eyes. She cradled my face in her hands, and we kissed.

It was a while before I realized Pagdorat was standing above us, fretting to me that the antlered king would toss me from the plank many times for this. I told him to lower his voice and sit down, but it was only Eniri's commanding tone that calmed him. Even then, he would not sit. He continued through the chamber apparently on some errand, looking over his shoulder at us.

I regret placing Pagdorat in a difficult position. The Teshi has been a good friend and teacher, and I hope he will obey the wishes of the princess. I can't help but worry that he sees me as treading too far down a forbidden road.

Frostfall 20

We await the arrival of the Gallerlander chiefs, and Harsen grows impatient. He wants us to leave Nalembalen at once. He had agreed to be my guide into Gallerlandia, he said, but did not want to die fighting for them against the Donovards. I said he was right, that I had not intended for this to happen either. So I released him from all obligations and sincerely wished him a safe journey home.

This angered him greatly, and he retorted that he had no intention of wandering alone in the black forest. The Gallerlanders, he said, should escort us to the Donovards, who would surely grant us safe passage to New Lorin. He added that the natives should send us off with electrum gifts in appreciation for all I had done to help them and as recompense for beating and imprisoning him. We could also make a plea with the Frontier Corps, he said, not to be too harsh with the natives, and perhaps even persuade Hilsingor to spare the tree city.

Our argument grew heated as I rejected his ideas as foolish and impossible and called his own desires greedy. "Have you learned nothing in the wilderness or here among the original peoples of Aprelaebos?" I asked. He again insisted that we leave "before it's too late," and that I "come back" to my old self. Then his temper flared like I had never seen it: "I do not want to die a wilderman among these green-painted beast men!"

We parted ways without making amends, but I doubt that he will leave on his own yet. I do realize that I have inadvertently led my dear friend into more than he bargained for back in New Lorin. But I never promised him treasure, and certainly not the natives' sacred metal, which he has apparently learned to covet.

The dangers of the wilderness aside, I had never dreamed I would find myself in such an enchanting place, dining with the chiefs of this woodland race, learning their peculiar language, or falling in love with their most beautiful princess. And I feel that I'm on the cusp of unraveling the most ancient and important mysteries the world has ever hidden from the eyes of man, a mystery that wise old Orren would have sacrificed everything for a glimpse of. In fact, he did sacrifice his life while teaching me what he knew to be the truth.

I am torn. I know the forgotten fate of the Agnesci lies here among their Gallerlander sons, their histories and secrets buried in the Graparin scrolls. Surely it would be a noble pursuit to find a way to reveal to my own people that these original peoples of Pemonia are our ancient brethren, not the children of Memelos as so commonly believed.

And I know there is much the Brintilians could learn from a people who do not value metal for its abilities to purchase, take lives, and accumulate power. Their practice of choosing kings from among the best of men, rather than all men being slaves to the whims of dynasties and their endless feuds, could change the bitter Old World.

But I know I must restrain my optimism. The idea that this former knight could change the hard hearts of men like Hilsingor and Hiltsfrad is folly. The dream of serving as a bridge between the peoples of the Old World and the New is simply that. I would be burned as a heretic instead.

So I will stay here with the Gallerlanders, come what may. I may not be able to change the course of the earth-ripping ship of the Frontier Corps, but I will do what I can to help these stone-bladed natives resist.

Frostfall 21

At last, the great council was convened today after the arrival of the important chiefs and the kings of Goyn-land and Umbyrland. Harsen and I were permitted to observe their meeting in the great hall from the margins, and Eniri has instructed me not to be too far from Gratgofa's call at any moment. And all the while more refugees trickle into Nalembalen.

Debate in the high king's hall formally began after the midday meal and continued into the night. Gratgofa heard from every chieftain present. Their stories of encounters with the Donovards and defeats at the hands of the Frontier Corps in the north were many and similar. The raiders employed brutal tactics of fire and steel, rode swift beasts, and had unnumbered strength in men. Many Gallerlander warriors had been lost and their families with them.

Whole villages and swaths of forest across northern Um-byrland were burned and laid to waste. Precious electrum was stripped from bodies and hovels and tombs, stolen from every corner of the land. One Gallerlander who had been taken prisoner but escaped reported that the Donovards are filling chest after chest with electrum ornaments and sending them by the boatload down the river to the sea.

This man proposed to Gratgofa the formation of their own raiding party to reclaim these sword shards of Wurumnak, but he was gently reproached by the council.

Although all lamented the loss of the sacred metal, such an attempt would be hopeless and wasteful. All agreed their present focus should be on the common defense, for which every able-bodied man and woman would be needed. The matter of recovering electrum would have to wait, perhaps indefinitely.

After every clan and family had said their piece, the council sat down to a solemn banquet finer than any I have yet witnessed in my new forest home. They digested the many reports and observations that they had heard throughout the day as they now sated their appetites on roasted venison and boar, quail egg pies, baked afban of many shapes and varieties, mellonberry tarts with pepper, skewered woodland hen, and, to my delight, a rich mushroom stew slurped straight from the bowl.

Many other hearty dishes of simple but satisfying flavor dotted the tables alongside wooden flasks of golden mead, spiced ale, and their plentiful black currant wine. Although the convocation of the grand council was a worthy event, I suspect that Gratgofa's cooks spared nothing for what could be the last great feast of this hall before blood is shed.

In the midst of the feasting and drinking, Gratgofa introduced me to the council as the "former ambassador from Newlorn," saying that none should count me as their enemy. I was appreciative of this description and glanced at Eniri, who smiled. Clearly she has significant influence over him. Gratgofa finished his introduction by asking me to advise the council about what could be done about the invasion of the Frontier Corps. Every eye turned upon me.

I saw no reason to hide the bitter truth. First I described how the Donovards would likely have the best steel weapons and armor the Brintilian Empire could supply. One of the chieftains, who had just witnessed this in battle with his own eyes, testified as to the strength of this "wicked" metal to Gratgofa.

Pagdorat told me that the chieftain described steel in terms opposite of Wurumnak's holy electrum, that it was "evil gray sharpness" like the fangs of Demfrebra. I added that the steel was refined from iron ore mined from the earth, like the electrum found under the roots of Galler-landia.

Pagdorat said this prompted many questions in the hall about whether Ominchar had buried his own fiendish sword in the earth for his followers to gather. The high king summoned Talimnat, his chief Graparin, for advice. The warrior-priest's words were whispered to Gratgofa, so no one was able to hear his secretive counsel on this matter.

I continued, telling Gratgofa that the steel was only one of many advantages that the Donovards had. Aside from the experienced colonial knights, the crusaders were disciplined and well organized, experts in fighting in effective formations. And all of them would come on horses into battle. Although mass cavalry would be less effective in dense forest, the deployment of many small mounted units could easily confuse and overwhelm his warriors.

Gratgofa, never having seen a horse, again was educated by the northern chieftains who described them as "dark beasts who fly upon the land." Through Pagdorat, I attempted to explain that horses were in fact noble creatures useful for not only cavalry but also for transport, work, and companionship for every lonely traveler. The high king sniffed, saying that if horses were revered by the colonists then their use would be forbidden to Gallerlanders.

I continued to press him, saying that in our modern times victory in battle often hinged on the effective use of cavalry. The Frontier Corps would be nigh impossible to stop with weapons of stone and wood alone. I recommended that the Gallerlanders attack the crusader camps stealthily at night to catch the soldiers unaware and steal their horses—even if only to deprive the corps of them—and said he should consider adopting their steel as well.

Gratgofa and his chiefs would have none of it. The northern chiefs countered that they had been able to channel the horsemen into traps or otherwise draw the Donovards off their horses and out of formation, thereby isolating and ambushing them from the trees and other hiding places.

Urgamdir acknowledged that their problem was the number of mounted knights and soldiers that had flooded over them, but that this would be solved by the greater number of tribesmen in Nalembalen. Another chief, apparently from a rival clan, scolded Urgamdir and the northerners for endangering the capital by not staying to fight in the north.

Urgamdir tried to ignore him, telling Gratgofa that he himself would be willing to capture and ride the horses if it provided an advantage. He had seen the strength of the Frontier Corps with his own eyes, adding, "My clan will reach out with our weary arms and strike them in the night as this foreigner suggests, while you low Umbyrs rest your weary ears here in the comfort of the city!" The frustration among the chiefs exploded, with fingers jabbing blame and curses in all directions.

I made a last effort to persuade them by shouting in my broken Gali, which gained their attention. If the Gallerlanders did not unite and merely waited for the Frontier Corps to arrive, then the tactics that failed them in the north would fail them here. And if we fought them here in the treetop city, the ruthless Donovards would not hesitate to set fire to the capital and burn the whole forest to the ground.

The chieftains burst into a loud outcry. I think most had fled to Nalembalen believing that their great capital would afford them protection and that their high king would lead them to victory. Pagdorat said some of the chiefs and the king of the Umbyrs now rebuked me as an infiltrator. Like Gratgofa, the Umbyrking had a crown of ivy, with tiny curled vines that quivered with his rage.

A few other chiefs, notably Urgamdir, were willing to try other tactics. Gratgofa watched me intently, presumably still testing whether I could be trusted. I stood defiant against the shouting, hoping the Gallerlanders would adapt to an enemy with fighting tactics I once taught.

One chief barked that the Gallerlanders' advantage was that this was their home and they knew their own land. I agreed with him, saying the enemy also understood this. I explained that the colonists built their best fortifications with stone to stand strong and resist fire. And these were often protected by layers of walls and moats.

I pointed out that Nalembalen had none of these defenses and everything—even Gratgofa's own throne—was made of wood. Once the raiders came, they would surely burn

Nalembalen rather than fight house to skyward house, because that is what they did to stubborn enemies in their own lands. It would be no difficult feat for the Frontier Corps, and the Gallerlanders could not fight the fire.

So I repeated that the Frontier Corps would have to be stopped before they arrived, and to stop them meant surprising them, taking their horses or otherwise disabling their cavalry, and adopting steel swords. The chieftains' only answer to this was more outrage. Urgamdir glanced at me despondently.

Gratgofa held up his hand to silence them. He said he had never seen the fortifications of the foreigners or the manner in which they fought, but that he believed what I and the others had said about their advantages. He said again that he had never seen a horse, but repeated his prohibition against even touching the "evil beasts." He similarly condemned the use of steel.

Gratgofa said he did not doubt that the corps would use fire. It had been a long time since Nalembalen had faced such a serious threat, but in dire times the "tree tunnels" had provided shelter and tactical surprise. Gratgofa declared that his people were the people of the tree, from crowning bough to deepest root. He wanted the chiefs to consider how using the tunnels could create an advantage for the Gallerlanders against this new foe. A decision would be made in the morning, when the council would reconvene after sleeping with their thoughts.

The court and his guests then dispersed for the night and sought out the places of rest that had been prepared for them in the chalet apartments stocked with fur beds and in the houses of relations throughout the city.

Before Harsen and I could retire to our chamber, the high king approached us. I was to follow him, alone, to the outside balcony. I complied, and Harsen sulked off to our quarters.

It was the same platform from which the Hral and Siglef were hurled to their deaths. Gratgofa and I stood together, looking out over the timber rail and down through the leafless branches to the snow-blanketed forest floor below. Flakes continued to float down from a pale night sky above, the light of the moon clouded by the snowfall.

It was cold, but the great Gallerlander did not shiver. His face was solemn and darkened behind the snow that accumulated in his green-streaked silver beard. The branches of his antlered helm were dusted white before he spoke.

Gratgofa began by saying that he did not doubt my intentions. He judged that I was genuine in my attempt to help his people. He still thought it was odd that a colonist would brave the deep forests just to scribble in a book, but accepted me as I was.

He knew Harsen, however, was a thief. Hearing no denial from me, he added that the kindness of Eniri had purchased his mercy for us both from the beginning. But he said her tender words about me in particular since that time convinced him I was not a threat to his people, though possibly to his own wishes that she wed one of his chieftains, he said with raised eyebrow. He was responsible for her well-being after she was widowed. He reminded himself aloud that he would not have known his son's fate were it not for me.

Gratgofa acknowledged that Eniri had grown fond of me, but he asked me to promise that I not involve myself with her. She too often followed her heart and not her head, he said with a fatherly chuckle. But even if Nalembalen burned down around him, it was his sacred duty to preserve her for a chieftaincy. Although he thought me genuine, he believed there would never be understanding between my people and his, however much we might want it, and that I should not make it harder for Eniri by loving her.

I hesitated, caught off guard by his gentle candidness, and was unwilling to make a promise I could not keep. Eniri was the loveliest woman, and the wild softness of her eyes had captivated me from the start. But I sensed that if I did not make this promise to the high king, I risked losing his trust. So, reluctantly, I agreed.

Gratgofa was satisfied and seemed compelled to compensate my faith. He said he genuinely wished for peace but that the time had not yet come. Regardless of whether some colonists, like me, had taken different paths in the New World, we shared the same foreign Almeric blood. He said the people of the Agnesci blood, his people, must restore the balance between these original bloodlines by removing the colonies from Pemonia, though he conceded that he did not believe the time of balancing had arrived.

He did not share my belief that the Gallerlanders needed to adopt the tactics of the Frontier Corps to defeat them. And he was disgusted by the idea of riding or in any way using an animal in battle, saying his people would fight using their own ancient ways.

I recalled watching the graceful, quick techniques of Yelgoram and his men, their simple stone and wood weapons easily fending off a pack of wolves and later saving me from the clutches of the Hral during our journey to the treetop city. Owerdir could run up a tree, but could such techniques defeat a mounted knight?

Gratgofa continued, assuring me that tomorrow the chiefs would agree that using the tree tunnels was the best option, and he was confident this approach could repel the crusaders. "These are the walls and moats of our city," he said, explaining that the roots of Nalembalen spread far and wide under the forests outside the city. The ancient Maluram had dug the tunnels and lined them with stone, with the roots serving as living ceilings, for the defense of the city.

He said many of the tunnels led to stairways up into the roots and into the hollows of the great trees. The Gallerlanders would move "like unseen winds within the earth," striking the enemy from all directions, then disappear to strike again elsewhere. This, he said, was how the Gallerlanders had defeated invading Rahlampians and Welkars and other tribes throughout the ages. Like them, he said, the foreigners' impending failure in Nalembalen would forever haunt their dreams, and they would not threaten the treetop city again.

I was uncomfortable with a strategy that waited for the enemy to arrive, but Gratgofa knew his lands and their history. I also reluctantly accepted that Gratgofa would not use horses and steel, but I remained worried about the divisions among the clans. I asked how he would unite them, but he was unconcerned. The Graparins had counseled him that Wurumnak would save Nalembalen and its people, yet the priest-warriors had no answer for his retort that Wurumnak had not saved the Agnesci from nearly being destroyed by the Almerics long ago. Instead, Gratgofa drew comfort from a vision.

He claimed he had foreseen the fate of the treetop city in a dream weeks before I had arrived in Nalembalen, and that the dream had only grown clearer since. In the beginning, the electrum of the great hall and his own helmet had been reddened by flame and melted back into the earth, and the giant trees uprooted and fell deep into the ground, causing rivers to form in the ravines that flooded the realm until it was a vast burned marshland.

Gratgofa said he had puzzled over what seemed like a premonition of his failure to stop this mysterious future destruction, which would certainly forfeit his chance of sitting among the Thuraniparin, Wurumnak's most glorious kings reserved to lead the last battle at the End of Days.

But each time the dream returned, there was a flame of white that flickered up from the stones of the earth, and the trees drew up from the ravines and reattached themselves to their roots. The electrum leaped up from the ground, and the burned lands faded back to green forests, as if the destruction of Nalembalen had never occurred.

His throne still sat empty, save for his antlered helm, but his people were at peace. He interpreted the dream as meaning that an approaching doom would be averted only by his own sacrifice, signaled by the arrival of a white flame. Events which he said the sky omens confirmed were now upon us.

I was struck by this mighty figure, tall and antlered like a great beast of his realm, standing on this terrace overlooking a majestic city of which there was no equal. The Agnesci race had proven resilient through sturdy men like Gratgofa.

I told him that my little book was filled with the bravery of his people and the wonders of their great forests, and I agreed they would not easily perish under the boot of foreigners. I also conceded there could be great advantage to using the tunnels to surprise the enemy then hide again, limiting the usefulness of their cavalry and forcing them to fight in dark and unfamiliar places. He nodded, saying the chiefs would conclude the same, but he had not wanted to reveal his prophetic dream to them, fearing his fate would stir sorrow in their hearts.

As we departed, I asked why he had told the dream to me. He replied that he admired my courage and appreciated my willingness to help. But he also wondered if I was the white light that flickered from the stones in his dream. He was unsure of this and studied my unpainted face, saying that the Gallerlanders had resisted the colonies for some time, but it felt different now.

Gratgofa quickly added that Eniri apparently thought I could keep secrets. Then the high king asked a final question of me: "What have you been told of the Agnesci since arriving in Nalembalen?" Nothing, I instinctively lied. I knew of the Agnesci only what I had brought with me, I said.

"It should stay unknown," he said, "because there is nothing more to know." He must have known about my interests and Eniri's telling of the tales, so part of me wished I had not lied to protect her. Regardless, he no doubt sees me as unworthy of the Graparins' secret knowledge, even if he does trust me enough to share his vision.

And now here I sit in my bedchamber within the high king's grand chalet, faithfully recording the day's events. I have wondered whether this journal will ever be read by anyone, or whether it will remain hidden or destroyed in these verdant depths.

My last thoughts are of the decision I know will be made tomorrow and how the battle must be waged despite the winter. The snowfall outside has grown heavier with the onset of night.

Frostfall 22

Everyone was roused early this morning with the ominous predawn arrival of a messenger from a village not two days' walk north of Nalembalen. He brought word that Donovard scouts had been caught lurking in the woods on the fringe of that town. The scouts were killed at once, but their presence indicated the main body of the Frontier Corps could be as close as two or three days from the capital. The final council was assembled.

It was a scene to behold. Anxiety hung in the hall as thick as the snowfall, which had not slowed with the dawn. I had hoped that the deepening of winter would slow the pace of the Donovards, but I remembered that Hilsingor was unlike any other. I wish I knew more about his corps to better counsel Gratgofa.

Once the high king reined in his chiefs, he laid out his thinking. Most of the chiefs were behind him, though Urgamdir and a few others still wanted to try stealing horses or otherwise disrupting the cavalry. But Gratgofa denied their request. They would defend Nalembalen the same way their ancestors had done in previous wars, said the high king, including "when the black-painted Rahlampians invaded Gallerlandia long ago from the east, and the red-toothed Welkar folk before them." (I made a note to ask Pagdorat later about these people, since it is clear that yet more tribes lay beyond Gallerlandia's sprawling forests.)

The chiefs were tasked at once with preparing the warriors for the tunnels. The wounded, sick, and frail were crowded into the underground shelters as well, or huddled in the hollows of the great trees. All food was stuffed into sacks so that provisions could be moved quickly, and heaps of furs and rough-grass garments were piled around every shoulder.

When the council concluded, I found Eniri on a footbridge on her way to tend to the newly arrived casualties from the north. She understood the worry in my voice. What would become of us?

She took my hands in hers and smiled with a warmth that shunned the flakes of snow around us. I told her that she was the greatest discovery of my expedition into Gallerlandia. Would she be safe? "Not be sad," she said in Brintilian and sealed her encouragement with a soft kiss. For a moment there was no winter and no war around us.

Frostfall 24

Yesterday, the 23rd, amid chaotic scenes of yet more refugees arriving and many others escaping southward, Eniri found time to come find me.

Harsen and I have repaired our friendship enough to talk as I donned what passed for armor among the Gallerlanders. He is again searching for ways to persuade me to surrender to the Frontier Corps and not fight alongside the natives, but I will not yield to his plea. I told him that my life back in the colonies lacked true direction and purpose, as when I wandered aimlessly in the wilderness for a time. But now I had found my purpose, here with Eniri and her people.

When Eniri arrived, she explained that there was little time, that I should follow her at once. Harsen huffed as I left.

She spoke on our way to the great hall, saying the Graparins were bundling all the electrum and would soon take it into the root tunnels to hide away; they would do the same with the ancient scrolls next. I begged her to find a way for us to have time to read the Agnesci histories. She already had, she said proudly.

From the great hall we approached the adjoining chambers that housed the twelve Graparins and their secret rooms. All doors therein were shut, and we heard no sound behind them. We silently crept toward the scroll room, as we had before. But this time Eniri tapped her slender finger on the little door.

It cracked open, revealing the worn, wrinkled face of an old man. He whispered a few words and moved to close the door. Eniri placed her hand in the gap and whispered a terse protest, then motioned toward me. The old eyes, topped with bushy white brows, peered over at me expectantly. For a moment he gazed in the distance before returning to Eniri. A few more faint words, a nod, and the door closed. We would meet tonight. And so we waited.

In the midst of a somber feast in the great hall, the two of us quietly made our way down to the forest floor. It felt odd to be on the snow-covered ground again after so much time swaying on bridges and platforms. Eniri led me through the snow and brush with her lamp. I looked up behind us as we passed out of sight of the chalet, seeing a figure looking down from a bridge. I could not be sure that someone had seen our departure, given all the Gallerlanders moving about to make preparations.

Once in the bush, we trudged on through the snow drifts as Eniri explained how she had persuaded the old Graparin, Hegdir, to help us. Rildning, she told him, was like a Graparin among his own people, seeking to learn and also protect the ancient tales to preserve the people, especially now in the face of danger. She had relayed my whole story to Hegdir, who was impressed with my foray into the black forest and my twice surviving the snakes.

Eniri noted that Hegdir was too old to fight or flee and would remain in Nalembalen, so he knew death would come soon for him. He agreed to share the scrolls with me, but only in secret. I was excited but also worried that without Pagdorat, my Gali would not be good enough to understand everything.

We soon arrived at a small waterfall, with frozen leggy columns stretching from its ledge into the glassy snow-swept pool below. The silence of the place was eerie, but I could envision that its waters would soon flow again with the intense heat of burning giant trees. Eniri had arranged for old Hegdir to meet us here, far enough from prying eyes but close enough for him to make it in the cold.

We huddled around the warm glow of the lamp. I suggested we make a fire but Eniri declined because it would attract attention. I countered that the forest was full of campfires because of the refugees, but she insisted. So we shivered, staring at the sparkle of the sealed water arches.

After a short time, another light twinkled in the falls, followed by footsteps crunching the snow. Following our path was Hegdir, his hunched body wrapped in giant furs and his balding head nearly invisible under three hoods. He clutched a tiny light that swayed as he shuffled toward us. He smiled as he approached, most of his teeth long rotted away. He was ancient, but moved with decent vigor. As he sat he told Eniri to make a fire. She shrugged and did so.

Hegdir held out his hands to Eniri in greeting, then did the same to me. He held mine longer and spoke. He said that he believed me to be a mysterious gift from Wurumnak. Hegdir said his people had long tended the forests but that the seasons had changed. The arrival of the "unpainted men" was not a surprise to him as it was to the others. For he knew the Agnesci visit to Cedelaebos in ancient times would one day spark the visit of the Almerics to Aprelaebos.

Hegdir said the Gallerlanders and the other tribes of Pemonia were the original brothers of the Almerics, and they must welcome those of the Almeric blood and not repeat the evils that the Almerics inflicted upon the Agnesci. Thus, Hegdir believed that one day both peoples would inhabit both continents together and share Wurumnak's created world in peace. He believed me to be a sign of that new era, the hope of a foretold peace between the ancient bloodlines.

I was astounded at the old Graparin's swift acceptance of me and his forthright telling of his belief and prophecy. If only the visionary Orren could have heard his words. Messengians like me are taught that God purposefully separated the Almerics and Agnesci into Cedelaebos and Aprelaebos, respectively, to prevent them from being united against God. If Hegdir's words are as authoritative as they must be, the Gallerlander religion has no such prohibition. But I had to ask him, why was the prophecy of peace a secret to his own people?

They are not ready to know these truths, he declared. The ancient pain of the Agnesci was so great and so deep that those terrible events, the expeditions, and even the existence of Cedelaebos and the Almeric peoples were buried so that future generations would not be roused by vengeance or curiosity until the proper time had come.

As an example, he pointed to Gratgofa and his chiefs. Like all high kings before him, Gratgofa was shown the histories and knew the truth. His eldest son, Gofalnig, and his widow princess, Eniri, were also told. But the chiefs and their clans do not know.

Unlike nearly all his predecessors, Gratgofa was now confronted with the arrival of the Almerics' descendants, explained Hegdir. The high king was undecided whether he should seek peace or defend the realm, but the ruthlessness of the crusaders and the suffering of the northern clans convinced Gratgofa that there would be no peaceful fulfillment of the prophecy.

So Gratgofa will seek nothing less than the complete expulsion of the Almeric race from Pemonia, even if he believes he is doomed to perish. The high king is a great leader but he will not accept the truth, added Hegdir, so the hour when all will learn of the prophecy has not yet come. The Graparins will remain the keeper of the keys.

I asked Hegdir why, if the prophecy of peace must come true, did the first Agnesci encounter with the Almerics not result in peace? He replied that the Agnesci Seafathers had crossed the seas too early, for the Almerics were too primitive in their knowledge of the world and too misguided in their religion to accept their Agnesci brethren. They viewed the Agnesci as demons from the sea, like the colonists see the Gallerlanders as demons from the forests today. Hegdir conceded that there would be many years of hardship until the colonists accepted that the inhabitants of Pemonia were truly their brethren and sought peace.

How, I asked, could the colonists and natives come to this understanding or seek fulfillment of a prophecy that neither side knew existed? Hegdir responded that the prophecy's fulfillment did not depend on our knowledge of it. Peace was naturally in the heart of every man, Almeric or Agnesci, and Wurumnak would guide.

Hegdir had decided to break his solemn oath to reveal these things to me because he saw peace in my heart and considered me a seed. He said I would grow strong in the truth and my branches would spread the knowledge to the Almeric peoples. Similarly, the future Gallerlander high kings would be forced to do so among their own peoples now that their secluded woodland home would be changed forever.

Hegdir warned me, however, not to share the ancient knowledge with anyone I did not trust, for the secret prophecy could be undone by wicked hearts. The knowledge, like the roots of a tree, would spread broadly but slowly, searching and feeling for waters that would sustain and not poison it. This burden that he now placed on my shoulders would extend well beyond my lifetime, to others in which I would plant the seed.

As I tried to comprehend all that he had said, Hegdir reached into his bulky furs and produced a vellum scroll, stained and torn with the wear of ages. He carefully unfurled it and pointed to a heading that read *The Cataclysm*. There were symbols that I recognized at the top as 312 and 522.

Hegdir said the first number showed that the information contained in the scroll dated to the 312th generation, and the second number showed that this particular scroll was written during the 522nd generation, meaning it was a copy of the earlier original. Hegdir said the original scroll is kept preserved while copies are penned every four or five hundred years for study and handling. Hegdir made this copy himself when he was a young Graparin.

Eniri explained that the Gallerlanders did not count the seasons and the years as the colonists do, but rather the generations of their offspring. Since generations vary among families, the generation number is kept by counting the generations of the high king, regardless of which family sits on the tree throne. It's clear to me that there is a deep ancestry of the peoples of Pemonia of which the Brintilians know nothing.

Hegdir continued, saying the tale contained in the original scroll was written at the behest of the greatest surviving Agnesci chief who had stayed behind and did not voyage to Cedelaebos with the others. The hand that wrote it belonged to one of the Seafathers, Agimdir, who had survived the

Cataclysm—the massacre in Cedelaebos—and returned home to tell the tale.

The chief became high king and charged Agimdir with the safekeeping of his knowledge by writing it down and keeping it secret from the new generations. Agimdir was the first Graparin, one of the few from the voyages who was not banished from the land.

Hegdir said the spoken word of the Agnesci had evolved and splintered many times since the days of Agimdir, but that Graparins had kept the old language when copying new scrolls. Thus, only they and the new generations of scroll-keepers that they trained could read them.

The tale was written as poetry. Hegdir read it, translating the old tongue into Gali, while Eniri helped me with some of the words as I scribbled it down. It is far from a perfect rendition but is now provided here in readable form. It was also impossible for me to capture the chant and rhyme of his words, but I have done my best to capture the tale.

And so the three of us hunched over the symbol-etched Cataclysm scroll by lamp and fire, and watched the light play behind the outstretched vellum whose primeval verses we consumed as eagerly as those ancient Agnesci Seafathers braved the seas.

❧

Arasemis's Note: This lengthy poem was written in Rildning's journal hastily. At times the scribble is ambiguous, but there are clearly two sets of revisions, which also trail into the margins of later pages. One is the hand of Rildning, but the other is someone else who had knowledge of the Agnesci tale and yet could write in Old Brintilian. Assuming this second hand is as credible as it appears to be, these revisions allowed me to piece together the complete poem.

❧

The Agnesci of Aprelaebos,
Bold and hardy of spirit.
Ever blessed by Wurumnak

To tend fields and forests,
To fish seas and streams.
Builders and shapers of woods, stones, and metals.

Glad be they in fair
Lands of Aprelaebos.
Brave hearts be kings of men,
Good clans arm in arm,
And peace among families.
All evil of Ominchar and his folk cast out asunder!

But half-fulfilled
Were Agnesci without
Brethren afar across the sea.
What became of the Almerics
In afar Cedelaebos,
Made also from Wurumnak's crafting hand of life?

Wurumnak wisemen bade
Great king to set the sails,
Prophecy to be fulfilled
Of greatest fleet of peace!
Long would be the voyage,
But waves and wind no longer to divide the brothers!

Wood-shapers and metalsmiths,
All clan builders tasked.
Heavy fell the hammers,
Quick chewed the saws,
Carefully laid the keels.
Ships laid down in harbors soon outgrew the stars.

Stocks of fish and meats,
Live forest hens and sheep,
All fruits and roots,
And herbs and grains packed,
For unknown the stretch of seas.
No room for weapons, and not needed to visit brethren.

Final look at sky omens,

All gathered on beach and plains,
Where once stood there
Asgemdirhar, forest of giants,
Harvested for ship sides.
After many years of work the time had come at last!

Many people young and old,
Whole clans and families.
Unnumbered villages emptied
Into the grand sea vessels,
Cities built for sail.
Unnumbered peoples boarded,
Gleaming, hopeful eyes set upon the afar blue horizon.

Joyous were the days,
Much merriment aboard ships!
The endless fleet
Seen in all directions,
Far as the eye could see.
All were part of the glorious quest for holy prophecy!

Stormy gales and sky fire
Attacked the fleet of peace.
Sails torn and hulls ripped,
Whole clans swept
Away under dark waves
Tall and hard as the snowcapped mountains of home.

Forward bravely
All sailed on.
Then no wind at all
Kept all ships still.
Slow they bobbed,
Drifting in the hungry deep at the edge of the world.

Countless suns and moons
Arose and fell on the ships.
Long-lasting the journey,
Food stores dwindled,
Hunger ravenous, thirst sharp.

Dead were cast away, shiploads merged to gain full crews.

Thankful prayers to Wurumnak
On day land first sighted,
Songs of praise
Across the soft waters
Spread from ship to ship!
Fleet still so large, ships behind could not yet see the land!

The distant land grew larger
And greeted the travelers
With bow of clouded
Mountaintops and sun.
Not long before
Weary feet would step to shore and touch dry land again!

No sign of brethren
When they landed on the beaches.
Ships anchored and
Small boats came in.
Shelters built with boards
And sail, food gathered in ponds and plains

Brethren on long-legged
Beasts soon appeared,
Found the beach camps.
Envoys were sent warily
To assure peace prophecy.
No common words were known but kind smiles found.

The brethren marveled
At the sea of weathered ships.
Never had they seen such labors
As great those broad voyagers.
We took them out to see them,
To their king we gifted many, food was given in return.

Our king and chieftains
Dined with those high brethren.
Our settlement on the beaches

They approved, for teaching
Them of our shipbuilding.
And so began the learning of speech and customs.

More of our kin came
From across the seas,
No knowing our fate.
But seeing our warm welcome,
They stayed with us.
The voyages flowed as we wondered if any still at home.

Yet not one generation
Passed before the cataclysm:
Brotherly relations soured by
Fears and warnings from
Foul priests and men of greed.
Unarmed, we sought Arukans' protection on the beaches.

Battle and war,
Much blood was spilled.
Cedelaebos itself divided!
And we ourselves,
Untrusted and trusted not,
And so we secluded ourselves to the beachside havens.

But we found our ships
Burning and washed in waves
Upon a bloody shore!
No escape from the evils
That pursued us,
No haven at the beaches, nor anywhere in Cedelaebos!

From place to place
We fled, but no help.
Women and children
They pursued first,
So no new generations
Birthed there, while our generation was fast dwindling.

Escape was craved.

The gales and famines
Of the sea seen better
Than death at the hands
Of the most evil brethren.
They had no prophecy, only blind fear of "bad sea folk"!

The only escape was
For the blood that was freed
To water's edge.
Imprisoned were the rest,
To face priest trials.
All condemned to death, no understanding of our people!

The earth screamed forth
And took our dead.
None survived
Of that great voyage,
Save one handful,
Aided by Arukans who often paid their own life price.

With a stolen gift ship
We sailed the seas again,
Sure to perish under waves.
But swift winds and strong currents
Carried us homeward,
Visions of unequaled pain and loss were carried with us.

Soon the winds died
And we were left adrift,
But saw sailing ships
Bound for Cedelaebos.
They saved us from dark waters,
And we saved them from darkness at their destination.

Together with others
That we encountered
Along the way,
A small fleet
Returned home.
Dark the day we carried news of the cataclysm home!

Mourning was great,
The king took his life.
A whole people writhed
At the slaughter and generations lost.
The burning of Haldembalir
And the ascent of the black serpent seemed near to us.

But hope still lay
In the ground-hidden
Electrum, much there still,
The priests assured.
Still time to find and forge
Wurumnak's sword, and souls to win for Thurondsogon!

But priests were downtrodden:
Mistimed our search for prophecy!
And our bringing of the lamps of truth
To that stony cold shore:
Those brethren were not ready
To unite with us for Wurumnak against the evil Serpent.

The seers of Cedelaebos,
Survivors of that red land,
Fulfilled they the tasks,
Released of all duties.
And protectors be they now,
And holders of the secret voyage of those fateful days.

No more
Will we
Repeat and seek
Across the sea!
Wait we will for their long travel here.

Only then
Will prophecy begin,
When they master
Sail and sea.
Peace seeking,

We will welcome them.

And only then
Will our own
Generations know
The truth
Of the brethren,
And the secrets that saved the vengeful and curious.

The Graparins
Will protect the tale
Of our folly,
The famous fleet,
The brethren, and the war,
Until united we prepare together for Thurondsogon!

I thanked Hegdir and Eniri for their patience during this urgent time and for the risks they had taken, then we were startled by a sound in the snow-caked bushes behind us. As I cautiously approached, I could hear the sound of short breathing and teeth ticking. It was Pagdorat, hunched in the snow and shivering uncontrollably. He had not taken the time to properly dress in several furs before following us, and he carried no lamp. I quickly brought him to the fire.

Eniri scolded him, but Hegdir wore a knowing smile. Pagdorat confessed to hearing our whole conversation after we helped him regain his warmth. Eniri fumed, but Hegdir calmly told Pagdorat that he had breached sacred knowledge that was not meant for his ears. Pagdorat was ashamed and resentful, saying that he worried Eniri and I would get into trouble. He did not wish us any harm, and now he wished he hadn't heard Hegdir's tale.

Hegdir surprised all of us when he replied, "The love between these two is only a trouble for those who do not know the prophecy or the potential for the ancient bloodlines to unite." Seeing the shock on our faces, Hegdir said our love could not be hidden from the eyes of the wise, and that others would accept it in time. As for Pagdorat, Hegdir asked if he desired to be a Graparin, since he had essentially begun training in the secret knowledge. Pagdorat vigorously shook his head. So he made the Teshi swear an oath of silence, which he willingly did.

I no longer worry about Pagdorat. Watching him there in the firelight convinced me that he remains my friend.

Arasemis's Note: At this point Rildning's journal becomes more difficult—and in some places impossible—to decipher. He made no other notes about the Agnesci voyage, the resulting Cataclysm, the old Graparin Hegdir, or what occurred soon after his meeting with Hegdir. Rildning's remaining entries are undated and quickly scrawled. Many of the pages are smeared and sprinkled with burn marks, likely from falling ash and embers from the burning of the giant trees of Nalembalen. His written word becomes increasingly hasty and abbreviated, but I have done my best to piece together what were likely their final hours in the treetop city.

Gratgofa's scouts tell us that the Donovard raiders draw close now. Messengers say the Gallerlander warriors sent out through the tree tunnels to the outskirts of Nalembalen are hard-pressed. We also know that some Frontier Corps units have circled around Nalembalen and are headed south, perhaps to cut off our escape. Gratgofa has ordered everyone to take up positions in the trees or in the tunnels. Eniri is caring for the people down at the roots.

No refugees arrive now. Any survivors have fled further south. Gratgofa remains on his throne, in command from his great hall but preparing to go fight at the front. We hear that his warriors are doing well at the city's edge, where the Frontier Corps has tried to penetrate with infantry. The Gallerlanders' tunnel tactics are working, and others leap from shadowy bush and glade. I will be permitted to join the fight when Gratgofa does. The high king is confident of victory. No reports of much crusader cavalry.

∼

I was helping to gather arrows and stone blades when Pagdorat was taken. Boarmaster Arbardir must have suspected something. Eniri saw the ugly brute and the chief Graparin, Talimnat, snatch my friend. Eniri is frantic, I cannot understand her words.

∼

Unable to find Pagdorat.

∼

At night a Gallerlander unknown to me came into my chamber to kill me. Luckily Harsen heard our struggle. I was cut with an electrum knife, the first metal blade I have seen among this whole people. I suspect it is a ceremonial dagger, given its many etched symbols, perhaps a Graparin tool? But the attacker fled. Harsen again insisted we flee because this war is not ours to fight . . . but I cannot.

∼

Safe for now in a tree hollow . . . Earlier, Eniri brought me to Gratgofa to seek help. Unfortunately, Arbardir and Talimnat were already with the high king. Pagdorat was bound and kneeling. He had been beaten severely. Seen with the bloodied electrum knife in my hand, Talimnat accused me of sacred theft and murder. Pagdorat said they knew all about Hegdir's oath breaking. An evil fire burned in the eyes of Arbardir and Talimnat. The chief Graparin urged Gratgofa to cast me off through the arches.

We heard a windy, rushing sound and looked through the windows. Thousands upon thousands of flaming arrows leaped up into the trees from the many figures on the ground far below. The heat of the red volleys could be felt upon our faces, turning the falling snow into a soft rain. I shook off the grip of the Graparins, and we ran.

Gratgofa shouted orders for all the tribesmen to fight. The Gallerlander archers shot down into the crusader masses below. Arbardir obeyed the call to arms, but Talimnat seized me. An arrow bit him in the face as flames chewed into the great hall. Pagdorat, tightly bound, could not move, and we could not reach him. Harsen, Eniri, and I forced our way down to the ground, flaming tree-hovels and branches falling all around us. We saw Pagdorat cast himself from the platform as the great hall fell after him. We carried Eniri away.

We have joined with Arbardir down in a root tunnel where he organizes the attacks on nearby raiders. We hear heavy thuds in the walls as the burning houses of Nalembalen crash to the earth. When we spring from the tunnels, we can see the fires have warmed the ground and melted the snow, so that thick mud now mixes with blood and ash. Eniri's beautiful face is tear streaked but determined.

It felt painfully good to shove a stone blade into the fissures of the crusaders' armor. The tunnels are a good defensive weapon. Even more so now that their cavalry has arrived.

We rest now down in the earth. Many of the tribesmen are sleeping or eating in the lamplight. We lament those whom we've lost, but carry on. Many people have fled through the tunnels toward the south. I'm uncertain of our position, but Eniri knows her way. Scouts say we are not far from Gratgofa and the Umbyrking, so we will join them when all have rested. Not being able to see the sky omens from the tunnels has added to the anxiety of the Gallerlanders.

Harsen was given a spear, but he does not want to fight. He knows it is too dangerous to surrender, but he keeps telling me that he will try when the moment is right. He knows he cannot persuade me to come with him. I am glad brave Urgamdir is with us. He complains about the tunnels and he wants a horse, but the other chiefs have forbidden it. I wish Yelgoram and Owerdir were here to help us. And I cannot help but wonder if they returned safely to their village.

The main body of the Frontier Corps has moved. We are still harassed aboveground and the fires are still burning. Some brave knights have entered the tunnels, but they did not live long.

❧

I told Eniri that I will stay with her even as the trees come down. The time has come to put down the quill and again pick up the spear and stone sword.

❧

Arasemis's Note: This concludes Rildning's handwriting, as he likely focused on surviving the battle at this point. How long they fought before being forced to flee is unknown, but Rildning certainly dropped or somehow lost the journal because an important Brintilian commander scrawled a note on the back page of the book:

This Rildning is a known heretic and traitor to the Almeric race. He will be found. I hereby claim this property in the name of His Imperial Majesty, to be used as evidence against the accused.

Sir Hilsingor of Ned Gollen
Marshal, Frontier Corps

EPILOGUE

Thorendor Castle, Wallevet Ministry
Harvesteve, 3032

"What happened?" Marlan asked. "Did they escape?"

"When you're ready, your next lesson will come from the second book I dug up from the dunes of Aggarwal," Arasemis said.

"The one you said was written in Gali, by the man named Enildir?"

"Correct. But I will say that Rildning escaped. The colonists were more concerned about carving out new provinces than chasing after one man. In fact, the journal does not bear a stamp commonly used by Donovard magistrates of that period to mark judicial property, so it was probably never sent to them by Marshal Hilsingor."

"And what happened to the marshal?"

Arasemis pointed to a shelf behind them. "The colonial records say that Hilsingor was killed under mysterious circumstances later in Aggarwal in the same region where I dug up the books." He smiled impishly.

"Did they assassinate him?"

"Don't get ahead of your training."

"You have the original colonial records?" Marlan asked.

"I was younger than you when I began searching out the secret histories of the natives of Pemonia, and stealing key documents from treasuries and archives across the continent to fill in the gaps. For every stone used to build Thorendor Castle, I have a book or scroll to clutter the interior."

"What happened to the rest of them: Eniri, Harsen, Gratgofa, and the others? I doubt they considered the secret Agnesci prophesy of peace to have been fulfilled."

"In due time, Marlan."

The pupil turned Rildning's journal in his hands. "Quite remarkable that this survived."

"The books of Rildning and Enildir are the only firsthand accounts of not only Rildning's expedition, but the Agnesci's secret histories. I think Rildning's depiction of the Frontier Corps' siege of Nalembalen, though fragmentary, leaves no doubt that the Gallerlanders' written histories could not have survived the burning of the treetop city.

"Indeed, several Brintilian chroniclers of that era recorded that the Donovard raiders found the remains of the Gallerlander histories, but the Donovards put all of it to the torch in an attempt to 'expunge all writings of the tongue of Memelos,' as one scribe put it. Thus, Rildning's journal provides the only known copy of the Cataclysm scroll, and therefore the only account that the natives of Pemonia were in fact the descendants of the Agnesci."

"But the Messengian Church has never accepted that view," Marlan said.

"Yes, and the rival Congregant Church has always sought to avoid the debate over Rildning. But now you see for yourself that Rildning was legendary and controversial for good reason. His journey from honored colonial knight to wilderman to defender of the natives was quite radical in his day, as was his falling in love with a green-tattooed native princess, a daughter of the primeval Agnesci."

"Can we begin Enildir's book?" Marlan asked. "I want to know what happened."

"The second book is very different from the first. Much understanding is required. And Garion is not here to participate."

"I've come a long way in my training," Marlan said. "I've mastered running up walls, as the Gallerlanders did. I can identify the medicinal herbs and craft stone blades. And I can read some Gali now."

"So be it. I suppose you have earned it. But I don't want to get too far along before recruiting more students. The revival of Candlestone will take more than a one-armed warrior-scholar and two eager pupils."

"Let us at least start Enildir's book."

"Very well . . ."

SNEAK PEEK

The story of Rildning continues. Step out of his journal and back to character perspective chapters, into an age of conquest and exodus across the New World that would set the stage for *Lords of Deception*...and for what comes next.

A Light in the Depths

Suffering heavy losses in a widening war, Rildning and his Gallerlander companions fan out across the continent to persuade other tribes to join in a common defense against the Brintilian Empire. But Rildning discovers that ancient tribal rivalries die hard and many still suspect him of spying for the empire.

And Rildning has another problem: his journal now lies in the hands of Marshal Hilsingor, imperial commander of the Frontier Corps. Knowing his enemy well, Hilsingor is determined to undermine Rildning's efforts and eradicate the remaining tribal enclaves.

ACKNOWLEDGMENTS

Thanks and appreciation to many for lending an ear, providing encouragement, and mending my scribbles. To my mother, who taught me to love books and to explore the art of writing. To my father, who taught me hard work and perseverance. And to my editors Anne McPeak and Tricia Callahan, for their talents and guidance.

ABOUT THE AUTHOR

Christopher C. Fuchs writes the Earthpillar novels and half-tales with flavors of fantasy, historical fiction, adventure, and steampunk. His debut novel, *Lords of Deception*, is the core of a nonlinear matrix of books that allow readers to wander and explore an epic alternative Earth that blends new continents and peoples, political intrigue, fictional materials, and customized medieval and early modern technologies.
He writes from Virginia.

To stay informed of upcoming books and receive discount codes, subscribe to the mailing list at
EarthpillarBooks.com.

www.ingramcontent.com/pod-product-compliance
Lightning Source LLC
Chambersburg PA
CBHW050341190726
48284CB00007BB/2105